SUFFER THE DEAD

A BLACK BEACONS MURDER MYSTERY

DCI WARLOW CRIME THRILLER #4

RHYS DYLAN

WYRMWOOD
BOOKS

COPYRIGHT

ISBN 978-1-915185-07-5
eBook ISBN 978-1-915185-06-8

Published by Wyrmwood Books.
An imprint of Wyrmwood Media.

EXCLUSIVE OFFER

Please look out for the link near the end of the book for your chance to sign up to the no-spam guaranteed VIP Reader's Club and receive a FREE DCI Warlow novella as well as news of upcoming releases.

Or you can go direct to my website: https://rhysdylan.com and sign up now.

Remember, you can unsubscribe at any time and I promise won't send you any spam. Ever.

OTHER DCI WARLOW NOVELS

THE ENGINE HOUSE
CAUTION DEATH AT WORK
ICE COLD MALICE
GRAVELY CONCERNED
A MARK OF IMPERFECTION
BURNT ECHO
A BODY OF WATER
LINES OF INQUIRY

NO ONE NEAR
THE LIGHT REMAINS

EPIGRAPH

"Suffer the dead a voice, so that they may be heard, and a vessel, so that they may seek answers from the living. For in that voice is the spear of retribution, and in the vessel's hand is the hammer of vengeance."

Anonymous.

CHAPTER ONE

POLICE COMMUNITY SUPPORT Officer Hana Prosser rarely drove this way to work. Still, these were not normal times. And though today's route was a detour from her usual commute, this was no early morning jaunt to Aldi.

Today she was on the clock five minutes after leaving home. She smiled. Conscientiousness could be a curse. No change there, then. And with that thought, the smile died. It was not the first time she'd driven these byways. This was her backyard. And the last time she'd been up here it had been to investigate a killing.

Her father, whose land she now skirted as she headed up towards the isolated Hermon Chapel on a rarely used lane, blamed the tourists. The price of milk, most of his farming woes, sheep on the road; he blamed tourists for more or less everything. Well, bloody tourists and their dogs. But then he had a special place in his farmer's black book for interlopers and their mutts. His opinion was that the increase in sheep attacks – the 'killing' she'd previously investigated had been of three sheep – directly resulted from naïve people clamouring to own cuddly canines that quickly turned into ravening beasts at the drop of an ewe's hat. The majority, in his not so humble opinion, had no clue about dog etiquette in the countryside.

And a dog could do a lot of lethal damage in a very short time faced with a flock of bleating sheep.

Despite all the signs her father, the other local farmers, and the local council had put up reminding people to keep their dogs on a leash, there'd been some nasty, atrocious incidents. Sheep terrified and mutilated, lambs slaughtered, dogs destroyed. No one wanted to see that, least of all Hana, who loved dogs and had a soft spot for sheep, stupid as they were.

Having been brought up on a farm with a flock of 700 scattered over 150 acres in this quiet corner of Powys close to the border with England, she knew all about the horrors that resulted from a dog attack. And now, as part of one of Dyfed Powys Police Service's Rural Crime Teams, she also had to investigate these things.

But dogs were not the reason she was winding her way along the edge of the Berwyn Mountains in North-East Wales this cool morning. A call from an old school-friend first thing had alerted her. The woman, mid-twenties like Hana and living in a house near St Cadwaladr's Church, heard the gunshots a little after 1am, she'd said. Probably nothing, but she thought someone ought to know.

Hana might have noted it down and written it off had she not taken a call from her sergeant in Rural Crime based in Newtown an hour ago. He'd rung to say he'd received a call from a fraught farmer's wife whose husband and son had gone out late the night before but had not returned.

'Gone out late means sniffing about for rustlers,' Sergeant 'Tomo' Thomas had muttered in the call Hana'd taken at 7.15am as she set up breakfast. Iestyn, her teacher husband, had still been in the shower, but Hana, disturbed already by her friend's earlier call, was in uniform and sipping her second coffee as she listened to Tomo's gripes. 'You know what these buggers are like. Probably met up with another lot and gone over for a quick whisky in a barn. They'll turn up in a minute, I daresay.'

She told him then about the gunshots.

Tomo didn't give it much thought. 'Yeah, well. Probably them taking a pot shot at a stray dog or a fox. Most of that lot are equal opportunity cullers.'

Hana pondered the "that lot" and wondered if Sergeant Thomas ever considered he might be putting his size eleven foot in it by referencing "that lot" in discussions with her since she was from "that lot" stock. She doubted it as Tomo was not known for his emotional intelligence. But he knew the patch and the sort of things the locals got up to having grown long in the tooth patrolling it. In that way, he was wise enough.

'Since you're up there, might as well check it all out. Any idea where the shots came from?' he'd asked.

Hana did have a rough idea. She knew how sounds travelled across the valleys and given where her friend lived, she'd worked out a rough area that might fit the bill. She'd started to explain but realised Tomo's attention span would not last the distance, so she'd shortened the answer to something simple. 'I'll pop up there now before I come to you.'

Tomo grunted his approval.

They were working out of Welshpool this week and her journey to work took about half an hour on a good day. Otherwise, the base was Newtown station. Only thirty miles but on these roads a good hour's journey if traffic, or the weather, was bad. Far more likely to be the latter than the former now that the bypass had opened, thank God.

The Rural team were carrying out traffic stops on forestry roads, targeting illegal use of off-road motorcycles as well as investigating two cases of animal theft in the surrounding areas. Rustling remained a real problem with gangs targeting lambs especially, as well as some premium cattle. But it was a big patch to cover, and they were thinly spread. Even so, the experiment with establishing a Rural Crime Team a couple of years before seemed to pay off for the Dyfed Powys service and it delighted Hana to be a part of it.

As soon as Tomo rang off, she'd stuck her head into the bathroom and kissed a naked Iestyn on the cheek with a playful grin before setting off. She'd toyed with asking her dad to come with her, for the company and because of his familiarity with the land, but he'd be busy with feeding now. Besides, this was police business.

She climbed north out of Llanrhaeadr towards the border with Gwynedd and, after a couple of miles, took a lane that did not appear on any Google map. She stopped at a gate and parked the car, frowning on seeing the gate unlatched and open. There were no sheep nearby but there were on the hillside not half a mile away. This gate should have been closed.

Looking south, she spied a cluster of houses where the friend who'd alerted her to the noise of the supposed shotgun lived. A cluster of five perched on the hillside, pale regular shapes in the broad sweep of the valley. Behind the houses, the land rose again and Hana had concluded that with a north-easterly wind, noise would have carried from this direction.

She stood on the high ground, breathed in the air and looked out across the landscape. God's own country, as her dad would often describe this little corner of Powys. God's forsaken country as Sergeant Thomas preferred to describe it. Few tourists came this way even though she was not that far from Pistyll Rhaeadr, a 270-foot waterfall that attracted visitors from across the border and beyond.

But not this grey morning. A mist hung low, mercifully

not low enough to obscure her friend's house, but blurring the line between horizon and sky. These hills were flat-topped, but on a day like today, it would not be difficult to imagine they reached into the clouds, like the bottom of a giant's staircase.

As her eyes swept across and down to where the land fell away, another open gate led to a small feed shed. From where she stood she couldn't make out if there were any vehicles parked behind it though it would be the only logical reason to leave the gates open.

Hana's Skoda had four-wheel-drive; even so, the suspension bounced and squeaked as it navigated the rutted lane down towards the sheds. When she got to the bottom of the hill, she pulled up next to the crumbling walls of some old sheep pens and got out.

Spring had arrived, and the hedgerows were filling out. But the sun sulked in its blanket of grey and the chill wind spoke more of the end of winter than the beginnings of summer.

She could still see the tops of the houses on the other side of the valley. Noise would definitely carry up from here well enough.

Hana walked towards the building. The Randals, whose land this was, put a new steel roof on the sheds last year, but the wooden walls had gaps and cracks that allowed Hana a murky inside view when she put her eye up to them.

Empty.

But what she saw through the cracks was the shape of a vehicle on the other side of the building.

A vague apprehension gnawed at her insides. Hana walked around to find a Land Rover Defender with two of its doors open but no sign of driver or passenger. She scanned the number plate. Definitely the Randals. She called out their names.

'Hello? Aeron? Joe?'

No one answered. All she heard was the moaning of the wind rising and falling through the gaps in the feed-shed walls.

Even though she was warm in her thick coat, she shivered.

Slowly, and for some reason trying to make as little noise as possible, Hana crept around to the shed doors. They were big and heavy and one of them stood open to reveal the shadow-filled dark space beyond. Spilled silage from the plastic-coated bales stacked at the rear littered the floor. Nothing unusual in that. She took all of this in within seconds before her darting glance focused on the other, closed half of the doors.

The half with two dark-red smears spattered over the bleached wood. One at about chest height that had run down towards the floor. The other, higher by a foot or two. This one with something lighter at the centre of the darker smudge. Something still glistening.

The gnawing sensation in Hana morphed into a swooping dive. She didn't want to get closer, but she had to know. Three steps before she stopped, leaned forward and stared, suddenly losing the ability to swallow. The some-thing pale was no more than an inch square and more a light ochre than white. But Hana had seen more than enough death on the farm she grew up on and knew what she was looking at. The little folds and ridges outlined by congealing blood only meant one thing.

Brain.

Hana stepped back, suddenly acutely aware of where she stood. Of how isolated a spot this little feed shed occupied.

A fresh gust added another mocking chorus to the wind's dirge. She could not see her friend's house across the valley from here, and the houses would not see her. Her breathing sped up, and she forced air out slowly through pursed lips in an attempt at slowing her respirations as she fumbled with the Velcro flap of the pocket that held her phone, all the while blinking at the scattered remains, aware that what she was looking at had no right to be plastered to a door.

Finally she got the phone into her hands. No signal.

'Shit.' She hurried back to the car and stormed back up the drive, tyres rippling and roaring over the stones to the open gate on the higher ground. Hana got out, glancing down to where she'd come from before turning her attention once more to her phone.

Two bars now. Her trembling fingers pressed buttons until she found the number and called it.

'Find them?' asked Tomo's bluff voice when he answered.

'Oh, Sarge,' Hana said, her voice barely a whisper.

'Hana—'

She forced out the words before he could say anymore. 'I think I have found them. Or at least what's left of them.'

CHAPTER TWO

Evan Warlow stood on the banks of the Daugleddau Estuary, within sight of some picturesque tearooms, his phone to his ear.

'How long is she likely to be in?' The question, he hoped, sounded genuine enough, even if its subtext contained a selfish undertone.

'A few days, the docs say. She's been rough since Wednesday with this pain in her stomach, not being able to keep anything down.'

Not even a vodka and tonic? Warlow stamped on the catty remark before it could escape his lips. Instead, he added, 'What do they think it is?'

Martin Foley, the man on the other side of the phone conversation and Warlow's ex-wife Jeez Denise's current partner, grunted noncommittally. 'Good question. They need to do some tests is all they've said so far.'

'Right.' The warm breeze swept over Warlow's face. Not quite summer in the far west of Wales, but today had been a rare, fine day with plenty of sun. The estuary was flat calm, the moored boats mirrored in the dark water.

'I thought you'd want to know.' Martin delivered this as an apology.

'I do.' Warlow hoped he'd camouflaged the lie. 'Did you contact Tom?'

'I did. He was going to text Alun.'

Good, Warlow thought. His sons, Tom and Alun, remained close and the younger son was good at keeping in touch with his older brother, even if they were separated by thousands of miles. He glanced at his watch. 4.10pm on Sunday in the UK, early hours of Monday in Western Australia where Alun lived.

'So they don't think it's appendicitis or anything like that?' Warlow probed a little more. He couldn't help himself. As a policeman it had become an ingrained response and Martin had never struck Warlow as someone detail orientated. Had he been he might have seen through Denise's more obvious attractions. Attractions which persisted, albeit in a more drawn, less luminous form, as a shell for the dark, self-destructive heart of the woman who had slowly and inexorably replaced the one that had once been Warlow's world. Easy-going Martin, a man who'd sold his business and lived comfortably on the proceeds, was a self-made man who deserved a medal. Not in his nature to be confrontational. Warlow had early on concluded that as a partner to a manipulative, high-functioning alcoholic like Denise, he'd been the wrong man in the wrong place at the wrong time when Warlow had stepped aside.

'Okay, well, give her my best,' Warlow said.

'She didn't ask me to ring, by the way.'

'Right.' No surprises there, since Warlow and Denise were no longer contractually obligated as someone put it, following their divorce. Not even on each other's Christmas card list, either. Unless you could send one written in poisoned ink. Still, there were the boys, the kids that had grown into men and remained the tacky glue that held Warlow and Denise in an uneasy alliance. Martin had been right to call.

'I wanted you to hear it from me and not from Tom,' Martin elaborated. But too quickly, revealing it as an afterthought.

'You're right, there. I appreciate it. Which hospital?'

'Prince Philip.'

'Keep me informed, then. I'll see if I can pop in.'

He wouldn't. Mainly because it might make Denise worse if she saw him. It would certainly put her blood pressure up. Both men knew that and neither of them needed to say it. Warlow killed the call.

Behind him, the road curved away past the boatyards towards a caravan park and a woodland walk. But his attention was drawn by some young men leaning against the side of a Toyota pickup with a custom zebra-stripe paint job. They were loud, and two of the three were drinking from cans of lager.

Some kids were playing nearby and when one of the men swore loudly, Warlow sent over a pointed look. One drinker who happened to also be smoking something hand-rolled caught the look and smirked.

Warlow sighed. Maybe they'd move on. He had no appetite for a showdown. Denise was a black hole when it came to mood. Even thinking of her took all the wind out of his sails.

He turned towards the tearooms as a couple of geese took off from the water with honking exuberance, leaving a line of ripples in their wake. His eyes focused on the little terrace. Every seat was occupied and he headed for the last line of picnic tables and the two women who sat there.

Warlow checked himself. Molly, at seventeen, occupied that grey area between childhood and adulthood. Still a schoolgirl, but also a young woman. That would be how she'd identify herself, he was sure, even if today she looked very much the child in a baseball cap and jeans. The woman sitting opposite her wore identical attire, and the similarity didn't end there if you added in the dark hair and olive skin they shared.

The Allanbys, mother and daughter, had walked with Warlow over the river stepping-stones at Cresswell Quay and out along the riverbank to Lawrenny on the Pembrokeshire coast after a lunch at the Allanby's house in Cold Blow. Both women had tall glasses half full of bubbly water in front of them, and both seemed preoccupied by something under the table.

As Warlow approached, the something, a black Labrador called Cadi, emerged, tongue lolling and tail wagging to observe her master's approach. Warlow calmed the dog by fondling her ears and took a seat on Jess Allanby's side of the table.

'Problems?' Jess asked.

'My ex-wife is in hospital.'

'Sorry to hear that.' Jess put down the water in a flash of pink. The colour her daughter had insisted on choosing as the plaster cast on her mother's fractured wrist.

'Her partner wanted me to know.' Warlow shrugged.

'Serious?' Jess asked. As a DI to Warlow's DCI, she too had the curiosity of a copper.

'Not sure yet.' He didn't add that Denise, with her astonishing capacity and appetite for alcohol, was at risk of many unpleasant illnesses. Instead, he picked up his glass of non-alcoholic beer and drained it. 'Shall we? It'll take a good hour to get back to the car.'

Molly got up, and Cadi followed her down across the terrace to the water's edge.

'Come on, girl, let's see if we can find a dead seagull.'

'Don't you dare,' Jess said.

Molly turned, her face registering appalled disbelief. 'Mum. As if.'

Jess shook her head but smiled at Warlow. 'Thanks for this. It's been delightful.'

Warlow looked around at the crowds. 'It's nowhere near as busy on weekdays. Sometimes I've walked this and seen not one person.'

'Amazing. It's good to get out.' She pushed a finger up under the cast and rubbed.

'How's the arm?'

'I'll be glad to get this damned plaster off. I keep knocking it against things. I swear we'll need to get a carpenter in to fix the kitchen table. Molly thinks I'm doing it deliberately.' Her phone chimed a notification, and she glanced at the screen. 'Hmm. From Catrin.'

Warlow waited. Sergeant Catrin Richards was a member of the team that Warlow headed for the Dyfed Powys Police Service. Jess's broken wrist had sprung from a murderer in their last case shoving her into a workshop full of spilled nitrogen. An episode Warlow still had nightmares about, though it hadn't seemed to dent Jess's enthusiasm for the job. Her enforced sick leave seemed to bother her more than the injury.

Jess read the text and frowned. 'She's had the heads up from Buchanan that West Mids are going to interview her tomorrow and she needs to make herself available.'

Warlow nodded. West Mids were in to investigate the involvement of a deceased colleague in organised crime. The whole of the team would need to be interviewed, Superintendent Buchanan included. Given Catrin's involvement with Sergeant Mel Lewis – the officer under investigation – stretched back a few years, it made sense that she be first. Still, it would not be something she'd relish.

'She worried about it?' Warlow asked.

'Enough to text me. But she'll be fine. You know Catrin.'

Warlow did. And he had no doubts Jess had every right to be confident.

Out of the corner of his eye, Warlow noted one man lolling against the Toyota push off and head diagonally across the parking area towards the corner of the tearoom terrace. He wore shorts and tennis shoes with no socks and his branded polo shirt looked a bit too small for him. Either that or his lager consumption had gone up a few gallons a week since he'd bought the top. The other two men grinned and shouted loud encouragement of the "Go on, mate. Get in there," variety.

'Looks like they're having a fine afternoon,' Jess said.

'Too much sun, I expect,' Warlow agreed, knowing full well that sun had bugger all to do with it, but that an excess of cold lager did.

Jess stood up. 'I need the loo.'

Warlow finished his drink. 'We'll wait for you near the notice board.'

Jess walked into the cafe. Warlow kept one eye on the man from the Toyota as he closed the gap between him and the girl and dog standing on the sandy bank. The DCI got up slowly and meandered through the seated tea drinkers on the terrace to stand in the shadows.

———

MOLLY HAD TAKEN Cadi away from the crowds about fifty yards from the tearooms to a spot where the dog was free to chase the birds and splash in the water. Toyota man stood on the edge of the bank, turning his head with the exaggerated bounce of someone under the influence of alcohol. Warlow didn't like any scenario where drink was involved. He'd seen far too much of it in his time, and now he despised it with a vengeance. Car crashes, domestic violence, murders; alcohol could be the fuel of mayhem. It didn't matter to him what anyone did in their own time, so long as they did it alone. And he was not some kind of teetotal zealot. But alcohol had no place anywhere near these tearooms on a Sunday afternoon.

Warlow took out his phone. He was not an iPhone whiz, but he knew how to use the camera. He pointed it now towards Toyota man who stepped off the concrete edge and strode unsteadily towards Molly and the dog.

'Hey luv, what's your name?' Toyota man asked. He looked to be at least ten, if not fifteen, years older than Molly. He had spent none of those years perfecting his conversational skills.

Molly ignored him.

'Oy, come on. What's your name? Not foreign are you? Speaka de English?' Toyota man grinned.

Molly glanced at him, frowned, and carried on playing with Cadi. Warlow sloped behind a family of four trying to skim stones over the water. He didn't think Molly had seen him. Toyota man decided on a different ploy. He whistled. Cadi, one of the friendliest animals Warlow had owned, looked momentarily confused.

Toyota man whistled again and called to the dog. 'Come on, here boy.'

Cadi bought in to this new game. Podgy Toyota man held his hand out, fist clenched as if holding something. The dog ran over. When she was within reach, Toyota man grabbed her collar roughly and picked up a handful of fur and flesh behind it.

Cadi yelped.

'Let go of my dog,' Molly said. She didn't shout, but the words were forceful enough for Warlow to hear.

Toyota man tilted his head but did not let go of the dog

whose tail had dropped low. 'I will if you tell me your name.'

Molly ignored him and walked towards man and dog. 'You're hurting her.'

Toyota man shrugged. Again the gesture looked slow and exaggerated. ''S only a fucking dog.'

Molly kept walking, eyes on the dog. 'It's okay, Cadi. I'm here.'

'Cadi, what sort of name is that?'

'The only one you're getting, mate.' Molly knelt and put her hand on Cadi's head.

Toyota man grinned. 'You've got a nice arse, did you know that?' It was then that he made the last of several mistakes that had begun with opening his eyes that morning and deciding to get out of bed. He reached out and grabbed Molly's arm with his free hand. Molly didn't recoil. Instead she leaned forward, pushing her arm towards Toyota man's body so that his wrist flexed and he had to let go. Cadi danced away. Toyota man let out an angry yelp as he stumbled backwards. 'You fuckin' bit—'

He got no further as an upward punch from Molly caught him between the legs. Not a forceful blow, but enough to clatter his meat and two veg against his perineum and trigger an involuntary wince from Warlow. Toyota man's hips swivelled back, and he doubled over, the only sound coming out of his mouth now was the stuttering, high-pitched squeak of a man in deep, visceral pain. He staggered back and fell to his knees on the floor before leaning forward and depositing the contents of his stomach in a spattering pancake on the little beach.

Molly put a lead on Cadi and walked past Warlow. As she did, she turned to him and smiled, showing no teeth.

Toyota man's two friends were hurrying over to help their poleaxed friend. Warlow, pretending to be a helpful bystander, joined them. Up close they were walking clichés.

Toyota man had tear drop tattoos on his neck, his drunk pal flaunted sleeves of red and blue ink. But Warlow spoke only to the designated driver holding a can of Coke.

'See that? She fucking hit him,' the driver said.

Toyota man's drunken friend joined the conversation as he leaned over the prostrate man. 'We'll sort her out, Deano, I'll fucking twat her.'

That was when Warlow took out his warrant card.

'No, you won't. You'll take Deano back to the car and get away from here as quickly and quietly as you can.'

'Who the fuck are you—' Deano's drunk friend began, but the driver, eyes on the card, put up a hand to stop him.

Warlow waved his phone. 'I have Deano here on video harassing that young woman and physically assaulting her. My guess is that if Deano went to court he'd know all the officers there from many a previous visit. Assault and sexual harassment of a defenceless young woman would mean prison.'

'She's hardly defenceless.' the driver glowered down at Deano, whose face was now almost matching that of the green verge a few feet away.

'That's not how the court would see it.' Warlow played them the video clip and saw the driver's face harden. When it had finished, Warlow asked, 'What's your name?'

'I don't have to tell you nothing.'

'True. But I can find that out from the plate of your safari vehicle in two minutes flat. I'm going to have a quiet word with the tearoom owner. If she ever sees you or that monstrosity of a truck here again, she's going to ring me, and several unhappy police officers are going to drive down here when they should be doing more important police work elsewhere. Who knows, they might decide to amuse themselves by playing the bongos on your heads. Now, I may be able to convince that young woman not to press charges, so when Deano can speak again, tell him he owes me one. But if I ever hear his name in connection with any violence, I will be down on him like a ton of pointy, shit-covered bricks. The extra-heavy engineered kind. I generally recommend a bag of ice on the crotch area for the next two hours. There'll be no charge for the medical advice.'

Both the sober driver and the second drunk man nodded. Warlow noted the latter looked far less glassy eyed than he had a few minutes before, and the sulk had long gone. The DCI turned and moved away quickly. A small crowd had gathered to watch the proceedings. What most of them had seen was a drunk man throwing up and being helped by his friends. Warlow saw no reason not to keep it that way.

When he got back to the cafe, Molly and Cadi were standing next to the notice board while the dog drank from a silver bowl of water kindly supplied by the cafe.

'You don't have to protect me, you know,' Molly said when Warlow joined her.

'Who said I was protecting you?' He added emphasis to the "you".

Molly held his gaze, spoiling for a fight, but then shook her head and grinned.

Warlow watched the three men hurry back to their vehicle. 'Who taught you that stuff? Mum or dad?'

'Mum.'

He nodded sagely. 'She's a good teacher. Remind me never to let her practise on me.'

Cadi, water dripping from her mouth, put a wet tongue on Warlow's hand. He fondled her ears. 'And you're a great guard dog.'

'That git hurt her,' Molly spat.

'She's forgotten about it already. I doubt whether Deano will though. Even when his voice comes back from being soprano'd.' Warlow took a fish-shaped treat no bigger than a five-pence piece from his pocket and gave it to the dog. Her eyes shone as she crunched it.

'What did you tell them?' Molly asked.

'To bugger off back to Mordor and never let me see them here again.'

Molly grinned her approval. 'Lord of the Rings reference. I like it.'

Jess appeared, waving her hands. 'Sorry, there was a queue. And they're out of paper towels.' Her brows knitted as she took in Molly's smile and Warlow's exaggerated air of innocence. 'Alright, what did I miss?'

'Someone threw up on the beach,' Molly explained.

'Is that all?' She looked at Warlow.

'More or less. I'll let Molly fill in the details.'

Molly sighed. 'Do I have to?'

'Mol?' Jess's question held a smidgen of warning in it.

Warlow took Cadi and set off with the Allanbys a few feet behind so that they couldn't see him grinning.

CHAPTER THREE

WARLOW FINISHED the return leg of the walk with the Allanbys and dropped them off at their rented house before heading back to his cottage in Nevern, overlooking a different estuary, but still on the Pembrokeshire coast. On the way, he stopped off at a Tesco service station that had just about everything in its large retail area, including, on weekdays, a hot food counter. Warlow often thought that if he asked for one, someone would nip out back and return with a kitchen sink. He bought milk and bread – wholemeal sourdough from a local bakery – and filled up the Jeep with fuel.

The newspapers on the stand were promising a heatwave. The woman behind the counter caught him glancing at the headlines and then out of the window at the grey clouds building in the west.

'I know,' she said. 'I'll believe it when I see it, too.'

At the cottage, Warlow fed Cadi and put the kettle on, letting the day's unresolved issues simmer in his brain. Front and centre was Denise. He chewed his lip. He could make the hospital this evening if he tried. But if she'd been throwing up for three days, perhaps now was not the time to pitch up with half a pound of grapes and a tube of Pringles. He knew, too, that he could talk himself out of it by thinking this way. And knowing Denise like he did, if he turned up, she'd undoubtedly think it was to gloat. He'd never do such a thing, but so poisoned had become her attitude towards him he would not put it past her.

He'd often thought about that. The poison. To begin with, there'd been rows, of course there had. She could be very difficult when she was drunk. Violent and vitriolic. Even when sober, the regret, recriminations and stygian moods were almost as bad. Eventually, Warlow realised that her addiction, psychologically at least, could only be interpreted as an illness over which she had little or no control. Towards the end, before he decided to leave for his own sanity's sake, he adopted a change of attitude. There was no way to stop her, she had too many secret ways and hiding places for that. Instead, he'd tried to be supportive, encouraging her to find her own answers and treatment. Bizarrely, without him to spar with and forced into looking at herself rather than inciting criticism, her attitude towards him hardened. She'd accused him of gaslighting her, amongst a slew of other things, until, eventually, Warlow had no option other than to leave.

And, of course, he knew he'd be criticised for taking a coward's way out. But sometimes, retreat ended up the only sensible move in a battle there was no way of winning.

Still, a vengeful Denise took every opportunity of slating him to anyone who would listen.

But Warlow had talked with Tom and Alun. Explained his position, and though his older son had reservations, they both saw the sense of it. The inevitability of it.

That did not make the decision any easier.

But he'd come to terms with it and, a little shamefully,

had breathed a sigh of relief when poor Martin took up the cudgel. He had warned him. One night he'd picked up the phone and done his best to explain without sounding as if he was some kind of jealous idiot trying to warn someone off. Yet Martin saw who Denise was and still chose to accept the challenge.

Mission bloody Impossible if ever there was one. But then Martin was no Tom Cruise.

Warlow had never known whether to feel sympathy or admiration.

He ought to speak to Tom about her admission, but the text he'd received that afternoon told him Tom was on a late shift and had not yet had any sensible news from the hospital where Denise had been admitted. One other advantage of being a doctor was that you got to talk medic to medic with those involved in care. Tom said he'd discuss it all with the consultant tomorrow.

Fair enough, thought Warlow.

He glanced at his watch. Still time to go to the hospital though.

Cadi appeared at the door, tail wagging in gratitude for the meal she'd been given. Warlow turned to the fridge. The walk had given him an appetite, and he found a pear and some cheese and crackers. Still six inches or so in the bottle of Appassimento he'd opened mid-week, too.

A meal fit for a king. Well, a DCI at least.

He'd quartered the pear and nibbled at some cheese when his phone rang.

Sion Buchanan's name appeared in the caller window. Warlow put the phone on speaker.

'Sion.'

'How's your Sunday been, Evan?'

'Great. Walked Lawrenny with our incapacitated DI and her daughter.'

'How is Jess?'

'Bored.'

'Alright for some.'

'Gives her a chance to work on what she's going to say to the West Mids team. I hear Catrin's up for a grilling tomorrow.'

The Buccaneer snorted. 'It won't be a grilling. Catrin's involvement, like Jess's, is background colour. They're really after the people Mel Lewis worked with over the last five years.'

'People like me, you mean?'

'Hardly, though they will want to talk to you. I'm talking about drug squad officers and vice. That's where the trouble usually is in this sort of thing.'

The Buccaneer was right. Evan pictured the big superintendent doing the polite thing and asking after his staff and decided to put him out of his misery. 'But you didn't ring to talk about the inquiry, I'm guessing.'

'No. It's not the only thing on the menu, as I've taken a call this evening from Selena Cook, the BOSU commander up north. They're very depleted of any senior detectives and a nasty one has surfaced.'

Warlow listened as the Buccaneer explained about the missing farmers and the finding of two sets of remains on a storage shed door. 'I said I'd send someone up there who knows the score. A safe pair of hands.'

'So why are you talking to me?'

The Buccaneer laughed. 'Nice try, Evan. I don't yet know how depleted they are, but I suggest you take Harries up with you and I'm sure I could spare Gil Jones. Once they've finished with Catrin I'll send her, too.'

'But won't West Mids want to talk to me and Rhys Harries?'

'They will. But they'll have to work around us. Crime doesn't stop for an inquiry.'

All thoughts of visiting Denise had now disappeared. 'How far north are we talking about?'

A valid question since Dyfed Powys had the largest land area to police in the whole of England and Wales.

'Short of the Arctic circle, but about as far as we stretch to. Know where Rhaeadr Falls is?'

'I can't say I do.'

'Okay. How about Oswestry?'

Warlow imagined a map in his head. 'That's in England.'

'It is, and where you're going is a stone's throw from the border. But also just a few miles from Gwynedd. Shoot an arrow west from where you'll be and you'll probably hit Snowdon.'

'Doesn't sound commutable.'

'It isn't. We'll sort out some accommodation for you. I've told them to expect you bright and early tomorrow at Newtown.'

Warlow glanced at Cadi wistfully. 'Have the bodies been taken for post-mortem?'

The Buccaneer let out an empty laugh. 'They don't do post-mortem on jam jars which is about as much of the remains they managed to scoop up.'

'So no bodies, then?'

'No bodies. Finding them will be your job.'

Warlow hung up and ate some cheese and a slice of pear. He put away the Appassimento without pouring any. Then he texted DC Rhys Harries:

We are off to the north. Bring snowshoes. I will pick you up at 7.30am

He waited.

Rhys texted back:

7.30 confirmed. I don't have any snowshoes, sir. Would wellies do?

Warlow smiled, enjoying the angst his frivolous

mention of snowshoes will have caused the young DC who had trouble reading Warlow's level of teasing, momentarily regretting it as childish, but then rolling into it because Rhys was an easy target. He texted back:

Wellies fine. Bring change of underwear too.

Warlow had a feeling this was going to be a rough one.

CHAPTER FOUR

RHYS HARRIES STOOD in the doorway of his parents' semi-detached in the village of Nantgrug as Warlow pulled up bright and early the next morning. The DC wore a shoulder bag and held a hold-all in one hand and a large sandwich cool bag in the other. He turned and shouted some goodbyes before closing the front door and hurrying down the front garden path to where Warlow waited.

'Stick the bags in the boot,' Warlow said through the open driver-side window. Rhys levered his long legs into the passenger seat a minute later, the sandwich bag held firmly in his hand.

'What's in there?' Warlow nodded at the bag.

'Snacks. It's a long journey. My dad said he takes two hours to Machynlleth and where we're going is a lot further north.'

'I don't think we'll need Huskies and a sled, Rhys.'

'No, sir, but snacks help the journey pass more quickly.'

There was no arguing with that because it smacked of maternal wisdom. And if one thing a long career in the police had taught Warlow, it was that you ignored such wisdom at your peril. Unless you wanted the smack to turn into a full-blown haymaker.

'Fair enough. The plan is to stop off at Newtown first and check in with their Incident Room. I think the crime scene is a good hour from there though, so you're right.'

Rhys held the sandwich bag on his knees while he buckled up.

Warlow narrowed his eyes. 'You will not do my kids' trick and eat those before we get to Llandovery, will you?'

Rhys tapped his flat stomach. 'Muesli and a bacon and egg sandwich already on board, sir. No. I'll be fine for a couple of hours. But I don't want to get crumbs in your car. I'll wait until we stop.'

'So long as they're not cheese and onion crumbs, feel free to graze at any time.'

A tiny flicker of doubt appeared and then disappeared on Rhys's face. Like a mouse peeping out from its hole to see a big black cat waiting for it. 'Not cheese and onion…'

'But?' Warlow side-eyed him a glance.

'I have marmite and I know some people don't like marmite. But my mother hedged her bets and went variety pack.'

Warlow did a double take. 'Hang on, your mother hasn't made sandwiches for me, has she?'

'Of course she has. Her usual mix. Egg and cress, ham and tomato… and marmite. I like marmite. There's tea in a flask, too, but that's in my bag.'

Warlow let out a wheezy laugh. 'Christ, we're not going on a bloody safari, Rhys.'

'You try telling her that.' Rhys put the bag in the well between his big feet and folded his arms as Warlow pulled away from the kerb.

In the bay window of the property a curtain twitched to reveal a waving hand. Mrs Harries's face appeared, baring a smile more dangerous than a charging rhino. A smile that said look after my boy, DCI Warlow, or else. Rhys ignored it with a little shake of his head. Warlow raised his in acknowledgement and stifled a grin. 'Any thoughts on getting your own place, Rhys?' Warlow asked.

Rhys sighed. 'I'm saving for a deposit, just like everyone else. And I offered to pay rent but my parents won't hear of it. Now I put some of what I earn into a holiday fund for them. It's a good deal. Accommodation and meals for a river cruise up the Danube.'

Warlow tilted his head appreciatively.

'It's the sort of thing they wouldn't do themselves because they think it's too expensive,' Rhys explained. 'But they went on one last year and loved it. They don't know it yet, but they're cruising the Elbe next.'

Warlow's European river geography had never been brilliant, and he half shut one eye in concentration. Rhys put him out of his misery.

'Berlin, Meissen, Dresden all the way to Prague. They'll love it.'

'Nice,' Warlow said with a nod.

The A40 took them along the valley within sight of the River Towy, past low-lying fields and castles on hills. Warlow loved this road and every single person he'd spoken to who travelled it for the first time was astonished by the quiet beauty of the landscape and the tantalising views of the Black Mountains to the east. They travelled in silence for a while, taking in the early morning sun reflecting off the snaking river on their right, Warlow allowing his thoughts to meander along with the road. Rhys, too, kept his eyes on the passing fields, but Warlow couldn't help noticing the little grin that never strayed too far from the younger man's lips. He was like a kid on a Sunday school outing.

'How's PC Mellings?' Warlow threw out the question as a teaser.

Rhys's nostrils flared, and his grin widened. 'Gina's fine, thank you, sir. She'll be chuffed to know you were asking about her.'

Mellings had worked a couple of cases with Warlow as a Family Liaison Officer. She was competent, oozing empathy and warmth. When he thought of her, he saw sunshine and smiles in his head. 'So this deposit you're saving for, is it a joint thing?'

A couple of spots appeared on Rhys's cheeks. 'Ah, well, that's… a possibility.'

Warlow stirred the pot. 'Really? Catrin said you'd been seeing each other.'

Panic widened the DC's eyes. 'I haven't told my mother yet, though. About the deposit, I mean. I'd be grateful if you kept that information to yourself, for now, sir.'

'What, you mean I can't put it in my weekly column for the Western Telegraph?'

Rhys snorted. 'Not yet.'

The road bypassed Llandeilo where Warlow had once rented a property. Shame, he'd have enjoyed driving through its narrow main street to see what new cafes and galleries had sprung up. Beyond the town, the road opened up on long straight stretches much beloved by leather-clad motorcyclists on a Sunday morning, some of whose riders came all the way from the Midlands. An opportunity to open up their throttles and wake late risers with their whining engines. Unfortunately, not all of them made it home as more than one had met his or her end in this sleepy corner of east Carmarthenshire at a hundred plus miles an hour.

Less chance of that on a weekday though, and Warlow kept the car at a steady sixty while they made good time to Llangammarch. From there, as expected, the journey snagged on the winding road north to Llandrindod as tractors, feed lorries, and a variety of slower vehicles frustrated progress. Warlow remained sanguine, and Rhys provided enough conversation for the time to pass quickly. The boy was an open book when it came to his hopes and expectations, constantly probing Warlow for any anecdotes of his long police career. The DCI recounted one or two, appropriately edited, much to Rhys's obvious enjoyment.

They stopped in Llandrindod for some tea and a sandwich. And though it was no picnic, Warlow had to admit that Mrs Harries's ham and tomato between slices of nutty seeded bread and salted Welsh butter made it almost feel like one. After one bite, he understood why Rhys seemed in no hurry to move out without good reason. But then Gina Mellings had a lot more to offer than marmite sandwiches.

––––––––

NEWTOWN POLICE STATION looked more like an airport hotel than Dyfed Powys Police's mid Wales enclave. Big bare lawns, pale brick walls and a steel and glass portico added to the impression that Warlow had of this being somewhere they should book in for a conference rather than turn up for work.

He and Rhys followed directions and walked into an almost empty and much smaller Incident Room than they were used to. Warlow couldn't help but feel a pang of disquiet. No buzz of voices. No clack of keyboards. In fact, the only noise that greeted them was a voice.

'Hiya. You're not from IT by any chance?'

Warlow turned to see a head pop up from behind a monitor and glare hopefully at Rhys. The face it belonged to was about the roundest Warlow had ever seen. When Rhys did not respond, a pair of plucked and arched eyebrows slowly shifted towards Warlow, the face registering a kind of dawning horror.

'Don't look at me,' Warlow said. 'I'm about as IT savvy

as a troglodyte, though Rhys would fit the bill, knowing how much time he spends on that Nintendo Swatch—'

'It's Nintendo Switch, sir.'

Warlow gave the DC his 'whatever' look.

The woman with the round face blinked several times. 'Oh. Then you must be DCI Warlow.'

A chair scraped, and the woman stood up behind her desk. She was about as tall as Catrin Richards, but there the similarity ended. DS Richards looked and behaved like an athletic cat, whereas this officer... didn't. Warlow struggled for the right words because the ones that popped into his head wouldn't do in this day and age. Chunky perhaps, heavy-set, as the Americans favoured, troubled by a sub-optimal BMI, as his doctor son Tom sometimes preferred. If she'd done a recent bleep test, the medical officer's stopwatch must have broken. Still, none of that mattered. Not really.

'Detective Constable Lowri Fellows, sir.' She had a great smile on a pleasant face framed in short red hair that looked carefully gale-blown. Warlow stepped forward and shook her hand.

'And the IT guy here is DC Rhys Harries.' Warlow nodded towards the DC.

Rhys crossed the space between them in two long strides. 'How's it going?'

Warlow glanced around, frowning. 'Where is everyone?'

Lowri took her hands away from her thighs and let them fall again with a slapping noise. 'This is it, sir. For now. DI Massey went off on stress two days ago and DS George is down with the flu as of yesterday.'

'Christ, it's a bloody plague ship. Let's hope it's not catching.' Warlow whipped around. He liked to have a Gallery for photos and a Job Centre for actions and pinned notices. Here all he saw at the end of the room was a single whiteboard with 'Expect DCI Warlow' written in a wonky hand with three exclamation marks attached.

'So you're the team?' Warlow turned back to Lowri.

She grimaced. 'Sort of, sir. We have other people in an adjacent room, indexers and the like.'

Warlow growled. 'When were the remains found?'

'Yesterday morning, sir.' Lowri tried to swallow, but it got stuck somewhere around her Adam's apple and she had to have three goes before it passed through her gullet.

No wonder Buchanan had wanted him to help out. Though this was hardly helping. This was starting from sodding scratch. Warlow sighed.

'Sorry, sir,' Lowri whispered. 'I'm normally in uniform but they've asked me to help under the uh... circumstances.'

Tricky word, circumstances, thought Warlow. Innocent enough when taken alone, but sticky and difficult to shift when you got trapped underneath it. Warlow angled his head towards the young officer. 'What were you doing when we came in?'

'Writing up my daily records, sir, adding to the case notes where I could.'

Warlow nodded. He tried to guess if she was a Welsh speaker. Both he and Rhys were, and sometimes you could tell from the way people intoned vowels and the odd word. But they were a long way north here and there'd be no trace of a West Wales accent. 'And you did that with no input from an SIO?'

Lowri grimaced and gave a brief nod.

'Good. You seem to know what you're doing. Thank Christ someone up here does. So you'll be with us for the duration.' Warlow leaned forward and grabbed a notepad from one of the many empty desks. He sat in a chair, pondered for a moment and then scribbled something down. He ripped the sheet off and handed it to Lowri.

'Find someone in CID. Tell them I'm asking for these and tell them if there's a problem to ring the mobile number on the bottom. That's DS Richards in Carmarthen. She'll be able to help them out.' A ghost of a smile formed on his lips when he imagined the response Catrin Richards would give when someone rang her to outline the lack of facilities. Her polite put downs were sharper than a Samurai's sword, and equally as cutting. Then Warlow cleared his throat. 'And get back here as soon as you can.'

'Nothing I can do, sir?' Rhys asked.

'Sniff around, find out where the nearest facilities are.'

'You need the toilet, too, sir?'

Warlow sent him a disparaging glare. 'I'm not a three-year-old, Rhys. I meant tea-making facilities. Has DS Jones not taught you anything? Simple physics. You need to fill a vessel before you can empty it.'

'I can show you. It's on the way,' Lowri said with half a smile. 'Where the kettle is and the men's.'

'Great.' Rhys blew out air.

'That's what I like to see,' Warlow grinned. 'Multi-tasking. And hurry up the both of you. I want to get up to the crime scene as soon as possible.'

CHAPTER FIVE

BECAUSE THE REMAINS were plastered over the feed-storage-shed door, the crime scene bods had constructed their evidence protection tent as an awning, using the wooden structure's roof and side walls for support. Outside of the tent, techs in light-blue paper suits knelt or strode around an area that now extended perhaps forty yards around the shed.

With no room for vehicles at the bottom of the rutted track, Warlow parked the Jeep on the verge near an access gate behind a slew of police and crime scene vehicles. He signed the sheet the crime scene duty officer held out to him and stood at the open gate. Stood on almost the identical spot where Hana Prosser had stood to phone in her grisly findings the previous morning. He took in the same view and inhaled the same air and noted how isolated a position this was.

No other habitation in sight except for a line of distant houses. Very convenient for the killers.

Early spring had not yet shaken off the vestiges of winter up here and a cold North-westerly whistled down from the hills, searching for and finding every gap in

Warlow's clothing. He pulled his coat around him and zipped up before turning to Lowri, who'd wisely come in what looked like a wearable duvet, and glancing back at where they'd come from and then forward to where the lane created a hill ahead. 'Where does this road lead to?'

Lowri stepped forward. 'Nowhere, sir. There's a chapel half way along but it's mainly a link between the B roads north and south. No one lives up here and other than the three farms there are no houses.'

'What about the officer who made the finding?'

'PCSO Hana Prosser, sir.'

'Where is she?'

'She's out with the Rural Crime Team but I did message her to say you were here. She's on her way.'

Warlow nodded, impressed. She'd done that without his asking, too. Things were looking up. 'Good.'

Lowri's mouth split into a momentary smile before her expression defaulted to rabbit in the headlights terror.

'Are you okay, Officer Fellows?'

'Yes, sir.'

'Because you don't look okay.'

'I am, sir, honestly, it's only… um, I'm a bit nervous. I've never been to an actual murder before, sir.'

'Hmm,' Warlow grunted. 'They're overrated.' He turned and walked down the rutted track, careful to avoid the puddles, and stuck to the ridges sculpted by tractor tyres. Two days of dry weather and the wind had dried off the surface. But one wrong step would earn you a muddy shoe with a matching sock and trouser hem to follow.

They'd set up a second tent as a mobile Incident Room in a field next to the feed shed. Some techs glanced his way as he approached and Warlow tried to make out someone he knew. Always a lottery when the technicians were tyveked up to the eyeballs like this, with only a few inches of flesh showing between mask and the cinched tight hoods on their crime scene onesies. He caught the eye of a man whose dark and bushy eyebrows marked him out.

'Ah, Dominic, who's running the scene?'

'Kapil. He's around here somewhere.'

'Povey couldn't get a visa for up here?' Warlow retorted.

The CSI shook his head. Alison Povey normally ran Dyfed Powys's serious crime scenes and nine times out of ten, whenever Warlow got called to one, she'd already be there.

Dominic's eyes crinkled. 'Alison's still tied up with the Llanelli drowning.'

Warlow nodded. A car had been driven into a reservoir with three bodies inside at Swiss Valley. It would take days to unravel and they'd only winched out the vehicle yesterday. Povey'd be up to her eyeballs in that.

The tent flap opened, and another Tyvek clad figure walked in. Kapil Rani stood taller than Warlow, but nowhere near as tall as Rhys Harries. However, he was thinner than both officers. He pulled his mask down and peeled off his hood to reveal a boyish face and a head that had long since lost the battle with baldness such that Kapil, still only slightly north of thirty, had opted to go the whole hog and shave off the residue in a full Vin Diesel. When he'd heard the Crime Scene Investigator described this way, Warlow had wanted to add Yul Brynner to the descriptive mix, but realised he'd be showing his age.

'DCI Warlow.' Kapil nodded acknowledgement, his words soft spoken as always. 'Good journey up?'

'Long journey up.'

'To the far-flung corner of the empire, indeed.' Kapil showed two lines of straight teeth.

As one of Povey's protégés Warlow had no worries about how thorough he'd be. The DCI got down to business. 'What do we know?'

They followed Kapil out along a marked path around the rear of the shed. 'The Randals' Land Rover was parked here, doors open. Nothing significant inside. We've taken it away for a full working over.'

Kapil led them to the front of the shed, a thin tape forming the cordon they could not cross, until they were in view of the doors. Numbered tags lay scattered all over the ground and on the bleached wood. Two blackening smudges drew the eye. Rorschach splatter plates that looked bad enough at first glance but which had a much deeper, more sinister meaning than their abstract form suggested.

'Shotgun?' Warlow asked, his voice a low growl.

'36 gram, number 1 shot.' Kapil said.

'What does that actually mean?' Rhys piped up from behind Warlow.

Kapil reached into a pocket and took out a clear evidence bag. Inside, a single small dark sphere sat at the bottom. He held it up for all to see. 'Grams refers to the weight of shot, obviously. The numbering system refers to the diameter of the shot. It's an inverse system, smaller the number, the bigger the diameter. Number one shot means a diameter of 0.16 inches. Anything bigger and a different system is used. It then goes to BB.'

Rhys frowned.

Kapil grinned, anticipating the question. 'No point asking because I don't understand why, either. There's probably some deep and dark historical reason.' He shook the evidence bag for emphasis. 'But these are big. For example, someone hunting small birds like pigeons would use a number 8 shot which has a diameter 0.08 inches.'

'What are you saying?' Warlow picked up on the fact that Kapil's point was important.

'It means that whoever had this shot with them knew they'd do real damage at close range. I've spoken to some hunters, and they said they used this for killing bigger game, like hares or foxes.'

'Oh my God.' Lowri's exclamation dripped with disgust.

'So, we are to assume that these were lethal?' Warlow asked.

'Difficult to be sure, but we also found traces of brain and skull on the right. I would assume extensive damage in that case.' He pointed to the floor. 'There's evidence that the bodies were dragged about ten yards and then removed. The blood trail stops there.' He pointed to a clear area to the left of the shed. 'Probably loaded onto a vehicle.'

'Treads?'

'There have been tractors down here and other vehicles.' He pointed back up towards the track. 'Well worn. We're getting input on tractor tyres. But there are several.'

'Shoe prints?'

'Again, many. But the ground has been dry down here for a couple of days.'

Warlow's eyes flicked across the killing ground, to the fields beyond and back up the lane. Kapil's voice brought him back to the doors.

'What we know for certain from DNA matching is that the blood spatter on the left comes from Aeron Randal, and that on the right including the brain matter, belongs to Joseph Randal, Aeron's son.'

'I thought DNA analysis took days?' Lowri's brows, carefully shaped as they were, crumpled into a frown.

Kapil nodded. 'You're right. But we've had some help from the boys in Shrewsbury. What you might not be aware of is that West Mercia has large ongoing investigations into stock theft. Rustling. They were good enough to offer us the use of their rapid DNA service. Ninety minutes as opposed to seventy-two hours.' Kapil smiled, his face registering a kind of longing. 'Amazing machines. Cartridge based. You can even bring them to crime scenes. Load the sample and away it goes. We're double checking of course, but as it stands, you're looking at the Randals.'

Warlow exhaled. 'So someone shoots them and removes the injured men... or bodies.'

Kapil nodded.

'When will your preliminary report be ready?'

'This afternoon.'

'Great.'

Movement at the gate near the top of the track drew their attention. A uniformed officer stood signing the clip-board sheet.

Lowri looked up. 'That's Hana Prosser, sir.'

'Excellent. Let's see what she has to say.'

———

QUITE A LOT, as it turned out. Lowri made the introductions as Warlow intercepted Hana Prosser at the bottom of the track. In contrast to Lowri Fellow's round-ness, Hana Prosser, even under the nullifying effect of the uniform and all its accoutrements, looked fit. As in athletic and slim as per Warlow's definition. Not Rhys's which, though the same word, had a whole different connotation when he used it. Hana exuded an air of capability and professionalism and, Warlow was glad to see, though clearly affected by the case, did not seem at all overwhelmed.

'I want you to walk us through what happened yesterday morning.' Warlow said.

And, in a refreshing matter-of-fact way, Hana did exactly that, beginning with the early morning call from her friend about hearing gunshots in the early hours, to arriving at the gate and noticing it open and seeing the

Randals' vehicle parked next to the feed shed. She led them through what she found and exactly what she did, waiting around until support units arrived and then CID.

'Who subsequently buggered off on the sick,' Warlow pointed out.

'Is it them? The Randals?' Hana's blurted question seemed out of character.

Warlow didn't need to reveal anything to this officer, but she'd acted calmly under difficult circumstances, removing herself from the scene with minimal contamination and securing it until the cavalry arrived. She deserved to be told.

'The crime scene techs say it is them. We don't know if they're dead yet of course, but it's the Randals' blood alright.'

Hana put her hand up to her face and looked away. Warlow wondered if she'd need to sit down, but she recovered quickly. 'It had to be, with their car there and everything. And Joseph's cap on the seat.' She squeezed her eyes shut.

'You know them?'

The PCSO nodded with quick repetitive movements. She pointed to the fields. 'Beyond these three acres is my dad's property. The Randals are my neighbours. Or were when I was growing up. My dad still farms here. I live in the area.'

Warlow filed that away. Someone with real local knowledge.

'Have you any idea why this might have happened? Anything you can tell us about the Randals?'

Hana had blonde hair tied back in a ponytail, cheeks ruddy from a life lived out here in the open. A faint sprinkling of freckles dusted her nose. She was young, mid-twenties maybe, but at home here whereas Warlow looked around him at the fencing and the sheep and the vast spaces and knew he wasn't.

'I've been racking my brains all night. They were hard working. Joe was younger than me and he didn't go away to uni. He went to the college... the local agricultural college... but finished there last year and he's been working with his dad since then.'

Rhys nodded. 'So what do you think happened, Hana?'

She shook her head slowly. Though the question could not have been a surprise to her, it seemed she still had no answers. 'Perhaps they disturbed someone. Rustling is a big problem around here.'

'You say your friend heard gunshots after midnight. How many?'

'Two.'

Warlow turned to look at where markers had been set down to show where the Randals' car had been parked. 'You found the Land Rover's door open?'

'I did. That's why I wondered if they'd disturbed some-one. They got out quickly and forgot or didn't have time to close the door.'

Warlow ran it through his head. 'Randal's wife reported them missing. It's dark at around 8pm. Why would they be out after dark?'

'Looking for stray dogs. Patrolling—'

'Patrolling?'

'Yes. Looking for rustlers. My dad does it too. Park up somewhere with a good view and look for lights from a vehicle. These thieves turn up with big lorries.'

An image of the big stock transporter lorries they'd had to follow on the journey came to Warlow. Plenty large enough to carry off two bodies in. He took out two cards and gave them both to Hana. 'My number's on there. Write yours on the back of the second one. I know we're going to need to talk to you again, but this is very helpful. You did well under difficult circumstances.'

The PCSO's smile was thin-lipped. But the DCI's words were genuine. Hana Prosser was exactly the sort of capable officer they needed on this case.

He nudged Rhys's arm. 'Tell Kapil I'll talk to him once I get his report.'

Rhys trotted off, and the other officers walked back up the track towards the cars.

'You're with the Rural Crime Unit?' Warlow asked Hana, as they negotiated the track.

'Yes.'

'Enjoying it?'

'Very much, sir. It's good to still be a part of the community.'

'Has word got out about all this yet?'

Hana shook her head.

It would soon enough, thought Warlow.

He waited at the gate until Hana drove off and looked back to see Rhys trotting up to join him. While they waited, Lowri asked, 'Where would you like to go now, sir? Back to Newtown?'

He thought about the question. He'd need to set up a proper base of operations. Get the required actions in motion. But they were up here now, where the crime had taken place. Whatever had triggered this sordid episode permeated the air around him. It made little sense not to use the opportunity to do the hard stuff.

'No. Not yet. I think we ought to pay a visit to the Randals' farm.'

CHAPTER SIX

THE RANDAL FARM was called Wern Ddu, translated as the black bog. But Warlow had learned not to read too much into a name. It could be too easy to romanticise these things into something they were not and never had been. The countryside quite enjoyed taking a pot shot at expectations.

Take cows, for example, innocent grass-chewing milk machines, mostly. Yet walk through a field where there were calves at dusk and old Daisy could transform into 1500 lbs of trampling, crushing death. People died in the countryside from being scratched by thorns laden with tetanus for crying out loud, or woke up with a blood-sucking tick stuck on their backsides exchanging a little speck of their donor's Type 'O' for the parasitic arachnid's Lyme disease.

Bargain.

No, best not to take anything for granted out here, thought Warlow.

They'd driven a couple of miles north before the sprawling farm appeared on the hillside and any poetic resonance melted away like so much mist. If there was a black bog somewhere on the property, no sign of it existed on the drive in. Warlow knew little about farming and the bewildering array of big dark buildings scattered over the site were a mystery to him. What the hell could they contain?

A walled-off yard led to a whitewashed farmhouse; an upright rectangle with a couple of stone barns attached. They parked up next to a couple of cars. Behind, an open shed contained several mud-spattered tractors and other farm equipment, though the parking area and the hardstanding in front of the house were clean.

Two slinking farm dogs ran out from one barn as soon as they arrived, barking and circling the vehicle. Lowri eyed them warily.

'Do you think it's safe?'

'You're not wearing a woollen jumper, are you?' Warlow grunted.

'No, sir.'

'Then as long as you don't say, baa, you'll be fine.'

Once the officers exited Warlow's Jeep, the dogs stayed back, moving back and forth, heads low, watching.

A small garden in front of the house itself contained a few plastic ride-on toys and a net-protected trampoline.

Warlow sent Lowri a glance.

'The Randals have a grown-up daughter, sir. She has two small children. They don't live here.'

They took the concrete path leading to a black, glossy front door. No one needed to knock as the door opened when Warlow got to within a few yards. A woman in her fifties dressed in a sweatshirt and jeans emerged, greying hair hanging uncombed around her drawn face. Judging by the red rims around her eyes and the tendrils of veins standing out on her scleras, Mari Randal had slept little, if at all.

'Any news?' Her words trembled with emotion, and she shivered in the doorway.

Warlow knew that reaction. Fear of the unknown fighting a mental battle with the fear of knowing.

He turned to Lowri and muttered, 'Is there a FLO here?'

'No, sir. Not yet.' Her eyes darted from the DCI to the woman and back.

Not good. He realised he had no idea how much this woman knew, but she looked on the verge of collapse. Rhys took the initiative and stepped forward, warrant card in his hand.

'Mrs Randal, I'm Detective Constable Rhys Harries, and these are DCI Warlow and PC Lowri Fellows. Why don't we go inside?'

Mrs Randal's voice rose in pitch. 'Have you found them?'

'No,' Rhys said, his eyes never leaving her face. 'But we'd like to ask you some questions and tell you what we can.'

She half fell against the doorframe. Rhys took another step forward and grabbed her. 'Come on, let's get you a chair.'

Not the introduction Warlow had wanted or expected. Christ, what the hell had he walked into here? Five minutes later he sat on a high-backed chair with a cushion tied to the seat in a kitchen that was the genuine farmhouse article containing a black range with a stove pipe running up through the ceiling, an enormous oak table and six chairs. Lowri took charge of tea-making while Mrs Randal sat ashen-faced, her eyes flicking from face to face, fingers knotted. She didn't look quite there, as if the mundane activities taking place around her were a dream.

Warlow sipped his tea. Good and strong.

'Thanks for speaking with us,' he said. 'Can I call you Mari?'

Mari Randal frowned. 'Why are you here? Why aren't you out looking for Aeron and Joseph?'

Fair question. 'We have lots of people doing that, Mari. But part of that is us trying to understand what took place the night Aeron and Joe went missing.'

'You should be out—'

Lowri put a hand on the woman's shoulder and placed a mug of tea in front of her. It might have been a reflex response, but immediately Mari folded her palms around the mug and lifted it to her lips. It seemed to help.

Always did.

'They wanted to check the stock. You know about the rustlers?' She blinked up at Warlow.

'A bit. I heard there'd been a spate of thefts.'

Mari nodded. 'Aeron was anxious. We had lambs. We had a good year. The thieves like lambs.'

'What made them go out that night?' Warlow looked for a coaster to put his mug on. Mari saw the gesture and pushed one towards him.

'Someone had seen lights on the Chapel Road. We have a network. Anyone sees anything suspicious they tell the others.'

'Others?'

Mari squeezed her fingers until the tips were white. 'The three farms. Ours, Prosser at Caemawr, and the Gregorys at Deri Isaf. We've all had stock taken. Now, if someone sees anything, we tell the others.'

In his peripheral vision, Warlow saw Rhys take out his notebook and start scribbling.

'So, someone saw something that night and alerted Aeron?' He reiterated the point for clarification.

Mari nodded.

'Can you remember who?'

'No. Aeron might have had a text on his mobile. I can't remember. At five past ten he told me he was going out to drive up to the Chapel Road to check things out. They'll be up there somewhere.'

Bits of them still are, Warlow mused.

He took a sip and set his tea down on the coaster. This was the part he hated, but there could be no shying away from it. 'Mari, we haven't found Aeron or Joseph yet and we have lots of men still searching. But we have found something.'

Mari's eyes widened.

'At the feed shed off the Chapel Road we found evidence of violence. Blood and some other tissue.'

'Tissue?' She uttered the word as if she'd never heard it before.

'You'll remember that some officers came here to remove items belonging to Aeron and Joseph,' Warlow persisted. It was important she understood.

She nodded. 'A comb and a hairbrush.'

'That was for us to use in DNA matching. The blood and other tissue found at the feed shed match the DNA of Aeron and Joseph.'

'What does that mean?' Mari's mouth quavered.

'It means there is good reason to believe a violent act took place and that Aeron and Joseph were the victims. It does not mean that they are dead, but it means you should prepare yourself for the worst.' Blunt words. Horrible words. But Warlow saw no point in pulling his punches here. Not when brain matter stuck to a wall was involved.

'The worst? But… how can you say that? They're still missing, aren't they?' Denial came quickly, as Warlow suspected it would.

'No. And I'd be delighted if I was wrong. I'd give anything to be wrong. But as of this moment, I need you to think about anyone who might want to harm Aeron and Joseph. Is there anything or anyone that comes to mind?'

'Harm? Why would anyone want to harm us?'

She used the word 'us'. A tight family then. But there were questions that needed to be asked.

'Does Aeron own a shotgun?'

Mari's eyes were already glassy on hearing Warlow's words about harm. At the mention of the gun, her jaw seemed to retract with horror.

'Yes,' she croaked.

'Did he take it with him the night he and Joseph went out?'

'No.' Her face tensed at the implication.

'Can we see it?'

Mari nodded and stood up. 'He keeps it locked up in the parlour.'

'And the key?'

'In the drawer.'

Warlow's eyes flitted across to his DC, who picked up on it immediately. 'Can we see?' Rhys asked with a sympathetic half-smile.

Mari stood still, as if she didn't want to go any further with this. Warlow waited and nodded at Rhys. The young DC stood up, the movement galvanising Mari out of her paralysis. Warlow waited while they left the room. He turned to Lowri, who sat next to him and whispered urgently.

'We need a FLO out here. I don't want this poor woman alone.'

Lowri nodded but didn't move. Warlow wondered if she thought agreeing with him might be enough. But she came through.

'Should I get on to that now, sir?'

'Good idea.'

Lowri got up and took herself and her phone outside.

Warlow looked around the kitchen. Plates were stacked on a dresser above some framed photographs of a young man at a Farmer's Union rally dressed as a chicken with a number on his chest. He stood up and walked across for a closer inspection. A fun run, Warlow guessed. Next to that, there were other photos of a girl that had become a woman with a partner and two younger children. On the far right, an older image of a couple on their wedding day, the era betrayed by fashion and the grainy quality of the image.

He swung his attention back to a noise in the corridor and the door through which Rhys and Mari re-entered. Rhys nodded. 'It's there, sir. I haven't touched it and neither has Mrs Randal.'

It would be taken away and examined by the forensic team. Warlow doubted they'd find anything. But leaving it here would not be a good idea.

'That your daughter?' Warlow pointed at the photographs on the dresser.

'Almeira, yes.'

'Two grandchildren?'

Mari nodded.

'You've been very helpful. I'm sure we'll have more questions, but we'll get an officer to come and be with you until we find more answers. Would that be okay?'

Mari shook her head. 'I don't need company.'

'It's our policy in cases like this. The officer will keep you informed and help with anything you might need,' Warlow said, shaking his head.

As if on cue Lowri came back in, her expression apologetic. 'They can't get a FLO until five, sir.'

Warlow glanced at his watch. Too long. 'Is there anyone we can call for you, Mari? Your daughter perhaps?'

'She's taken Berwyn, that's my grandson, to the doctor. He's come down with an eye infection.'

'Is there no one else that can be here?' Warlow persisted. He did not want to leave this woman alone now. Certainly not with a shotgun in the house.

Lowri consulted her phone. Warlow was about to get annoyed when the PC looked up. 'What about your brother-in-law, Padrig? He rang this morning to ask about his brother. He was keen for you to know he'd called. He seemed—'

'Padrig,' Mari cut across her, uttering his name almost wistfully. 'Aeron hasn't spoken to him since their father died.'

Warlow's police instincts twanged like a plucked string. 'And why is that, Mari?'

Her shoulders sagged. 'There's some land over towards Mochteg. A patch of grazing that Padrig claims his father had always promised him. But there was nothing in the will. Padrig started accusing Aeron of changing the old man's mind and it turned nasty as these things do. Padrig felt cheated. I wanted Aeron to give him the land, but he's stubborn.'

Warlow leaned in. 'When you say things turned nasty, what exactly do you mean?'

Mari looked appalled. 'Nothing physical,' she blurted. 'Rough words is all. Bad words. Since then they've kept apart.' She glared at the DCI, the innuendo about her brother-in-law the final straw. 'You will tell me the truth, won't you?'

'I have, Mrs Randal. I've told you the truth.'

'You think they're dead, don't you?'

He held her gaze. Felt it burn into him. 'It's something we must consider. The violence I talked about earlier involved a gun.'

Mari's face crumpled and her head dropped to her chest like a demolished chimney stack. Then the tears came. She exhaled and then inhaled like she was drowning.

Rhys, still standing, pulled up a chair and put an arm around her shoulders. Once again, Warlow was impressed with the young detective's good nature and instincts.

'We will find them, Mrs Randal. I promise you that,' Warlow said.

But he could not be sure that Mari Randal heard him over the noise of her sobbing. Or whether she'd tuned in to the fact that Warlow had not promised he'd find them alive.

CHAPTER SEVEN

IN THE END, Warlow did the only sensible thing he could. He left Lowri with Mari Randal to await the FLO. He briefed the PC, ensuring she knew to keep a close eye on the woman and the gun. Rhys had already contacted Kapil to send a team to retrieve the firearm and carry out necessary testing.

As they drove away from Wern Ddu, Rhys opened the cool bag and took out another marmite sandwich.

Warlow's face registered incredulity. 'Did that bloody thing belong to Mary Poppins once?'

Rhys, sandwich six inches from his mouth, looked defensive. 'My mother likes to make sure she's made enough.'

Warlow scowled and navigated the narrow lane. 'Any ham and tomato left?'

Rhys peered into the bag. 'Two, sir.'

'Right, let's have one.'

The food helped settle Warlow's misgivings. Mari Randal seemed convinced that her husband and son had run into thieves. But there were other things she'd let slip that needed looking at, too.

'Thoughts?' Warlow threw out the question between mouthfuls.

Rhys pondered for a moment before answering. 'I doubt Mrs Randal wants to believe the worst, sir.'

'No. Who would? But did you learn anything else from our chat?'

'That we ought to look into this rustling business?'

Warlow nodded. 'And how do we do that? What's your plan of action?'

Rhys chewed slowly. 'Hana Prosser works with the Rural Crime Unit. She might be the best source.'

'Call her and find out where they're working. Anything else?'

Rhys chewed some more, letting the yeast extract fuel his thinking. 'Book into the hotel. We need to inform them if we're eating in the restaurant tonight since we missed lunch.'

Warlow shook his head, glancing at the sandwich in the DC's hand. 'I can see you're near starvation point, but try not thinking about your bloody stomach for five minutes.'

Rhys frowned and put the hand holding the sandwich on his lap. 'The brother? We ought to talk to him, too.'

'Exactly. We need an address. So give Lowri a ring and tell her to get on with that.'

Warlow drove on. Next to him, Rhys opened a packet of crisps and stuffed a handful into his mouth. They reached the Chapel Road but instead of turning back towards the crime scene, Warlow turned the other way. Half a mile further on, trees appeared on their left and after a slight bend, Warlow turned off and pulled up in front of an austere grey building. Hermon Chapel proudly displayed its history in black writing on the pale grey walls. Built in 1760, rebuilt in 1860. Warlow knew little about churches or chapels, only that some time after the civil wars, they banned Nonconformists from attending Anglican Church services. So they built their own. Less ostentatious and ornate than the medieval Catholic designs, these were more house-like in structure, emphasising the simpler relationship between worshipper and God.

Warlow got out for a better look.

The chapel distinguished itself from a house with the absence of a chimney and in the design of its long and narrow windows with rounded tops, two on either side of the porch door, and one above. All constructed to allow as much light as possible into the space. Lichen and moss crept over the facing walls, reaching up towards a slate roof. The grey solid building looked to be in reasonable repair and with the cemetery beyond it spilling down the hillside. Fresh flowers adorned at least four of the graves, even though some stones now stood at odd angles; a sign of their antiquity and of how the earth had shifted over decades of wet winters.

Warlow gave little thought to religion normally. He'd considered all the arguments about faith, the need to believe in something without hard evidence of its existence, and, being a copper, found it difficult to swallow. His whole professional life revolved around procuring evidence after all. He found it hard enough to believe in human compassion and tolerance after seeing the things people did to each other. So, when it came to creeds and theology and deities, all of which did about as much for understanding and fellow feeling as Genghis Khan did for cross-border relations, he remained unconvinced.

A small notice board, devoid of any notices, announced the chapel as part of the Baptist Union. He glanced at his surroundings. People would need to make an effort to get here to worship. Warlow wondered how many bothered to pitch up on a Sunday.

The Jeep's passenger door opened and Rhys began to get out.

'Don't bother,' Warlow said with a sideways glance. 'Nothing to see here. I'm curious, that's all. Stay in the car and finish those crisps. You have thirty seconds. And if I hear your mouth crushing another potato once I am back in there, there's a good chance I'll press the eject button and you'll have to walk.'

The look of panic on Rhys's face was ample evidence that the DC had not finished his salt and vinegar savouries yet.

Warlow strode towards the wrought-iron gate that led to a path next to a vine-covered stone wall leaning precariously outwards. Someone had bothered to cut the grass adjacent to the path. So the place had not been totally abandoned. He walked to the door, tried it and found it locked. They'd need to search it properly, obviously.

Satisfied, Warlow turned away and went back to the car. Rhys, mouth bulging, crumpled a crisp packet in his fist.

'Any joy from Hana?' Warlow asked as he buckled up.

Rhys nodded, trying to swallow quickly. Three times his Adam's apple bobbed before he could reply. 'She's sent me a pin.' The word sounded thick and clogged in his throat.

'Is it out of our way?'

Rhys took a swallow of water from a plastic bottle. 'Eight miles east towards Welshpool.'

'Good. Stick it into Google maps and let's find her. If you can stop feeding your face for five minutes, that is.'

———

THE RURAL CRIME Team had set up a couple of four-by-fours in a lay-by on a stretch of road running through a forested area near Criggion, close to the English border.

Hana Prosser waved them in to park behind the rear of the two cars. This was an unmarked forestry road but well maintained and travelled by the looks of it.

Two uniformed officers in Hi-Vis yellow were talking with a couple of motorcyclists holding on to large bikes. Both riders and their vehicles were almost completely covered in mud.

Warlow parked, and he and Rhys got out.

'You found us, then?' Hana grinned, walking towards them.

Rhys looked around and sucked in the air. He was a country boy at heart. 'Tough day at the office, I see.'

Hana raised her eyebrows. 'This will all need writing up in an office, don't you worry.'

Rhys nodded towards the motorcyclists.

'What's going on there?'

'A friendly chat. There are protected species in here and we've had reports of Enduro riders using cycle paths. There are areas where scrambling is allowed. A little reminder to these guys, that's all.'

Warlow wasn't sure what Enduro meant, but he was spared asking by Rhys doing it for him.

Hana nodded. 'Cross country motorbike races with obstacles and different skill challenges. But the bikes are specialist machines. Deep suspensions, that's why they're quite tall. And those big tyres, of course. They can make a mess of a cycle track. But that's not why you're here, is it?'

'No,' Warlow admitted. 'I wanted to ask you about sheep theft.'

Hana bared her teeth and sucked in air. 'We've had some. They took thirty sheep from a farm last month. And last year we had 140 taken from Cornel Cadno. That's only ten miles away. It's a big thing when that happens.'

'So what's the story? Gangs?'

'Tomo's the man you need to talk to. Sorry, Sergeant Thomas. He's up there with the riders.'

'Great.'

Hana grinned. 'Tea? We have an urn.'

Warlow looked at Rhys. 'Looks like you'll get your picnic after all.'

They sat on abandoned logs and drank tea, waiting for Thomas to finish up. May had been slow to heat up and the trees on the lower slope were yet to get their summer covering of leaves. Higher up, the dark green of a conifer plantation provided a backdrop. The vista to the northwest revealed hillier terrain, and thicker clouds seemed joined to the earth by grey sheets as cloudbursts spilled rain.

The riders took off on their bikes, and ten minutes after arriving, the burly sergeant joined Rhys and Warlow.

'Afternoon,' Thomas said. 'Welcome to my office.' He had a big grin on a big face. Something, a skin condition, sprouted a rash around his nose, which was also big.

'Thanks for seeing us.' Warlow held out a hand. 'DCI Evan Warlow.'

Thomas shook it and smiled. 'I know who you are, sir. Hana's filled us in. She said you wanted to gen up about the rustling?'

'Is it a big problem?'

'Big enough for the farmers who get hit. Whoever does this needs to be organised. It's never a one-man show. Someone to round up the sheep, load the transporter, drive the transporter.'

'What happens to the sheep?' Rhys asked.

Thomas's face darkened. 'What do you think? They're killed and sold as meat. Sometimes, the really nasty bastards will slaughter on the ground and take the carcasses. I've seen that. Two years ago an Albanian gang in Stafford were caught doing just that.'

'Is it worth it?' Rhys asked.

Hana sent him a quizzical glance.

'I mean, how much is a sheep worth?' he added quickly.

'Depends,' Hana said, shrugging. 'A pedigree ram might be worth thousands.'

'But the majority are fed into the food chain,' Tomo muttered. 'And now, we get organised crime buying and selling sheep at auction to launder money.' Thomas shook his head. 'That's the world we live in these days. Overall, countrywide, cattle and sheep rustling was worth three million last year. And it's on the rise.'

Warlow stood up and stretched his legs. 'And is violence a part of the pattern?'

Thomas shook his head. 'No. That's the thing. More often than not, these raids are planned. Farms are watched, targeted because of where they are. Fields chosen because they're near roads. Raids take place at night and usually with no one seeing anything.'

'When it happens, it's devastating for the farmer. These sheep are acclimatised to the conditions here. A lot of them are organically reared. It takes years to build a flock. The farmers don't know who to trust,' Hana said with feeling.

Rhys, suitably admonished, nodded in sympathy.

'What about surveillance?' Warlow asked.

Thomas shook his head. 'That's a growth industry. There are things like tracer dots sprayed into fleeces. Some farms have put wireless camera on remote buildings or even auto number plate recognition systems. But it costs money.'

Hana nodded. 'You should talk to my dad about that.

He's done some work with the Farmer's Union on this. They have a long list of suggestions.'

Warlow's tea was cooling. He took another gulp of the strong orange brew. 'What sort of things?'

'Common sense things,' Hana told him. 'Like padlocking gates and grazing livestock away from roads. Checking stock regularly but at different times of the day. As I say, my dad's the expert on all that. He'd be happy to chat, I'm sure.'

Warlow nodded and turned back to Thomas. 'Is it likely the Randals disturbed a gang?'

Thomas looked around at the forest. 'Five years ago, I'd have said there was no chance. These days, who knows. It's as likely a scenario as any other.'

Warlow nodded. He wouldn't cross it off his list. He thanked Thomas and Hana, but added one last thing. 'If you could mention to your father that I may want a word, that would be useful.'

The PCSO gave a brief nod and watched as the detectives made their way back to the Jeep. As they drove off, Rhys wisely kept the cool bag shut.

CHAPTER EIGHT

WARLOW SAW no point in going back to the skeleton-staffed Incident Room when he and Rhys finished with the Rural Crime Team. Better he shake that particular tree in the morning. It was gone six when they reached Newtown. DS Gil Jones texted to tell him he was on his way after a day spent on an operational review. Prior to joining Warlow's team, Gil had been heavily involved in Operation Alice, a multi-force Child Abuse investigation, sometimes involving care homes, though how much care ever took place in these homes was anyone's guess. And though he'd not had an active role for some time, its tendrils in the form of looming court cases still reached out to him.

The Angler's Lodge sat, appropriately enough, on the banks of the snaking River Severn on the northern edge of Newtown. A sprawling, old-fashioned inn, modernised at the rear with river-view rooms and the odd little romantic bothy for couples. Warlow and DC Harries definitely didn't qualify, though, to ensure the gnarled older gent accompanied by the strapping younger man did not raise an eyebrow at reception, the DCI flashed his warrant card as soon as he got to the desk.

Once they'd checked in, Warlow suggested they meet in the bar at seven to catch up with Gil before supper.

'That'll give us just under an hour's downtime.'

'Right, sir.' Rhys nodded. 'I think I'll take a walk around the town. Get my bearings.'

What it was to have the energy of youth. Warlow was stiff from sitting in the car all day. Be nice to stretch out on a bed for a while. They parted on top of a stairway and Warlow had a parting shot. 'Stay away from any dens of iniquity.' A throwaway remark that made Rhys pause with a look of genuine puzzlement.

'That's what my mother always says. She hasn't texted you, has she?'

Warlow didn't answer or turn around. Partly because such an absurd question didn't deserve an answer and partly because now that the opportunity had presented itself, he was quite happy to inject a soupçon of doubt into the young DC's mind. So he kept walking, an unseen smile on his face.

The room they'd given him was pleasant enough. It had a shower, a bed and a metal fire escape running past the window. He wasn't sure about the dark flowery wallpaper on the feature wall behind the headboard, but he could live with that. He was here to work.

He threw his bag on the bed, took off his jacket and his shoes and made himself a cup of hotel-room tea after first inspecting the kettle for suspicious items. There weren't too many hotels in the town, which meant that weddings and stag nights – if there were any – ensured occupancy. And young men were prone to pranking when they'd had a few drinks. What better way to surprise the next guest than to leave a few ccs of urine in the bottom of the kettle. Liquid a busy cleaner might be happy to not check or throw out because he or she might be hard-pressed for time. Or, and

Warlow had seen it and smelled it, leave something a little more biologically solid for the incoming occupant.

Either way, it had become second nature to check these things. Thankfully, apart from a little limescale, the kettle's element looked squeaky clean. While he waited for it to boil, he rinsed one of the ridiculously small cups, set it to dry, and then phoned Tom.

From the background noise – a buzz of people and distant sirens – Warlow surmised that his son was at work in the hospital. He got straight to it.

'Did you have time to talk to someone about your mother?'

'Yeah. I got through to the consultant. The differential diagnosis is cholecystitis, peptic ulcer of pancreatitis. Her amylase levels are up.'

Sometimes Tom forgot who he was talking to.

'Lost in translation, Tom.'

'Sorry, Dad. It could be any of those three. A gut ulcer, gall stones or a knackered pancreas. A scan will tell. Plus they're awaiting repeat amylase and lipase levels.'

'Is this an infection?'

Tom sighed. 'Inflammation more like. Gallstones can trigger pancreatitis for example.'

'What about her drinking?'

Tom sounded resigned. 'Yeah. That's a big contributory factor for ulcer and pancreas.'

'Does this mean they're keeping her in?'

'Definitely. She's on IV fluids until she stabilises and they get to the bottom of things.'

Warlow leaned forward in his seat to massage his toes. 'I'm still up in darkest Powys and will be for a while. But as soon as I'm done, I'll call and see her.'

'What are you doing up there?'

'Counting sheep.'

Tom snorted. 'Fair enough. Silly question. I suppose there are bad guys everywhere.'

A truism if ever there was one.

Warlow made the tea and while it steeped made another call to DS Catrin Richards. She, as always, answered on the third ring.

'Are you missing me, sir?' Catrin's upbeat voice made Warlow smile.

'When can you get here?' He imagined her grinning by return. Diminutive in stature, she nevertheless was no wilting flower.

'Oh, dear. Is it Rhys? Is he sending you a little bananas?'

'There are no bananas because he's eaten them all.'

'That boy can eat.'

'How did the interview go?' He didn't need to elaborate.

'Two Inspectors. McGrath and Cheesely.'

'Is that a joke? Mac and Cheese?'

'Well done, sir. It took three minutes for someone else to come up with that one when they turned up at HQ this morning.'

'And?' Warlow fished out a tea bag and looked for the milk.

'They're pleasant enough. They mainly wanted to know about the day Mel Lewis jumped.'

Warlow let that one settle. He opened a tiny plastic pot of milk and poured it in. The tea turned from black to slightly less black. But he hardly noticed because his mind had gone back to that day on the edge of the Pembrokeshire coast when he'd confronted Mel Lewis over his involvement in a drugs ring and murder case. They'd talked on a clifftop and Mel Lewis had seen no way back other than to step out over the edge.

Warlow could have asked Catrin what she'd said, but

there'd be no point. Lewis had fooled them all until Warlow had finally seen through the detective sergeant's bluster and subterfuge, and confronted him before he could harm someone else. In doing so, he'd saved a life. But losing a colleague like Mel, even though he'd bent under the pressures of money and debt, still ached.

'I'm talking to them again tomorrow, but then I'll be free to come up, sir,' Catrin added. 'Oh, and I sorted out some boards for the Incident Room. There should be a Gallery and a Job Centre set up now.'

'Good. All we need now is someone professional to decorate them.'

'Bit slow, is it, sir?'

'For now, yes.' Warlow tried the tea. It tasted of stale dust. He sighed. 'You know you have nothing to worry about in this Mel Lewis thing?'

'I do, it's just that it's weird being on the other side of an interview table. Mac and Cheese are good though. Professional, I mean. And feisty.'

'I look forward to meeting them.'

'I'm sure the feeling is mutual, sir.'

Warlow rang off. If he knew one thing about DS Catrin Richards, it was that she could look after herself. He abandoned thoughts of tea, emptied the cup into the sink and turned back to his phone. One more thing to do. He opened up WhatsApp and sent a message to Jess: *Hope the dog is not causing trouble. Evan*

He threw the phone on the bed, unpacked his bag, and changed into jeans and a polo shirt. By the time he'd splashed some water on his face, he'd had two texts in return.

The first, from Jess, read: *Dog is a dream. Same can't be said of daughter*

The second was from that daughter: *Dog is gorgeous, as always. Can I come and live with you?*

Warlow exhaled a rueful chuckle. The Allanbys were a close-knit family and Molly was a great kid. But being seventeen should come with a government health warning for those in the immediate vicinity. He resisted the urge to text that back for fear of getting caught up in something. Besides, by his watch, it was almost seven and he needed a drink.

———

IN THE BAR, Warlow ordered a pint of IPA. When he visited London with Tom, they'd go to pubs where there'd be an array of craft ales. Not that he was a big beer drinker, but when offered, Warlow favoured sour ales and beer, usually a Saison or a Gose, but the Angler's Rest offered no such choice. Instead, he opted for the brewery's frothy special and sat at a table in a leather bucket chair with his back to the wall. An old habit, but one that had served him well over the years. Most people entering the area had eyes on the bar itself, scoping out the drinks on offer and on tap before turning to inspect the room. It meant it gave an observer like Warlow a vital few seconds before a target looked at him. He'd used that to his advantage on many an occasion.

Rhys entered five minutes later, dressed in tight jeans and an untucked shirt. The barmaid, a short-haired girl with a nose ring and different coloured nail varnish on each finger, flashed him a smile. Warlow waved and said, 'Order what you want on my tab.'

He watched the exchange between the young detective and the woman whose smile never faltered and occasionally became a full-blown laugh. The DC's congeniality could be infectious. Particularly in heterosexual exchanges. It was one of the reasons Warlow saw his role in life as one of Rhys's gatekeepers. Such good humour and innocent exuberance in a man was unnatural. Still, it never ceased to amaze Warlow that age seemed to be no barrier. Females either wanted to date Rhys or mother him. Males too, maybe. In this day and age, all too probably. But that was outside of the DCI's sphere of knowledge.

When Rhys eventually strolled over to the table with a pint of something cloudy, Warlow peered at it suspiciously.

'Please don't tell me it's one of those bloody alcopops.'

'No sir. Cloudy cider. Locally made. I'm always game for that. It's a rule with Nant Seconds you should try a local brew whenever you're away.' Rhys took a gulp of his cider, made a show of swilling it like a sommelier with constipation, and let out a contented. 'Aah.'

'Did you get a chance to scout around town?'

'Yes, sir. Noted all the major landmarks and attractions. There's a fish and chip shop a hundred yards west and the Indian takeaway fifty after that.'

'Aren't we eating here?'

Rhys, already a third of the way through his cider, made a face. 'Yes, but it's early. Never know what we'll be feeling like at ten.'

'I'll probably be feeling the pillow on my bed,' Warlow muttered. His phone chirped a notification. He fished out some reading glasses and read the text.

'From Gil. Says he'll be here in forty minutes.'

Rhys looked anxious. 'Is that a satnav forty? Only it was half an hour out for us.'

'He didn't specify what method of timekeeping he's using,' Warlow said.

'Perhaps I'd better warn the restaurant.' Rhys put his hands on the arms of the chair, ready to push up.

Warlow creased his brows. 'What, in case we're fifteen minutes late?'

Rhys paused mid-raise, looking decidedly unhappy.

Warlow knew the signs by now and shook his head. 'For God's sake man, get some crisps if you're that hungry.'

The DC stood up, grinning. 'How about you, sir? Peanuts? Scratchings?'

'No, I think I can stave off collapse from starvation for another half an hour.'

Gil Jones turned up five minutes early. A big stocky man with a full face, Gil had been around the block more times than he could remember. His presence on the team added experience and a calming element, partly because his size prevented him from doing anything too quickly.

They convened, once Gil had dropped off his bag, in the riverside restaurant: Gil with a pint of bitter in front of him, Warlow with a half, Rhys on his second cider.

'Bugger of a journey. Got stuck behind a cattle lorry. I've got more manure on my bonnet and tyres now than on my roses.' Gil took a swallow of beer.

'Room alright, Sarge?' Rhys asked.

'Tidy. Nice view of the river.'

Rhys's face fell. 'How come you get a river view when me and DCI Warlow get the street?'

'Want to swap?' Gil offered.

'Can we?' Rhys sat up.

'Don't be so bloody soft.' Gil smacked his lips. 'So, how's it all going? Any sign of the bodies?'

Warlow shook his head and outlined what they'd done that day. 'Tomorrow, I want the Incident Room sorted out. Get some CID out and about. Everyone needs a kick up the backside.'

'How was your day, Sarge?' They'd put bread and butter on the table and Rhys had eaten half of the slices already.

'Operation Alice reunions are hardly ever fun-filled. Still, I caught up with a few old mates.' He reached for the butter, stopped and looked at Warlow. 'That reminds me, I ran into Owen Tamblin.'

Warlow grinned. 'How is he?'

'Counting down the days to retirement. But he gave me a message for you.' Gil fished out his notebook.

'A written message.' Warlow's eyebrows went up.

'Oh, yes. Too much detail and too many names. You know what it's like, trying to remember stuff as you get older. My father had a short-term memory problem. It must run in the family because my father had it too.'

Rhys paused mid-chew, thought about what Gil had said and then let out a Muttley-style laugh and promptly choked on a crumb. He followed this up by going red in the face and had to sink half a pint to clear both the crumb and his blushes.

Gil looked on, all innocence. 'Something I said?'

Warlow shook his head. 'It's beginning to feel like I'm the one in charge of a day-centre outing.'

Gil found the page. 'Here it is. The Geoghans. Mean anything to you?'

Warlow scowled. 'Unfortunately, yes. I helped put them away for manslaughter and fraud. One of my better days at the office. But Derek Geoghan, a definite waste of human DNA, recently got released on medical grounds.'

Gil nodded. 'Well, Owen Tamblin says that they've disappeared. Said Derek Geoghan failed to turn up for a medical appointment and his parole officer went to visit and found they'd abandoned ship. No sign of them. Owen said for you to keep your eyes open. They're not in your fan club, it appears.'

Warlow thought about this. Neither of the Geoghans was getting any younger and unpleasant trash though they were, he hardly considered them a viable threat. Still, Owen had a point.

A waiter arrived with their starters, and Rhys actually rubbed his hands together.

'So, tell us about these Geoghans then, sir.'

'I will. After we've eaten. No point spoiling a good meal.'

CHAPTER NINE

When Warlow, Gil and Rhys walked into the Incident Room at Newtown the following morning, the skeleton staff had doubled. Now there were two officers sitting at desks. Warlow wasn't surprised to see Lowri Fellows already there, but the other female officer who met his eye with a defiant glare brought an immediate grin to his face.

'Well, well, DS Richards. You are a very early bird.'

She stood up. Rhys, all smiles, walked over to her desk where he loomed almost a foot taller than her. 'I thought you were being grilled by Interpol.'

Catrin ignored the sarcastic barb. 'Superintendent Buchanan had a word with Mac and Cheese last night and they agreed to let me join you lot up here.'

'Mac and Cheese?' asked Rhys. 'Wouldn't say no.'

'Polite nicknames,' explained Catrin.

'So they're done with you?' Rhys asked.

'No, but they said if they needed more they'd come to me, since DCI Warlow is up here, too.' A loaded statement if ever there was one. Explanation over, Catrin turned and pointed towards the back of the room where one white and one hessian covered board had been set up. The Job Centre and the Gallery. Photos had already been posted on the beige Gallery.

'That's more like it,' Warlow said, unable to hide his admiration as he turned to the DS. 'What time did you leave to get here?'

'Just after six, sir.'

'Did you fly?' Rhys looked sceptical.

'No. I used my advanced driving cert skills and quiet roads.' She sent him a triumphant grin.

'We're glad you're here,' Warlow said. 'I see you've met PC Fellows.'

Lowri blinked and nodded looking slightly overawed by the fact that he'd remembered her name.

Warlow turned an open palm towards the burly man behind him. 'This is DS Gil Jones. He's normally our Incident Room manager but since you know the lay of the land so well, I'm going to ask you to assume that role for now.'

Fellows' index finger crept up to her chest, pointing inwards. 'Me, sir?'

'For now. I need Gil out and about since we're short a DI.'

Lowri nodded again. 'Thank you, sir. I'll do my best.'

'Good. Mind you, if I need your local knowledge you'll be out with us and we'll sort out a different OM.' Running the office was a big responsibility. Warlow had no doubt that if the investigation escalated into anything other than the missing-persons-under-suspicious-circumstances job it currently was, they'd need more help and experience. But he was all for moving forward and so he'd make do with what he had.

'Right, first things first. Rhys, get the kettle on and we'll have a quick catch up of what we know.'

Ten minutes later, armed with mugs of lubricant tea, the stuff that oiled the wheels of any case, the team stood in front of the Gallery. The photographs they had were, for once, not the usual crime scene gory snaps. Yes, the spattered remains on the feed-shed door left little to the imagination, but all the others were of faces. At the top, Catrin had placed the missing Randals: Aeron and his son, Joseph.

Warlow studied the images as Rhys flicked through his notebook. He'd asked the DC to precis the case for the others while they waited for him to ready himself. Both photographs drew Warlow's eye as he tried to assimilate whatever information he could from these two-dimensional images. The snap of Aeron Randal had been taken at an agricultural show, judging by the backdrop of tents and stalls and a big Shire horse. He'd turned to the camera, smiling to show off a snaggle-toothed grin and a face tanned from the weather. Despite the obviously fine day, he wore a check shirt and a woollen tie.

Joseph Randal's face looked remarkably different. Another candid shot in an open-necked shirt, his hair short, with a well-groomed look. If he'd been asked, he would not have pinned the label 'farmer' on Joseph, whereas Aeron could have been nothing else.

Beneath, Catrin had pinned Mari Randal and a photo of the daughter, Almeira, who Warlow recognised from the images he'd seen at Wern Ddu.

Rhys cleared his throat and began the recap with a finger pointing towards the images on the Gallery. 'Aeron Randal, aged fifty-one and his son, Joseph Randal, aged twenty-four. Both reported missing two days ago by Mari Randal after leaving the farm at 10pm last Saturday night. The following morning, while responding to a report of gunshots heard in the early hours, a PCSO from the Rural

Crime Team discovered the Randals' abandoned vehicle near a feed shed in the hills near Rhaeadr. She also found blood and tissue spatter against the feed door. Crime scene have confirmed this is consistent with a shotgun blast at close range. And, as you know, we've had confirmation that the blood is that of Aeron and Joseph Randal and that some of the other tissue also belongs to Joseph Randal suggesting a serious injury was sustained.'

'Why did the Randals go out at that time of night?' Catrin asked.

'There have been a spate of livestock thefts, sheep mainly, over the last twelve months. The three farms have a watch system, and someone had seen lights on the Chapel Road,' Rhys answered.

'Lights on a road?' Catrin asked.

Warlow explained, 'It's a remote location. They keep an eye out for that sort of thing.'

Gil stepped forward, mug in hand, and pointed to the existing crime scene snaps and the car with its open door. 'So they left their car. Are we assuming they've been taken by another vehicle?'

Rhys sent Warlow a questioning glance. 'The lane leading to the shed is used only by farm vehicles, tractors, four-by-fours. Kapil wasn't hopeful they'd find much. But yes, we assume they've been taken somewhere else.'

'And I suppose there's no CCTV anywhere around?' Catrin asked in a forlorn tone.

'Be worth you paying a visit to see for yourself,' Warlow answered. 'Go on Rhys.'

'We've visited the Randals' farm and interviewed Mrs Randal. She couldn't give us much information, but we do know that there is a brother who has had reason to fall out with Aeron Randal over a contested will. But at present, our working theory is that the Randals disturbed some rustlers in the process of stealing livestock and things went bad.'

'Has someone counted the sheep?' Gil's question, logical as it was, made everyone turn and look at him. 'To see if any are missing, I mean?'

'I don't think so, Sarge,' Rhys replied. 'Who would know the numbers? Mrs Randal?'

'She's our best bet,' Warlow agreed.

Catrin, who had been listening with a pad in her hand, stepped forward and posted an action on the Job Centre. On it, Warlow read in the black Sharpie ink she preferred, 'Counting Sheep'.

'Better have a couple of coffees on board before we take that one on. In case we drift off, you know…' Rhys said. Four sets of eyes drifted slowly back from Catrin's note towards the young DC's face, baring, as it did, an expression of glowing smugness.

'That's very good, Rhys,' Gil said, though no one was laughing, so stunned were they by this attempt at humour from such an unlikely source.

'Tumbleweeds,' whispered Catrin.

'Thank you, Sarge,' Rhys replied to Gil, ignoring her.

Lowri Fellows stifled her guffaw with a hurried cough.

'Right, that's enough of that.' Warlow brought them back to the matter at hand. 'Let's get into gear. There's no sign of Aeron Randal's phone, so we'd better get on to the providers for records. Standard stuff. Let's make sure there's nothing here that we're missing.'

Catrin posted another note.

'Then there's the brother, Padrig. Lowri, have you got any information on that?'

Lowri nodded. 'We have an address in Welshpool, sir.'

'Good. We need to talk to him. Catrin and Gil, why don't you find him. While you're out you can call in to the crime scene, too. See what you think.' Warlow had a sudden thought. 'Oh, and there's a chapel up there. I have no idea if it's been searched, but you might as well call in there as well.'

Gil nodded, making a note.

'So that leaves the rustling side of things.' Warlow stepped up to the Gallery, staring at the SOC photos, talking out loud with his back to the team. 'We had a chat with the Rural Crime Team yesterday but it's all a tad woolly.' He turned suddenly, making Lowri flinch. None of the others did. They were used to it. 'Catrin, let's get a map up, check on where the nearest livestock thefts were and dig out reports. Rhys, you chase up the mobile records. I'll chat with CID and get some more help. We need an Exhibits Officer and some secretarial sup—'

From somewhere outside, an amplified voice thundered through their ground-floor open window, stopping Warlow in his tracks.

'POLICE   INCOMPETENCE.   WHERE   IS ROBERT? WE DEMAND ACTION. POLICE INCOM-PETENCE. WHERE IS ROBERT? WE DEMAND ACTION. POLICE INCOMPETENCE—'

'What the hell is that?' Warlow walked to the window and peered through the glass. Outside, on the sweep of lawn between the building and the pavement, stood a woman holding a placard in one hand and a megaphone in the other.

The placard read:

MISSING 12 MONTHS. CLUELESS POLICE. WHERE IS ROBERT LLOYD?

From this distance, it wasn't possible to see what the woman looked like, what with her beanie hat and the thick coat she wore and the megaphone in front of her face. And even as Warlow watched and heard her deliver the same three sentences over and over, a couple of Uniforms made their weary way towards her from the front of the building.

'POLICE INCOMPETENCE. WHERE IS ROBERT? WE DEMAND ACTION. POLICE INCOM-PETENCE—'

Traffic slowed down to watch her. But, as the police neared, the woman dropped the megaphone and walked quickly away, holding her placard even higher than before.

Warlow turned and stared at Lowri Fellows.

'What's that all about?'

Lowri crinkled her nose. 'That's Julia Lloyd, sir. Her son went missing twelve months ago. We think he up and left, but Mrs Lloyd is convinced something happened to him. It's still an open case, but as you know, often mispers remain mispers because they want to. Especially young twenty-somethings who think the grass is greener in Liverpool. The last anyone saw of him was in Shrewsbury train station, heading for Crew. There's CCTV of him in Lime Street station that same day. After that, nothing.'

Warlow had to think about this. Why Liverpool and not Carmarthen or Cardiff? But then he realised that Merseyside was closer to where they were than Cardiff or Carmarthen. Or at least no further.

'Every day she turns up here before work to make a nuisance of herself. She's been warned off, especially for the megaphone. But she isn't the type of person to give up. In fact, she'll walk up and down now for a good half an hour. To remind us. Ignore it. It's normal, sir.' Lowri shrugged.

Warlow turned back to the Incident Room with a little shake of his head, muttering, 'Normal?'

Before anyone could reply, the door to the Incident Room opened and Hana Prosser walked in and made directly for Warlow.

'Morning, sir. Apologies for the interruption, but my dad had to come to town today on some NFU business and

I've cajoled him into coming to see you. That is if you still want to?'

Warlow's expression brightened. 'Someone who knows about the thieving? Perfect.' He looked at Lowri Fellows. 'Is there somewhere we can have a chat with Mr Prosser?'

CHAPTER TEN

WITH THE REST of the team busy getting to grips with the actions Catrin had posted, Warlow met with Hana and her father, Elis Prosser, in the SIO's room, which was nothing more than a portioned-off area of the Incident Room and even smaller than the one he was used to. With barely enough room for the three of them and only one chair on each side of the desk, Hana grabbed a second chair and placed it before nipping out to fetch her father.

Warlow hadn't seen Hana without her police baseball cap before. But today she had not yet tied her hair back, and it fell to her shoulders in yellow bangs. She moved confidently and picked the chair up with ease. A testament to her upbringing on a farm, no doubt.

She came back three minutes later with Elis Prosser, who immediately shook Warlow's hand. The shake was dry and firm, the skin like old leather.

'Good to meet you, Detective Chief Inspector.'

'It's Evan.' Warlow motioned for him to sit. Hana took the seat next to him. Elis was not a tall man, with only an inch on his daughter, but the family resemblance stood out.

A full head of curly hair had greyed at the temples, but a fresh shave and ruddy features lent a clean-cut appearance. Like his daughter, Elis had a full mouth, a good smile, and a spark in his eyes. Unlike his daughter, he wore glasses in a snazzy square frame.

'Can we offer you some tea?' Warlow asked.

'No. I'm off to a meeting and there'll be plenty of coffee there, so I won't.'

'Dad's a Union rep,' Hana explained.

'Does that mean you work for them?' Warlow asked.

Elis shook his head. 'The whole of farming is a kind of trade union. We elect representatives at all levels. I'm a county delegate. Today's meeting is with local government and the council.'

'Sounds enthralling.'

Elis grinned. 'I'll need that coffee, I expect.'

Warlow nodded. 'Thanks for sparing us the time.'

Elis glanced at his daughter. 'I'd be in for it if I didn't cooperate with the police.' His smile slipped away. 'And this business with Aeron and Joseph is... well, it's mystifying and very upsetting. Anything I can do to help?'

'You've known them a long time?'

'Aeron and I were in school together. We both grew up on the farms. Hana and Joe were in school together, too. It's a small community.' Elis wore a blue striped shirt and a knitted tie under his chequered jacket. His trousers were pressed and, though they were hidden under the table, Warlow suspected he'd be able to see his face in the man's polished brogues. Yet there was a dash of the modern about him, which may have been something to do with his daughter's influence.

'I'm not at liberty to tell you everything about the case,' Warlow continued, 'but there are some things you can help with.'

Elis nodded towards Hana. 'This one tells me nothing. All I know is that Aeron and Joseph are missing.'

'That's no secret. Can you tell me about Saturday night?'

Elis's bushy eyebrows shot up. 'Yes. I got a call from Hari Gregory over at Deri Isaf farm at around nine-thirty. He'd been out checking stock. We all do that now, since the thefts. The Union suggests we check stock close to roads especially and we encourage people to avoid stocking those fields as much as possible, but it isn't always easy.'

Warlow had never noticed before but come to think of it, how many miles of farmland bordered a lane? Probably thousands.

Elis continued, 'Hari Gregory had seen some lights on the Chapel Road. He texted me and Aeron. My land only has a small strip at the south end next to the road. Aeron's fields border the rest. I went out and took a long route which comes to the Chapel Road from the south. Aeron could have come the other way. I don't know.'

'And when you do go out on these checks, would you take a gun?'

Elis clasped his hands together on the desk. 'Personally, no. But I know some men who do. There are foxes as well as thieves in the countryside, Evan.'

Warlow pondered that answer. City dwellers, looking in from the outside, made the big mistake of thinking that the countryside was a place you went for peace and quiet. But unlike the city, when things kicked off, the possibility for mayhem was so much greater. Mad cows could crush you. Rivers never had signs saying which were the deep and treacherous bits, and, as he was quickly learning, every bugger seemed to have a gun. 'What time did you get home, roughly?' Warlow asked.

'I got back at around ten-thirty.'

'Did you see any lights on the Chapel Road?'

'Nothing. No sign of anything. Of course, it's possible one of the locals had come through. Sometimes kids go up to the chapel to do what kids do. It's a quiet spot. They'd be undisturbed.'

'It's commoner in summer during the warmer weather,' Hana confirmed her dad's statement.

Warlow stole a glance at his notebook where he'd jotted down a few questions. 'So livestock theft is a big issue in this neck of the woods?'

Elis nodded. 'It is across the country. But we are close to some big population areas: Shrewsbury, Telford, Wolverhampton. That's where we think the animals go. For slaughter and meat.' Elis shook his head. 'Animals that have been bred for generations. Flocks that have been nurtured.' Elis's eyes looked suddenly moist. 'I know what people outside must think. That it's trivial to lose a few sheep. But if a farmer with a shotgun ever found a rustler, there would be blood. That's one reason I don't take a gun out with me.'

Hana reached out a hand and placed it on her dad's arm.

'So, do these thieves simply drive around until they spot a likely target? Close to a road as you suggested?'

Elis nodded. 'They could. Or they could use local knowledge.'

Warlow frowned and sent a glance towards Hana, who looked momentarily uncomfortable. 'Dad suspects some people might have been involved in selling information.'

'In what sense?'

'Damned drugs, is what sense.' Elis growled. 'Though sense doesn't come anywhere near it.'

Hana elaborated, 'Mid Wales has a drug problem like everywhere. During a big operation last year we found some maps with areas marked out. Farms with fields next to roads. Exactly the sort of thing a thief would need to know. No one accepted responsibility and a lot of people ended up in jail. Which was a good result.'

Elis rounded on his daughter. 'What about Hopkins? She's not in jail. She's still—'

'Dad!' Hana's tone held a warning. She dropped her eyes and then brought them back up towards Warlow. 'Sarah Hopkins. Small-time dealer and partner of an ex-farm worker who fell out with the farmer he worked for and ended up robbing the old man for drug money. He went to jail for that. He was involved in the ring that Operation Dresden broke up last year, too, but Sarah Hopkins somehow wriggled free.'

'It's her. It has to be her.' Elis seemed adamant.

'We have zero evidence,' Hana said with a little apologetic smile.

But Warlow filed the information away.

Elis looked at his watch and then at his daughter. 'I ought to be going.'

Warlow stood up. 'Of course. If we need any more information, we have your number.' He reached across and shook hands again. 'It's been a useful chat. Thanks.'

'You ought to pop over to the farm one day,' Hana said. 'My dad has it ship-shape.'

Warlow nodded. 'Is it you and your wife that run it, Elis?'

Something passed across both father and daughter's faces then. A momentary flicker as if they'd heard nails on a blackboard and Warlow knew instantly he'd said the wrong thing. 'No,' Elis said. 'It's only me at Caemawr now that Hana has her own place. I have help, of course. Hired hands. And Hana pops back now and then.'

'Right, well, I may take you up on your offer,' Warlow said. 'I freely admit to knowing very little about farming.'

'Well, you have an expert on hand if you need

anything,' Hana said. The pride in her voice spoke volumes.

———

WHEN THE PROSSERS HAD GONE, Warlow stayed in the SIO room and tried to evaluate that little tic he'd noticed at the end. It didn't matter, and it should be none of his business. But in this line of work, everything was his business. He stood in the doorway and called to Lowri Fellows.

'Got a minute?'

Lowri got up from her desk and joined him. 'Sir?'

'Something I said to Mr Prosser set off a little alarm in my head. He doesn't have a wife, am I right?'

'Yes, sir, you are. It's tragic really. Hana and her dad are really close.'

'I could see that.'

Lowri nodded sadly. 'It's because Hana's mum died when she was five.'

Shit, thought Warlow, inwardly cringing at recalling his assumption.

'A tractor accident,' Lowri explained.

Warlow sucked air in through his teeth. He'd driven behind enough tractors over the last twenty-four hours not to have to work too hard in imagining what one of the roaring monsters might do to a soft, unwary body. 'Christ. I put my big foot in it there, then.'

Lowri's shake of the head was dismissive. 'Oh, I don't think it's a raw wound, sir. It's years ago and Hana doesn't hide it. She doesn't talk about it much but it's no secret, either.'

Maybe not a raw wound, but a wound nonetheless, judging from the reaction he'd seen.

'Thanks, Lowri.'

She turned to go.

'Oh, one more thing. Is the name Sarah Hopkins familiar, to you?'

Lowri's shoulders sagged. 'It is, sir. Depressingly so.'

'Right. Pull her file. I'd like to see for myself.'

CHAPTER ELEVEN

By 9.30AM, Catrin and Gil had left for Welshpool and Padrig Randal's address. Repeated attempts to reach him on his mobile had failed and they were left with the old-fashioned approach of turning up and knocking on the door.

Warlow looked over Sarah Hopkins' PNC file. An exemplary citizen she was not. At twenty-four years of age, she'd been arrested twenty-two times on a long list of charges including assault, possession, shoplifting and several public order offences such as affray. The face that stared back at him from the screen could have looked attractive with a mane of red frizzy hair swept to one side, but the hard mouth and sod-off expression in the eyes combined with a pebble-dash of acne spots stubbornly persisting on her forehead had eroded the promise. The partner that Hana had alluded to, a wiry twenty-three-year-old called Mark Hallam, looked equally defiant when Warlow pulled him up.

The address on record for Hopkins said no fixed abode, but Warlow knew she'd have haunts and said as much to Lowri, who immediately suggested she talk to one of the team at Nightlight; a free drug and alcohol misuse service that saw to the needs of the addict community. Warlow nodded his approval and left her to it. Twenty minutes later, she came back in, smiling.

'Your luck's in, sir. She's at the drop-in centre now. Believe it or not, she's volunteering there. Do you want me to get some Uniforms down there to hang on to her?'

Warlow smiled at the way she said Uniforms. Until yesterday, she'd been one herself. But he shook his head.

'How far is this drop-in centre?'

'It's on Shrew Street. About half a mile from here.'

'She doesn't look the type who'd say much if we drag her in. And we don't have any reason to arrest her. Better we go to her.'

Lowri's eyebrows went up a notch.

Warlow smiled. 'I enjoy a challenge.'

He slid on his coat. 'Rhys, you're in charge.' Warlow got a silent thumbs up in reply because the DC was busy talking to someone on the phone. Accompanying the gesture though was an irritatingly exuberant grin and raised eyebrows. All Warlow could muster was a shake of the head.

Nightlight occupied an old building that had once been a book shop on the edge of a new redbrick development of townhouses and flats not far from the centre of the town. Funded through government budgets for drugs misuse and charity donations, it provided services for those on the fringes of society. Warlow'd thought about his strategy on the way in the Jeep. He could come across as heavy handed and aggressive. Or he could try the overly friendly approach. Turning up to thank the woman for her help in the recent arrests – because there were always some arrests when it came to drugs – and coercing her into cooperation or risk being labelled a collaborator. Funny word collaborator. Snitch or grass were commoner and collaborator sounded more like something that happened in wartime.

So, he mused, perhaps not that inappropriate after all.

Yet he was spared any play acting by a stroke of luck, which, on the whole, featured very little in his line of work. But for once, in Sarah Hopkins' case, the bread fell butter side up. The mean-looking photograph he'd studied not twenty minutes before had morphed into a young woman who met his eyes when he introduced himself and didn't spit in his face. A good start that got even better when she shook his hand.

She'd put on some weight and her sunken cheeks had filled out and the crystal tips hair had been tied back.

When she said, 'What can I do for you?' Warlow detected only a wary defiance, not the vehement avoidance he'd expected.

'A few quick sheep-related questions,' Warlow said.

Sarah's bottom lip came forward. 'Sheep?'

'You're not in any trouble.' Lowri quickly added the reassurance.

'I bloody hope not. I don't know anything about sheep.'

Warlow held up a placating hand. 'Five minutes, I promise.'

Sarah shrugged. 'Okay. I… like… need a fag anyway.'

Outside, they stood on the pavement while Sarah lit up. She'd put on a puffer jacket against the brisk wind, but at least it wasn't raining, though the promised heat wave had not yet manifested and looked about as likely as gravy-flavoured yoghurt. Lowri took out a notebook. Sarah stood, arms folded, while Warlow asked the questions.

'You are in a relationship with Mark Hallam?'

'Was.' Sarah took a toke from her cigarette and blew out the smoke through the side of her mouth.

'No longer?'

She shook her head. 'Mutual agreement. We both agreed he was a total bastard.'

'Good,' Warlow said.

That made Sarah frown.

'Well, isn't it? Looks like you're getting your act together.'

Sarah scowled, but then thought about it and shrugged. 'Suppose.'

Warlow grasped the offered olive branch. 'Lowri here tells me they found some maps when they raided Mark's address. Maps of farms with fields marked out. Do you know what they were?'

Sarah stared back at him unflinchingly, but with narrowed eyes. 'Why are you asking me this?'

Lowri answered, 'We're investigating a violent crime. We think it may be related to livestock theft. We know you're not involved and you're not under any suspicion.'

Sarah's eyes drifted between Lowri and Warlow. She hadn't been cautioned. She knew what she said could not be used. She inhaled another lungful of tobacco. 'Mark had this, like, thing going with someone in Telford. He didn't get involved himself, but they paid him for scoping out the farms. I've got no idea who they were. All I know is that they were, like, Romanians or Albanians, or some shit. He said it was free money. And he knew all the farms up towards Vyrnwy. He used to, like, work up there. I didn't ask what they did with the animals.'

'What do you think they did with them?'

Sarah looked unhappy.

'What they didn't do was send them on an all-expenses jolly to Abersoch, that's for certain. They slaughtered them and sold the meat.' Warlow didn't pull any punches on that one.

Sarah flinched.

Warlow followed up, 'Did he ever talk to you about these people? What they were like?'

She nodded. 'He said they were clowns. Who the hell steals sheep, he said. And it was rubbish money. Couple of hundred, that's all.'

Warlow shook his head.

'Did he mention them using guns?' Lowri asked.

On hearing this, Sarah took a step back. 'Guns? To steal sheep? No, never mentioned any guns. They'd go in at, like, three in the morning and any sign of trouble they were out of there like shit off a stick.'

An interesting analogy, thought Warlow, trying to remember a time he'd ever had recourse to fling a turd from a twig and failing. 'And you don't have a phone number or a name?'

'Sorry, no. If I did, I'd give it to you. I didn't like the idea anyway because they also stole, like, sheepdogs to help with the sheep. I like dogs.' She slid the hand not holding the cigarette under her armpit. 'Look, these people weren't big time. They were looking to make money by stealing sheep. Not exactly, like, Ocean's Eleven. Mark met them a couple of times and they paid cash for the maps. That was it.'

Warlow nodded. 'You using, Sarah?'

She shook her head. 'I got ill last year. Ended up in, like, hospital with pneumonia. No drugs or booze for seven weeks. I haven't, like, used since I got out. I come here to help the others. There's even a chance I'll get a job over at Millinghams, packing.'

'Sounds good,' Warlow said.

'First time since I was, like, sixteen. I've wasted, like, a lot of time. On drugs and on Mark.'

'You need to think about giving up the fags next.' Warlow let a smile play over his lips.

He noticed for the first time that she wore a little makeup that covered most of her acne scars.

'It's fucking expensive, I know that.' Sarah sighed and looked at the inch and a half of cigarette left in her hand.

'And it makes your clothes smell,' Lowri added.

'I haven't, like, had to think much about my clothes smelling for a long time.' Sarah shrugged. 'But you're right.'

Warlow handed over a card. 'If you remember anything new or think of something that might help us, ring me. Anytime.'

Sarah glanced at the card, then at Warlow, before tucking it into her jeans back pocket.

They left her to finish her cigarette. Back in the car, Warlow headed for the station, musing over the interview. Sarah Hopkins hadn't given them anything, but a box had been ticked.

'That was a surprise,' Lowri said. 'Sarah Hopkins actually holding a conversation without trying to rake your eyes out.'

Warlow kept his focus on the traffic while his brain flew back to an encounter with a Sarah Hopkins clone in the Eastgate Shopping Precinct in Llanelli, more years ago than he wanted to think about. An encounter that changed his life. Cerys McLean claimed, loudly, to those who would listen and, more often than not, to those who had no choice, that she was a drug freedom activist advocating the legalisation of just about everything that was bad for you. Warlow didn't like the word activist much. It sailed a little too close to anarchist for his liking. There were passionate people, often the young, whose enthusiasm he admired. And protests were fine so long as they stayed peaceful. But he'd seen too many colleagues injured by violent opportunists who had about as much sympathy and understanding of a cause as a cobblestone did.

Cerys McLean used her schtick as camouflage for a voracious drug habit. She 'protested' by sticking used needles in her lapels and hair pieces so that anyone touching her risked being contaminated by her taint.

Warlow took on that challenge and came away with the grand prize. Hepatitis C and HIV as a combination package. He'd had a hard job coping with that for a while. The worry over it, or at least the worry over the chance of him giving the same virus to his colleagues through bad luck or trouble, ended up with him opting for early retirement. It had taken the death of Mel Lewis, or more specifically the case that led to his death, for him to realise that he may still have something to give the job. It had taken Jess Allanby to make him understand that McLean's gift needn't be a death sentence.

Not physically nor psychologically.

He picked up on Lowri's stare and realised his silence was becoming noticeable.

'It happens. People can turn themselves around,' he murmured.

'Well, I think it's amazing. Even if she couldn't help us.'

Warlow threw her a side-eyed look. 'I wouldn't say that. It may be that this rustling lark has an organised-crime element, but these thieves don't go in toting shotguns. It's not like robbing a jewellery store. "Not, like, Ocean's Eleven," to quote an expert. And I bet none of them looked like Brad Pitt.'

Lowri smiled at his paraphrasing.

'It sounds to me to be all about stealth, this rustling lark.' Warlow indicated to turn off into the station.

'And that helps, does it, sir?'

'Perhaps.'

'So you don't think it's worth talking to Mark Hallam?'

'No, I don't. But we'll keep him on the back burner for now. Let's see what Gil and Catrin dig up first.'

CHAPTER TWELVE

CATRIN DROVE a job car up to Welshpool. She'd left her own at the headquarters in Carmarthen and the Focus smelled strongly of the two cheap pine air fresheners dangling from the rear-view mirror. She'd bought the scent in her first garage pit stop on the way up to Newtown yesterday. The aroma did a reasonable job of masking the underlying bouquet of stale food and sweat that had leeched into the seat material. One that no amount of valeting could quite remove.

Next to her, Gil sat thumbing through his phone, the seat belt bowing forward over his ample girth, chuckling to himself occasionally at something he read.

'My eldest grandchild says he wants a YouTube channel for his birthday?' He glanced across at Catrin. 'Is that some kind of swimming inflatable?'

She gave him an old-fashioned look. 'Hilarious. But seriously? A YouTube channel? How old is he?'

'Nine going on twenty. He watches this kid opening presents who gets three million thumbs up – his words – and says he can do that.'

Catrin's eyes went skywards. 'I know. There's even a tutorial on how to breathe.'

'But the *diawl bach's* only saying it because it'll mean he'll have to get a present every week.' Gil shook his head, but his eyes glinted. 'It was his birthday on Saturday.'

Catrin nodded. 'Smart kid. This is Bryn?'

'Bryn, yeah. But he must have told his sister because she's now texting me saying that she wants one, too, for face painting tutorials. Only she spells it 'tootoreos.''

'And she's what, five?'

Gil sent her a disparaging glare. 'Four and three quarters. I'll thank you to be as accurate as she always is.'

Catrin's grin widened. 'Keeping you busy, Gil.'

'Yeah. But no complaints.'

She knew what Gil had been doing before he joined the team. Operation Alice had involved all aspects of child abuse, including videos of the worst kind. Gil would have had to look at some of those. Catrin was prepared to forgive him for laughing at silly texts from his grandkids every day of the week. Well, to an extent.

Sighing, Gil flicked open another app on his phone. 'Eight minutes to destination according to this. I'll let the good lady Google take over from here.'

She did. Nine minutes later, they both stood outside the door of number 7, Livesey House. Padrig Randal's flat was one of four on the first floor of a nondescript council property, a stone's throw from Sainsbury's. Gil rang the doorbell, then he knocked, and rang the doorbell again. Either Padrig had become totally deaf or was not in.

'Could be at work,' Catrin suggested.

Gil considered this and shrugged. 'Then why isn't he answering his phone?'

'Might not hear it in the tractor.' The heavily accented voice came unexpectedly from behind and both officers turned to see number 4's door open six inches. A slice of female face, lined and topped with fine white – or was it mauve? – hair, peered out at them through the gap.

'Tractor?' Catrin asked.

'That is where he will be. In the tractor. He works for Selwyn Bute. They have the big Zetors.'

Gil stepped forward, only for the door to begin shutting as the woman withdrew.

'Hang on there, Mrs uh…' Gil protested.

'Do not come any closer.' The voice warned shrilly through a one-inch crack.

Gil stopped. The crack between door and frame widened again. The half-hidden face peering out looked at least eighty years old.

'I have the door on the chain,' the woman explained.

'Good,' Gil replied. 'Glad to hear it.' He fished out his warrant card. 'We're police. Here to speak to Mr Randal.'

The door opened another inch to reveal more of the face and a pair of eyes behind thick large-framed glasses squinting at the card. 'What has he done?'

'Nothing,' Catrin answered. She tried to place the accent. Definitely not local. The lack of abbreviations, the hard 'r' sound. Not Russian, but that neck of the woods. Polish probably. 'We're after some information, that's all.'

The big magnified eyes looked back at her. 'He will be out all day. This time of year it is cutting or spraying *błoto*, ah, muck. Contractors have to work around the weather. When it suits, they will be like the blue-arsed flies.'

'You know a lot about farming, Mrs…' Gil let the prefix title dangle, hoping she'd fill in the blanks. He remained disappointed.

'We used to rent farm, my brother and I. He died and I came here.'

Catrin resisted the urge to respond to Gil's can-you-believe-this look. 'Did you see Padrig go to work this morning?'

'No. But I hear him. Half five as usual.'

'Okay.' Catrin held up her card. 'I'm Detective Sergeant Richards. This is Detective Sergeant Jones.'

'Welsh names, yes?'

'Yes. Welsh names,' Gil replied.

She nodded. 'Wales had been good to me.'

'And you are Mrs…?'

'Miss. It is Miss.'

Catrin heard it as mees. She waited, like Gil, for the surname to follow. It didn't. Catrin took out two business cards. 'If you see Padrig, give him one of these and ask him to ring me or Sergeant Jones.'

She pushed the cards through the crack. The woman took them and read one. 'I may see him later. But if he is very late, I do not open the door.'

'Good idea.' Gil nodded.

Slowly, the door shut and bolts clicked home. The officers exchanged glances. Catrin shrugged and turned away.

'What the hell just happened?' Gil asked, as they made for the stairs.

'A wary resident. I'd be too if I clocked you lurking on my landing, no offence intended.' Catrin grinned.

Gil threw her a dirty look and shook his head. 'I do not lurk. I'm more of a loomer.'

'That implies height not girth.'

'You did say no offence intended, didn't you?'

'Come on.' Catrin tried appeasement. 'We could have been scammers after her life savings. Good she's being cautious.'

'Maybe. But she never gave us her name.'

They'd reached the little foyer, and Catrin hesitated for a few seconds as Gil opened the front door. 'Her name?' she said, nonchalantly. 'It's Nowacki.'

Gil turned back, mouth open. 'How do you know that?'

'I'm a detective. It's what I do.'

'And?'

Catrin raised one sculpted eyebrow and pointed to the communal post box under the stairs she'd clocked on the way in. The boxes had flat numbers and names attached. 'We need to get you out and about more often, Gil. Hone those rusty deductive and interpersonal skills.'

Gil nodded slowly. A warning sign if ever there was one. 'I'll try and keep up, but I'm not as sharp as I was. Especially when it comes to yaws.'

'Yaws? What's yaws?'

'Oh, that's very kind. Mines a double shot latte and a chocolate chip muffin. I noticed that Cafe Nero next to Sainsbury's too.' Grinning, Gil walked out of the door without giving Catrin a chance to reply.

———

IN FACT, as Gil waited outside in the parked Focus and Catrin ordered the takeaway coffees and muffin – singular, Padrig Randal was not spraying "*błoto*" over the fields to make the grass grow quicker and thicker. He should have been, but he'd phoned in sick, told the manager that he'd eaten a dodgy curry the night before and couldn't be more than ten yards from a toilet for the next few hours. Now he sat alone in his car on an abandoned building site in the improbably named Gobowen area of Oswestry. He'd parked there because he thought it unlikely there'd be cameras anywhere and he wouldn't be disturbed as he unwrapped the cheap Nokia he'd bought in Argos and the pre-loaded SIM card he'd bought in Asda.

Too stressed to go back to his flat, the thought of ten hours spraying cow-shit had turned his stomach. All he wanted to do was speak to her. The police would want to speak to him; be unnatural if they didn't, him being the younger brother of Aeron and Joe's mad uncle. But he wasn't ready. Not yet. Before he did, he needed to know what the hell was going on.

Only one way to do that.

Padrig slid the SIM into the phone, plugged the USB charger into the adaptor he used for the car's lighter socket and waited for the phone to fire up. It showed three bars of reception as he slotted it into a holder on the dash. Good enough. It took five rings before she picked up. She wouldn't recognise this strange number and her wariness was clear from her croaky, anxious voice.

'Hello?'

'Mari, it's me.'

'Pa—' The blurted name stuttered and stalled. 'No sorry, you've got the wrong number.'

He half expected the ring tone to appear when she finished the sentence but it didn't come. Instead he heard muffled voices, the sound of heels on a floor, a latch opening, and then Mari Randal's urgently whispering voice again.

'What are you doing ringing me?'

'Sorry, I had to. I had to know what was happening, Mari.'

'The police are here. They've sent someone to be with me.'

'What about Aeron and Joe? Are they back—'

Her sob cut him off. 'They found blood on the feed-shed door in the lower pasture of the Chapel Road. It's theirs.' Her voice caught on an intake of breath. 'Tell me it wasn't you.'

'Christ, Mari,' he protested. 'Of course it wasn't me. Jesus.'

Mari's breath came in sharp inhalations and long exhalations. 'I thought… I thought Aeron had found out, and—'

Padrig interrupted her flow before she said the damning words. 'Aeron didn't suspect anything. Neither did Joe. I swear. We've been careful. Whatever's happened, it has nothing to do with us.'

'Us?' Mari whispered. 'Is there an us now, Padrig?'

His heart stuttered. 'Don't say that. I wish I could be there. I want to be there.'

'No, no, you mustn't. Almeira will be here. And the police have this detective, Warlow. He'd know. You need to stay away, Padrig.'

'I can't. If I don't call to see you, it'll seem bloody odd. My own sister-in-law.'

Mari said nothing.

'What?' Padrig demanded.

'I told them you'd fallen out. You and Aeron,' she whispered. 'Don't be angry.'

'God, Mari. Fuck's sake, shit.' He massaged his shut eyes, squeezing until his retinas saw nothing but flashing lights. 'Where do the police think Aeron and Joe are?'

'They don't know.' Her voice fell to something low and desperate. 'But they told me to prepare for the worst.'

It hung between them, a harrowing silence weighted down with the awful implications of that sentence.

Eventually, Padrig spoke. 'You can't do that alone. You can't. I'm coming over.'

'No. No. Don't. It'll only make things ten times worse. Stay away for now, please.'

Padrig sighed. 'They'll want to speak to me, you realise that. What do I tell them?'

'Can't you go away?'

'How would that look?'

Mari's voice trembled when she spoke next. 'What a mess.'

It was. A bloody mess. 'I'll keep this phone just for us.

If you see this number texting, it'll be me. Pretend it's a scam text or say it's your bank or something.'

Another pause. But then she answered in a desperate voice, 'Okay.'

She ended the call and left Padrig sitting in his car, staring out of the window at the three layers of breeze blocks on some concrete foundations that had been like that for two years. Someone's shattered dreams, no doubt.

He knew the feeling all too well.

CHAPTER THIRTEEN

A COUPLE of Uniforms stood waiting outside their response vehicle when Catrin and Gil arrived at Hermon Chapel. The Uniforms had obtained a key from one of the deacons, one Hari Gregory, the man who had raised the rustler alert on the night the Randals went missing. Gregory had been too busy to attend but promised to pick up the keys later.

Catrin made a mental note. Be good to have him answer a few questions. She stood back as Gil fitted the key to the rattling door and opened it, trying to suppress the anxiety that churned inside her. She didn't like these old buildings. Irrational maybe, but her partner, Craig, loved horror movies and the kind of computer games where the undead leapt at you from every shadow. Hermon Chapel, isolated, old, dark and silent, was exactly the sort of location both films and games revelled in.

She shivered. Luckily, Gil didn't see it.

Inside, the chapel felt dismal and gloomy. Catrin suspected that the grey cloudy day didn't help. There were enough windows in this building to light it up when the sun shone, but today the big yellow ball in the sky had gone

AWOL and murky shadows lurked in the corners. It all added to the oppressiveness. Like many of the old places of worship dotted around the Welsh countryside, a sense of redundancy permeated the building.

An ornately decorated balcony ran around the rear and side walls, and the pendant lighting hanging on metal rods from the high ceiling did little to chase away the shadows when Gil flicked the switches.

'Bloody hell, this takes me back.' His voice echoed through the space. 'My grandmother, a staunch Methodist, used threats and bribery to make me attend twice on Sundays for too many years before I could plead home-work as an excuse. Education always trumped religion in our house. But for years I dressed in a jacket and tie, some-times a dickie, and sat pinned in a pew, bored and semi-comatose as some old fogey told us all what we already knew.'

'What was the bribe?'

Gil's face dissolved in recalled ecstasy. 'Ah, a ninety-nine from Domachi's van on the way home from the after-noon shift. In other words, Sunday school.'

Catrin shivered. 'I'm not a big fan of the supernatural. Why are these places always so depressing?'

Gil looked around, his eyes finally settling on the ornate ceiling with its fancy plasterwork. 'Pretty joyless, I agree. Give me a gospel choir or a bunch of happy clap-pers any day. Right, let's not hang about. You have a butchers down here, I'll go upstairs.'

Catrin bobbed slowly up the aisle, checking out the varnished pews and squatting to look underneath. She saw nothing except a chewing gum wrapper. Someone was going to hell for littering. Five minutes later, Gil came back down.

'Nothing,' he said, as he joined Catrin. 'Except a couple of moribund mice. Must have died of poverty.

Okay, it's a chapel, not a church, but I'm allowed a little artistic licence.' He waited for her to respond to his convoluted joke, but all he got was a shake of Catrin's head. He'd take that. Grinning, Gil turned and picked up a book from one of the pew seats. A black hymn book, shiny, the covers scuffed at the corners, words all in Welsh. 'I have to say I enjoy the odd sing-song. *Gwahoddiad* gets all the blood pumping, even if it is an American tune and lyric. The Welsh version adds a lot of *hwyl*.' Gil started to hum.

Catrin folded her arms across her chest. The angst from being told how to live your life that the congregations in this place must have suffered seemed to seep out and press down on her. 'A friend of mine lives in a converted chapel. It's amazing. Some people think it's wrong, but I think it's great. At least the old place has some life. Not like here.'

Gil put the book down and they turned to face the central pulpit at the back with its backdrop of pipes from the organ behind. Below and to the left, a single door led to whatever lay beyond. They worked their way towards it, checking the pews as they went until Gil reached the door and turned to his fellow sergeant.

'You Church or Chapel, Catrin?'

'Neither. My gran and mum might go to midnight mass at Christmas in their local church, but they're fair-weather worshippers. I never saw the attraction. I switch on the news and I always feel that religion has a lot to answer for.'

'Careful.' Gil made eyes at the ceiling. 'Never know who might be listening here.'

Catrin gave him one of her half-lidded stares and nodded to the door. 'Shall we get on with it?'

'We might need a torch.'

Catrin waved a black Maglite.

Gil grinned. 'I knew there was a reason I brought you.'

He reached out for the ancient Bakelite doorknob and twisted. The latch bolt moved easily, and the door creaked open on its hinges.

The room beyond had a low sloping ceiling and two sash windows that let in a good amount of light, such that Catrin didn't need her torch. The place smelled of old paper and dust. A table and chairs took up much of the space. Somewhere to sign a marriage register, perhaps? However, she doubted anyone had got married here for a good while, judging from the loose boxes and plastic bags piled on the shelves that lined the back wall and on the table itself. A few of the chairs looked small.

'Sunday school?' Catrin said.

'At one time. Not recently judging by the dust.' Gil walked around, lifting a few of the larger plastic bags and avoiding the enormous spiders he disturbed with a look of distaste. 'Feels like books. Nothing else here.'

Catrin nodded. She'd known as soon as the door opened. The absence of a smell gave it away. That and the total lack of blowflies. No bodies in the vestry today.

They'd dispatched the Uniforms to the cemetery to check for any fresh disturbances on the ground. But when they emerged from the vestry, Catrin took one step and stopped.

At the far end, the front of the chapel, in the murky space behind the last pew and the dark wood panelling of the inner wall of the atrium inside the front door, something moved. A darker shadow, half the height of a person. The skin on the DS's neck contracted from her nape to the small of her back. She reached out and grabbed Gil's arm, pointing into the darkness.

'There,' she whispered. 'See it?'

In her head, the blood spatter on the feed-shed door they'd visited not half an hour before came back in glorious technicolour. It hadn't looked to her as if anyone would have survived that. But what if they had? What if they'd crawled…

Something shuffled and let out a small groan.

'*Beth uffern—*' Gil began. *What the hell* in his native tongue. He never got to finish.

The hunched shape changed in front of their eyes. Elongated as it stood up and spoke. 'Hello?'

Catrin let out the breath she'd been holding.

'You alright, Catrin?' Gil peered at her. Luckily, the gloom was too dense for him to notice how pale she'd become. 'Looks like you've seen a—'

'I'm fine,' she chirped, feeling very much not so.

Gil, looking highly amused, tutted. 'And there's me thinking you didn't believe in all this supernatural stuff.'

'I said it had a lot to answer for.' It came out as truculent and only added to Gil's amusement.

'Here,' he called back to the spectre hailing them, and walked past his colleague cheerfully whistling the first few bars of the theme tune to *The Exorcist.*

All Catrin could do was purse her lips and shake her head.

'Hari Gregory,' sang the man, as he strode up the aisle holding a tissue between the big thumb and forefinger of his left hand.

Catrin exhaled quietly and composed herself before following Gil.

Gregory was a rangy man with close-cropped hair and large bulbous eyes behind his glasses. A crooked grin split his weathered face as Gil made the introductions and he shook first Gil's and then Catrin's hand, before holding up the tissue.

'Someone left this here from the last service. Spotted it as I came in.'

'When was that?' Catrin asked.

Hari looked crestfallen. 'Three weeks ago. We manage once a month now.'

'Much of a congregation?'

'A dozen on a good day. The preacher comes over from Llanfair.'

'Thanks for letting us have a look around.'

'Did you find what you wanted?'

The simple answer would have been no, but that would have been churlish. 'Yes, thanks,' Catrin replied. 'It's been very helpful.'

Hari shook his head. 'Awful, this business with Aeron and Joseph.'

Catrin took out her notebook. A gesture she'd developed as a signal to the person being questioned that she was here on business, not for a social chit-chat.

'Yes. Mind if we ask you some questions?'

Hari shrugged. 'Not at all.'

They walked to the front of the chapel. Hari sat towards the edge of a pew, Gil behind him. Catrin stood in front, facing the men, and it was she who posed the first question.

'From what I understand, you had a surveillance system set up?'

Hari shrugged again. It seemed to be his default response. 'I suppose, though surveillance is a bit of a posh word for looking out for each other. If we heard or saw something, we took it in turns to investigate. On the roads, that is. If something was happening on my land, then it would be up to me. But on the road, we had a rota.'

'And the night the Randals disappeared, it was their turn?'

Hari nodded. 'I'd been out to check the stock. I'm on the other side of Caemawr, but one of my fields is on the top. I was coming back from there when I saw the lights. Slow moving, that's what got my attention. I texted Aeron and Elis Prosser and Aeron texted back that he'd take a look.' He sighed and looked up at the pulpit.

Looking for answers that weren't there, Catrin thought. 'And you heard nothing after that from them?'

Hari shrugged. 'Nothing. Until someone called around to say they were missing. A police officer.'

'Was that unusual, not to hear anything back?'

'No, not if there was nothing to say.'

From behind, Gil asked a question. 'And nothing else. No gunshots?'

Hari shook his head. 'But we are down in a dip. Something happening this side, we wouldn't hear.'

'And are all three of you members of the congregation here?'

'Not all of us.' Hari sent a wistful glance up and around at the Gallery. 'Aeron is a deacon, like me. There was a time this place would be full. Easter and Harvest especially. We try to keep the old place going, but it's getting harder. No one wants to go to Chapel. None of the youngsters.'

'You said Aeron, but no mention of Elis Prosser?'

'Elis does not attend.'

Catrin noted the lack of elaboration. From the way he'd said those words, it looked unlikely he'd want to. She asked, 'And you haven't been aware of anyone threatening the Randals?'

Hari's face fell, and he swivelled back to face Catrin. 'Threatening? No. Do you think—'

'We're keeping all our options open, Mr Gregory.' Gil applied the usual balm.

But the sergeant's words didn't take the edge off Hari's shock and he stared at the officers in horror. 'You think thieves might have taken them? For ransom?'

Interesting choice of words. Catrin threw Gil a glance. 'What makes you say that, Mr Gregory?'

'I don't know. I've been wondering all sorts. We all have. I mean, where could they be?'

It was an excellent question to which neither officer had an answer. Gil's phone broke the ensuing silence with a sing-song alert. He glanced at it and stood up. 'That's from Rhys. POLSA wants to set up a search in the vicinity of the feed shed.' Gil walked around and addressed the seated man. 'You won't object if they stray onto your land, will you, Mr Gregory?'

Hari shook his head. 'Of course not. I'd be more than happy to help.'

'Good, I'll let them know.' He handed over a card. 'And if you can come up with anything else that might be helpful, anything at all, give us a ring.'

CHAPTER FOURTEEN

THE TWO SERGEANTS returned to the Incident Room in Newtown mid-afternoon. Having suffered half an hour's worth of Gil's merciless teasing and bad horror puns on the journey back, Catrin got straight back to work. She'd had more than enough of suggestions such as 'who ghosts there' for when she next confronted someone in a dark alley, or if she fancied coming over to play with his grandchildren in a game of 'Hide and shriek'.

At least they'd not returned empty-handed. When Gil walked into the room, he was carrying a large white box in both hands.

Lowri read the label on the box with a look of troubled disgust. 'Oh, my God. What did you find up there, Sarge?'

'Where?' Gil looked confused.

'At the crime scene. Is there something awful inside that box?'

Rhys extricated his long limbs from his chair and stood, all smiles. 'Camouflage working a treat, Sarge.'

Gil, still confused by this conversation, came around the desk to consider Lowri's viewpoint. The label on the side of the box, red on white, read: HUMAN TISSUE FOR TRANSPLANT.

'Ha,' he blurted. 'I keep forgetting.' He grinned at Lowri and then shifted his gaze to Rhys and jerked his head towards the door. 'Go on. Kettle time.'

Lowri, still unsure of this exchange and of how anyone could be so jovial in the presence of body parts, stood up. 'I'll do it, the tea, I mean. I'd rather not see what's inside.'

'Oh, you will,' teased Rhys. 'You will.'

Lowri had already crossed the room at a half trot when Catrin put her out of her misery. 'They're biscuits. Sergeant Jones's idea of a joke.'

'It's no joke,' Gil protested. 'It's a fool-proof way of keeping prying eyes and pilfering hands away.'

'You can still make the tea though,' Rhys suggested with an enthusiastic nod towards Lowri. 'Since you offered, I mean.'

Lowri's incredulous gaze flitted from one face to the other before she shook her head and left the room. Rhys, doing a passable impression of a Cheshire Cat, made a little fist.

'Don't get used to it,' Gil warned.

'Poor kid. She must wonder what's hit her with you lot.' Catrin fired up a PC and sat at the desk. She downloaded some photos from her phone and began printing them off onto A4. 'Where's the boss?'

'Talking to Kapil about the Scene of Crime report.'

'Okay. Let's wait for the tea and then you should give him a shout.'

———

GIL AND CATRIN'S presence came as a welcome sight to Warlow. They needed something to get things moving and another two minds would do no harm. He missed Jess and her way of looking at a case. Perhaps, when he had more to work with, he'd give her a ring. Still, when he emerged from the office, he found much to please him.

The Gallery was filling up with photos. Gil had one of his biscuit displays on show and hot tea steamed in a mug with I HEART Wales on its side and a post-it note saying DCI OWEN stuck to the handle.

'Now this is what I call a catch up.' Warlow grabbed a chocolate digestive and took a bite, chewed and sent Gil a slit-eyed look. 'The real McCoy, or should I say McVitie's.'

'Spot on.' Gil nodded. 'You're getting better.'

Warlow took a sip of tea. 'Don't know about better. Fatter, yes, since you joined the team.'

Gil held up his hands. 'May I point out, as I have on many an occasion, that biscuit consumption is a voluntary activity.'

Warlow glanced at the display arranged on the plate: chocolate digestives as an outer ring, bourbons as a fan leading to vanilla cream sandwiches in the middle, with a significant number of gaps dotted randomly around. Every member of the team looked guilty.

'Right,' Warlow sat. 'How did it go in sheep country?'

'Not baa'd,' Gil said and earned a scathing look from Catrin.

'There's good and there's bad, with one 'a', sir.' She stuck an A4 image of Hermon Chapel on the Gallery.

'We didn't find Padrig Randal.' Gil held a hand up in apology, partly for the sheep pun and partly for their failed mission. 'A neighbour says he's out "contracting". But his employer says he's rung in sick.'

'Hmm.' Warlow grunted. 'What do you make of that?'

'He may keep a low profile for all sorts of reasons,' Gil replied.

'If he's really sick, wouldn't he be at home, in his flat?' Lowri asked. 'It's where I would be. At home, I mean.'

'Maybe he has another bolt hole,' Gil suggested.

'Sooner we find him the better, I think.' Warlow narrowed his eyes and then pointed to the image of Hermon. 'What about the chapel? Did you get inside?'

'We did, sir,' Catrin replied. 'And managed to have a word with Hari Gregory, the other farmer. He's a deacon and a key holder.'

'Spoo-key holder,' Gil muttered.

Catrin jutted her lower jaw forward and shook her head. 'No sign of anything in the chapel. Nor the cemetery attached. But the little chat with Gregory turned out to be useful. He confirmed seeing some slow-moving lights on the Chapel Road last Saturday evening. That observation prompted him to alert the other two farmers.'

'Right, so that confirms what Mari Randal and Elis Prosser told us.' Warlow turned to Rhys. 'How are we getting on with phone records?'

Rhys reached for a pile of printouts on his desk. 'Yes, sir. There is a text message on Aeron Randal's phone at 21.45 on Saturday evening. I don't have Gregory's number yet, but I can get that. The message says: "Lights Chapel Road. Slow, could be lorry. Sorry, no more details."'

'Good.' Warlow nodded. 'Nothing after that?'

'No sir. No calls or messages after that. There are no tower pings after 10.55pm which means his phone went dead.'

Warlow stood up and walked to the Gallery to join Catrin. 'Right, so we have a timeline between when the Randals left their farm, and the phone went dead. Whoever did this wanted nothing to be traced.'

Catrin wrote 22.05-22.55 on the board.

Warlow stared at the figures. 'So in just under an hour, something terrible happened at that feed shed.' He pivoted to study the sombre faces of the team. All the joviality of before had gone. 'We have Kapil's preliminary report back from the scene. It's not that great. Too much animal activity around the shed for tyre identification. Sheep have been walking all over it. We already know it's Aeron and Joseph Randal's blood. The solid tissue on the wall is also Joseph Randal's. It's Kapil's opinion that neither men would have survived that degree of damage and blood loss. I've warned Mari Randal to expect the worst. But what I'd like to do is find her husband and son for her.' He flicked his gaze towards Lowri. 'Where are we with the POLSA?'

Startled by the question, she cleared her throat. 'They've set a mile radius around the shed, sir. Though there's only four hours of daylight left, they're going to start this afternoon because the weather's holding. They'll do what they can tonight and start again tomorrow.'

Anyone watching from the road would see a line of policemen and tracker dogs combing the fields. Warlow felt a strong urge to go up there and help. But he wouldn't. They were the experts. He'd just be in the way.

'Okay, then we'll do our bit here. Find out what Padrig Randal drives and get his plates out to patrols and ANPR.'

'What about Joseph Randal?' Lowri's question filled the little space that followed Warlow's instructions. Because it wasn't aimed at anyone in particular, it took a moment before anyone answered, which left the young PC blinking and trying to swallow. Something that seemed to take a lot of effort.

'What about him?' Once again, Catrin responded first.

'His phone. I mean, it would be good to know if his phone went dead at the same time.'

'Good point.' Catrin dipped her head and turned to Rhys. 'DC Harries?'

Rhys showed a lot of teeth in an apologetic grin. 'I've concentrated on Aeron. Joseph Randal's phone had a different service provider but it's on my list.'

'Okay.' Warlow addressed Lowri. 'We have a rule in

this team. You come up with an idea, you follow it through. Joseph Randal's phone records are now your responsibility.'

'Yes, sir,' she responded with a flurry of nods, her eyes bright.

Warlow added a half-smile by way of encouragement. That was the wonderful and priceless thing about enthusiasm. Until someone crushed it, as so often time and disappointment had a tendency to do, a prod of acknowledgement was all it needed. His team had thoroughness, determination and, with both Rhys and Lowri, enthusiasm as their wellspring. Add to that Gil's experience and Warlow's tempered cynicism and it all seemed to work remarkably well. They still missed Jess's smarts, but they'd have to work harder on that for now. And she was only a phone call away if needed.

He turned back to the Gallery and the Job Centre, pleased to see how the investigation was expanding. Yet something, a loose thread, needed pulling. He stared at the images of the chapel and of Padrig Randal. 'Did Gregory mention anything about Padrig Randal falling out with his brother?'

Gil shook his head. 'We talked about rustling, that's about all.'

Warlow tutted. A missed opportunity there. He hadn't briefed them about it. But there was someone else they could ask. He turned back to the waiting faces.

'Right, looks like we've all got enough to do. Rhys, give Elis Prosser a ring. See if you can get hold of him before he goes back up north. If he's free, you and I are going to meet him for a coffee.'

————

Elis Prosser opted for tea instead of coffee. Warlow joined him while Rhys took the latte route with a pile of whipped cream and chocolate powder on the top that looked worryingly like an iceberg covered in penguin crap.

They were in a cafe in the Bear Lanes Shopping Centre surrounded by people laden with bags.

'I appreciate you meeting us at short notice again, Mr Prosser.' Warlow eyed the scones on display on top of the glass counter and heard his stomach protest. He'd skipped lunch and was paying for it.

'No problem, Evan. Anything I can do to help.'

Warlow brought his attention back to the farmer. 'I'll get to it. We've had officers out to the scene and they called in to Hermon, the chapel.'

Elis nodded. 'Did they find anything?'

'No. But my colleagues spoke to Hari Gregory. He told them you don't attend.' Warlow sipped his tea. Too weak by far. He should have asked for an extra bag for the pot.

'I do not,' Elis replied. 'Blind faith lost its appeal for me when my wife died.'

Warlow nodded. The death of a loved one did indeed test one's beliefs in an all-seeing God. 'What about the Randals?'

Elis shook his head. 'Yes, Aeron is a deacon and he and Mari attend. Joseph, like many of the younger people, was not a worshipper.'

'And what about Padrig Randal?'

Elis's bushy eyebrows crept a little closer together behind the glasses. 'No, we no longer see Padrig, though he was baptised at Hermon like us all.'

Warlow nodded. 'Is there a reason for that?'

'He no longer lives locally,' Elis explained.

A good enough explanation. But not the one the DCI was after. 'I understand that relations between the brothers had become a little strained.'

Elis put down his tea cup. It looked ridiculously small in the farmer's big hands. 'An unpleasant business. So sad.'

'There has been a rift then?' Warlow kept up the probing.

'After what happened at the old man's funeral...' Elis shook his head at some painful recollection. He looked into Warlow's face almost pleadingly, but the impassive expression he found there made it clear the police officer wanted more. 'They fell out after the service. Words were exchanged, and they came to blows in the cemetery with their father's coffin waiting to be put into the earth. I will never forget it. We had to separate the brothers, there on the grounds of Hermon, "God's sacred place".' He delivered this last quote with a wry smile.

Rhys slurped some cream from the remains of his coffee and got a scathing glance from Warlow. Thankfully, Elis seemed not to notice as he carried on explaining. 'I don't think the brothers have spoken since.' He stopped, his frown deepening. 'Why would you want to know about Padrig? You surely don't think—'

'We're in the process of trying to discover as much as we can about the missing men, Elis. Most of what we'll learn will not be relevant. But every small piece of information adds up.'

Elis nodded.

Warlow continued, 'Are you aware of Padrig having threatened Aeron since that day?'

'Threatened? No.' Elis seemed definite. 'I don't think they've spoken since.'

Warlow risked another glance at Rhys and was relieved to see the DC had his notebook out.

'We've been trying to find Padrig. He's not at home. Any idea where he might be?' Warlow abandoned the insipid brew in his cup and it chinked loudly as it met the saucer.

Elis looked thoughtful for a moment. 'He contracts, but he also does construction when farm work is slow. As a digger driver. He's worked on sites in Oswestry. But I don't think he has a place there.'

Warlow smiled. 'Great. That all helps. Will you be back up to the farm now?'

'I will. There'll be plenty to do.'

'We won't keep you then.' He stood and shook Elis's hand then turned to Rhys. 'Right, let's shift our backsides.'

Rhys stood and drained his cup, only to almost collide with Warlow at the door. The senior officer held up a napkin.

'Sir?' Rhys looked confused.

'Whatever the hell it was you were drinking was delicious, I'm sure. But unless you're considering keeping some for later, you'd better wipe the remains of it off your upper lip. I've seen fussier five-year-olds. Next time make it an Americano.'

CHAPTER FIFTEEN

BY THE TIME Warlow and Rhys got back to the car, 6pm had come and gone and a text message from Gil announced that he and Catrin had gone back to the hotel since little more could be done that night.

Warlow reluctantly agreed. They were on the lookout for Padrig Randal, the organised search for Aeron and Joe was in full swing and everything else would have to wait until the morning.

'Meet in the bar in an hour, sir?' Rhys asked in the reception of the Angler's Lodge.

'Sounds good.' That allowed just enough time for Warlow to make some phone calls.

He rang Jess first and asked about Molly and Cadi.

'Both fine, thanks for asking. How about you? How's it going up there?'

Warlow sighed. 'Slow. Still no sign of the mispers. We've got a couple of leads, but nothing concrete yet.'

'What's your gut telling you?'

From his seat on the edge of the bed, Warlow eyed the kettle. He felt cheated by the insipid dishwater brew he'd had in the cafe. But the promise of a pint in the bar kept the idea of another cuppa at bay. 'Fresh air so far. But now that Gil and Catrin are here, I'm sure they'll shake something loose.'

After a beat of silence, Jess asked, 'You okay, Evan? You don't sound your usual acerbic self. You're not unwell?'

'No. I'm fine.' Jess and Buchanan were the only two people in the force, hell, in the world – apart from his doctors – he'd ever told about his HIV status. And though she was careful not to show it, since telling her, Warlow got the impression she'd become a little more sensitive to his health. As usual, he batted her concern away. 'Always a bit more difficult playing away from home. Nothing's quite as I'd like it. The bed, the tea, the Incident Room. If you can even call the box room we're in an Incident Room.'

'Yeah.' He heard the sympathy in her voice. 'Well, if you need to talk anything through, you know where I am.'

She was talking about the case. Of course she was. And even if she wasn't, he wouldn't dream of lumbering her with any of the baggage that, away from the cut and thrust of police work, played on his mind. He ended the call and changed out of his suit into jeans, aware that the button around his waist felt a tad tighter than normal. Bloody Gil and his biscuits. He needed to get back into a routine. He missed walking the dog more than anything. But, truth be told, Jess had been spot on in her assessment of his preoccupied status. He had something on his mind. A thorn that he'd keep worrying at unless he plucked the bugger out.

He eyed the kettle again. Very tempting, but he didn't need another tea. Boiling the kettle would only be another distraction from what he knew he needed to do. He stood at the window and looked out. No river view here, only traffic and pedestrians and lights from the cinema opposite. Warlow had no idea what was showing. Yet he'd have paid good money to watch anything as a distraction as of this moment. Well, almost anything. So long as it didn't have any singing in it.

But he still had his phone in his hand and half an hour to kill before he was due to meet the others.

No excuses, in other words.

He looked at the screen, called up his contacts, and found the name. The oldest in his book and one with no surname.

Denise.

The number rang for twenty seconds. He almost gave up, but then a voice answered, croaky and familiar. 'Hello?'

'Hi, Denise. It's Evan.'

Something rustled. Paper or some kind of material. But no words.

Warlow tried again. 'I heard you're not well.'

'And?' There she was.

He almost smiled at the familiarity of a passive-aggressive dagger thrust right up to the hilt.

'I'm ringing to find out how you are, that's all.'

Denise hissed out air. 'Why? So that you can wag that bloody finger of yours again?' Cigarettes and alcohol had ravaged Denise's voice, but even for her, it sounded raw. Warlow recalled Tom had told him she'd been throwing up for days.

But he had no interest in fighting this evening. 'I stopped wagging that finger years ago when I realised it did neither of us any good.'

Silence.

'You still there, Denise?'

'I am. I've walked out to the corridor so no one can hear me swear if it comes to it. Who told you I was ill?'

'Martin and Tom.'

'Huh. That must have made your day.' Once upon a time, Denise's bitter snipe might have triggered an equally poisonous response from Warlow. But he'd long ago tamed that beast.

'What are they saying there, Denise? Are you any the wiser as to what's wrong?'

His sincerity deflated her anger. Her conversations with him were always a verbal tussle, but for once it seemed that being in hospital had robbed her of some of that fight.

'Gall bladder, pancreas or an ulcer. Possibly all three. I've had a scan and I'm waiting for the results.'

In the street below, an idiot on a motorbike roared across the river bridge up Broad Street to a T junction. All of two hundred yards. For no other reason than hoping someone might notice his shiny new 250cc penis extension. In defiance, Warlow turned away.

'Do you feel any better?'

'The pain in my back and guts only goes away with the drugs but I've stopped throwing up as of mid-day. And now, since you've rung, the pain has moved right around to my arse. Does that count?'

Despite the words, most of her prickliness had gone now. Warlow sensed only desperation in her voice. He ambled away from the window and sat on the bed again.

Denise sighed loudly. 'Plus I can't drink in here, as you know.'

'That must be—'

'Dia-sodding-bolical is what it must be. Not even a solitary shot of vodka as an apéritif. Yeah, enjoy that one. You must be laughing like a sodding hyena at the thought of me going cold-turkey.'

Warlow tried to imagine her walking the corridors of the hospital like a caged beast. He saw nothing funny or satisfying in the image. He kept his voice low and soft. 'We both know that can't be easy.'

'Christ, is that the best you can come up with, Evan? That's the understatement of the sodding century.' Her breath eased out in a loud exhalation, catching a couple of times on the cogs of the anxiety he knew she'd be unable to hide. 'They say my liver enzymes are through the roof and that's all because of the booze.'

Warlow's eyes narrowed. This was very new. A Denise who actually admitted her problems. He supposed she'd have no choice faced with the doctors' examinations and their blood test results. But if he wanted real proof of her newfound fragility, it came in the next sentence. 'What the hell happened to me, Evan?'

The 64 million dollar doozie. Make it 64 billion dollar doozie. Of course, he didn't have an answer because the shock of it had numbed his brain. This was the first time he could recall her questioning herself. 'I don't know, Denise. I wish I did. But it's an addiction like any other. Something must have given you the craving. Or driven you to it. I hope it wasn't all me.'

A long beat followed. Outside, someone blew a car horn several times. A cheery blast followed by a yell. Someone out on the town, no doubt. Eventually, Denise answered her own question. 'A bit you, a bit the job. Mostly me not liking to be alone. But none of those are an excuse for what it's all led to. What it's made me. How it drove you away, poisoned the family, made you hate me. Don't think I don't know that, Evan.'

He didn't insult her by lying. Because he had grown to hate her. Or what she'd become at any rate. But separation had turned most of that hate into concern, if not pity. 'The boys think the world of you, Denise.'

'Do they?' Her rasping laugh sounded forced. 'Alun doesn't want me to go out to Australia. He's been upfront about that. And Tom refuses to meet me at a restaurant. Hardly unconditional love.'

'We both know why that is.' Two bottles of wine in and Denise became a loud and obnoxious drunk, demanding everyone in the place join her in a chorus of "*I Will Survive*", or asking for the music to be turned up so she could dance. Of course, the wine was only topping off the bottle of vodka she'd consumed slowly since breakfast, merely adding fuel to the fire. But his boys only needed to experience that once to want to avoid it like a pustular plague.

'Yes, we do.' Her voice broke. Suddenly, this was the old Denise. The tender, funny, reflective Denise he had not seen or heard for years. A few days of enforced abstinence had pried open a locked and self-aware door she'd slammed shut years ago. 'My dad drank. So did my mother, but not to the same extent. They encouraged me to have a wine with food from the age of fourteen. I thought it was normal. They thought they were preparing me for the world.'

Warlow remembered Denise's dad. Jack Grady lived life to the full and used booze to lubricate his way through it. Loud and brash, always the first to the bar and the last to leave it. 'They thought they were giving you a head start.'

'I could have done without it. And of course, I wish things had been different.' Denise laughed softly. It turned into a chesty bout of ugly, ripe coughing that went on for half a minute. When she wheezed to a stop, she said, 'See. I do have regrets.'

Warlow searched for a reply. All he managed was an anodyne. 'You could always start again.'

Denise laughed softly. 'Too late for me, Evan. Far too late.'

Her admission threw Warlow off balance. 'I'm up north on a case. When I'm done here, I'll call in to the hospital. Tom might be back on the weekend,' he said.

'That would be nice.'

She sounded tearful and emotional. Two words he

hadn't used to describe her for years. And suddenly, into his head burst an image of the old Denise. The one that stole his heart at twenty-two. The vivacious, naughty, do anything for a laugh, Denise that complemented so well the dry, considered Warlow.

'Right,' he said, an unaccustomed welling in his chest taking him by surprise. 'I'll see you in a few days. Look after yourself, Denise.'

'I'll try, Evan. I will try.'

─────

WHEN WARLOW JOINED the others in the bar a while later, a pint of IPA sat in front of an empty seat at the table.

'My shout,' Gil explained. 'Rhys is adamant that this is what you'd want.'

'He's right. Thank God some of those detective lessons are finally paying off.' Warlow side-eyed Rhys before lifting the glass to his lips. 'Just what the doctor ordered. Cheers.'

The rest of the team reciprocated. Warlow took a swallow and then licked froth from his upper lip. The beer tasted fresh. 'Any news from the search team?'

Catrin put down her glass of Coke Zero with ice. 'Lowri rang. They've stopped for the night, sir. Back at it in the morning. So far, nothing.'

Warlow took another couple of swallows of his beer. Gil looked on with wary amusement. 'Now there's a man in need of a drink. All okay, Evan?'

'As well as,' Warlow replied. 'What time is the restaurant booked for?'

Rhys looked over the rim of his glass. '7.45, sir.'

Warlow nodded his approval. 'I didn't have any lunch. Let's hope they do scabby horse.'

'I'll drink to that.' Gil raised his glass.

'Double helping.' Rhys raised his.

'So long as there's a vegetarian option.' Catrin eyed her fellow officers charily.

'Scabby turnip then.' Rhys grinned.

'How about I grab a menu?' Gil got up and sauntered to the bar.

'Good idea.' Warlow watched him go and attempted to push thoughts of his ex-wife firmly to the back of his mind. This would have to be a working supper.

CHAPTER SIXTEEN

A FINE DRIZZLE of the kind that demanded intermittent wiper action accompanied Warlow and Rhys's journey from the hotel to the Incident Room the following morning. Though possible to vary the speed, Warlow could never quite get it right so either the bloody things ended up dry wiping with an annoying scrape, or he ended up looking through a rain-spattered windscreen for two seconds longer than was entirely safe.

Driving conditions, however, did not seem to bother his companion a great deal. 'Great breakfast in the hotel, isn't it, sir?' Rhys grinned his approval.

'Surprised they didn't declare a famine after you and Gil had been at it.' He'd watched in awe as both men visited and revisited the food.

'You had your fair share, though, didn't you, sir?'

'I did.' He'd planned on sticking with muesli and yoghurt, but one look at the thick bacon and sausage Gil brought back to the table and the sautéed mushrooms Rhys had three helpings of put paid to Warlow's good intentions. He'd rationalised it by remembering he'd gone through the previous day with no lunch. The way his stomach felt under his belt now, he'd probably manage for a good twenty-four hours on water only.

Traffic slowed to a crawl thanks to some road works. As they waited in line to turn right into the station, Rhys pointed out of the window at a striding pedestrian almost matching their crawl.

'Ah, there's the protestor lady, sir.'

Walking purposefully along and overtaking them with no effort, placard in one hand, megaphone in the other, was the beanie-hatted town-crier he'd seen, and heard, from the Incident Room window the day before. Being only a few yards away, rain dripping off her waxed coat, Warlow stretched forward to sneak a peek past Rhys. Julia Lloyd had dark hair under the hat, and, contrary to the impression he'd got from what he'd seen yesterday, looked surprisingly normal. She had a long, strong, almost beautiful face tanned from the weather and looked slim. From all the protesting, he assumed. She glanced across and caught Warlow's eye in a defiant glare and delivered an upward thrust of her "MISSING 2 YEARS CLUELESS POLICE. WHERE IS ROBERT LLOYD?" placard. He responded with a toothless smile and quickly sat back.

She crossed the road in front of them and marched around the corner towards the station. Twenty seconds later, Warlow heard her voice.

'POLICE   INCOMPETENCE.   WHERE   IS ROBERT? WE DEMAND ACTION!'

Up ahead, traffic moved and Warlow eased the Jeep around the corner and past Ms Lloyd once again. But as he turned into the car park, she must have realised they were the enemy because she aimed the megaphone squarely at them and delivered a full blast of: 'POLICE INCOMPETENCE.   WHERE   IS   ROBERT?   WE DEMAND ACTION!' Just in case they hadn't heard.

Rhys clapped his hands over his ears. 'Someone should stop her.'

Warlow parked the car and grabbed his coat from the back seat. 'If they found her son, I expect she'd stop of her own accord.'

The accusatory mantra accompanied them as they headed for the entrance and dimmed only slightly once they were inside. When Warlow got to the Incident Room, he walked to the window to see a repeat performance of yesterday unfolding outside, another slapstick scene from the Keystone Cops with police approaching and the perpetrator marching off before they could get to her. He smiled at that, knowing full well if he gave Rhys the Keystone reference, he'd be clueless. He'd get a blank stare and one of the DC's special smiles. The one he kept for humouring old people.

Outside in the rain, Julia Lloyd lowered the megaphone, clamped the placard under her arm and beat a hasty retreat.

The Incident Room looked busier. As well as an Exhibits Officer and secretaries, other Uniforms and plain-clothed CID manned a few desks. Gil and Catrin had left the hotel a few minutes after Warlow and the door to the Incident Room opened now to reveal DS Jones shedding his coat. He threw a meaningful glance at Warlow and jerked his head backwards over his shoulder as a warning. A few seconds later, Catrin followed with two other people Warlow had never seen before. Both male, both suited and not fazed at all by their environment.

Cops then.

Catrin walked across to the window where Warlow stood, an apologetic and unhappy expression on her face. The two men accompanied her, all business-like.

'Uh, DCI Warlow, this is DI McGrath and DI

Cheesely. Apparently, they needed another word with me.'
Catrin's plastic grin told a different story.

Warlow shook both proffered hands and wondered
what time these poor sods got up to be here this early.

'So we thought we'd catch up with you, if that's okay?'
Mac, clearly a Brummie, did the talking, his supposedly
professional smile getting nowhere near his eyes. Cheese
looked around, taking in the Incident Room, lingering on
the Gallery.

'No, it isn't. There's a time and a place,' Warlow said.

'Agreed. But you lot are all over the shop. You're closer
to our patch here than your own HQ.' Mac's voice rose
and fell. It was true, you could get to Birmingham in ninety
minutes from where they now stood.

Cheese, however, spoke with a harder-edged accent.
More South Yorkshire or Derbyshire. 'Won't keep you
long. We just need a chat.'

Warlow realised he could be awkward about it. Tell
them to make a formal appointment through the Buccaneer, but he wanted to cooperate and find out what the hell
happened to Mel Lewis as much as anyone. 'You've got
fifteen minutes,' Warlow said. 'Follow me.'

He got Rhys to organise tea, but told him in a whispered aside to forget the biscuits. He didn't want Mac and
Cheese getting too comfortable.

'So, Mel Lewis,' Mac said, once they'd found seats in
the cramped room. 'You and him went way back, am I
right?'

'You are. We worked together on and off for years.'

Cheese started thumbing through pages in his notebook. After a while, he stopped riffling and looked up. 'His
involvement in the Engine House operation began after
yours, though, is that correct?'

Warlow went through it once more. Aware of how this
worked. They wanted to hear it from the horse's mouth, as

opposed to the horse's typed-up report. He explained that though he'd been the SIO in the initial search for the missing couple murdered by the gang who'd set up an illegal drug factory and distribution centre under the derelict engine house on the edge of the Pembrokeshire coast, Mel Lewis's involvement came much later. 'He did the review a couple of years after I got nowhere.'

'Did he try to influence you while you ran the initial investigation?' Cheese adopted a deadpan delivery. Meant to keep people on edge, no doubt. All it did for Warlow was to irritate him.

'No. He had nothing to do with that initial investigation.'

'But you were friends, yes?'

Warlow nodded. Mel Lewis tried several times to get him involved in his passion: sailing. And though that had not panned out, since the DCI's sea legs were wobbly at best, they'd remained friends, sharing an interest in rugby and work. Nothing strange or sinister in this. Yet Mel's capacity for hard drinking became the main reason they hadn't been closer.

The odd Saturday afternoon session during the Six Nations was one thing. Regular Sunday morning hangovers with a tongue like a rubber flip-flop all day were another. Weekends of heavy boozing had never floated Warlow's boat.

But the Engine House case had thrown up links to organised crime and Warlow's initial failure to find the bodies of the two missing walkers hidden away by the people who put them there had more than one interpretation. Depending on how suspicious you were. The same thought obviously occurred to Mac and Cheese.

'You're not a sailor, Detective Chief Inspector?' Mac asked.

'No. Not my kind of thing.'

'You enjoy renovating houses, so we hear,' Cheese said.

'Cottage, singular. And enjoy might be stretching it a bit. I retired once so I could spend more time doing the old place up. It's where I now live. But then you know all that, I'm sure.' Warlow's grin matched Mac's in the sincerity stakes.

'Expensive business, renovation.' Not a question, merely an observation. Cheese kept his eyes on his notes.

'Luckily, I had the property left to me by a relative. But yes, materials are bloody expensive.' They were digging, probing. It wasn't what he'd been expecting.

'That must have eaten into your pension pot, no?' Mac looked genuinely interested. Warlow knew he wasn't.

'It did. But like I said, I needed somewhere to live.'

'Yeah, you and your wife are divorced, and she got the house. We are up to speed on all that,' Cheese said.

Christ, these two were looking for a chink in his armour. Something to exploit. The bastards. He sat up in his chair, wanting to tell them that was none of their bloody business, but Mac asked another question before he could.

'Couldn't have been easy, realising you'd been played.'

Warlow sat back and seethed for a few seconds, remembering the gut churning moment he'd realised that someone on the inside had been involved in misdirecting the investigation into firstly the missing walkers, and then the engine house drugs farm. More than one witness had been murdered and he was pretty sure that he'd prevented more killings by his actions. Still, he forced himself to answer the question hidden in the statement. 'Lots of people had the wool pulled over their eyes. Me included. But coming back to the case afresh gave me a new perspective. As it often does.'

'Yeah. It's you we have to thank for opening things up,

isn't it?' Cheese asked, slowly letting his eyes drift up from his notebook to engage with the DCI's.

Warlow kept quiet, trying to work out where exactly they were going with this.

'Must be difficult knowing that a colleague was playing you right from the start,' Cheese added.

'What the hell does that mean?'

'If I found out a mate had been lying to me, I'd be really pissed off. Wouldn't you?' Mac looked at Cheese, who nodded in reply.

And then Warlow saw their little double act for what it was. Mel Lewis had jumped off a cliff within sight of the engine house. A derelict building, Lewis, and whoever stumped up the seed money for the marijuana factory, ran with the help of the two farmers who owned the land. But the only witness to that jumping had been Warlow. Jess had been nearby, helping an injured witness. But she'd been preoccupied. Warlow's word was all the inquest had to go by.

The coroner had accepted it unequivocally.

Mac and Cheese clearly did not.

The low rumble of anger ticking over inside Warlow ever since the two detectives had begun questioning him ballooned into a roar. He thumped the desk with his fist. 'Are you accusing me of pushing him?' He felt the colour rise to his cheeks, helpless to stop it.

'We're accusing you of nothing,' Cheese said.

Warlow leaned forward. 'Good. Because if I thought you were, I'd take exception. A very large exception. I've already given my statement to the Conduct Unit. I'm willing to help anyone nail the bastards that made Mel do what he did. The bastards who got their hooks into him. But I will not sit here and listen to you two throw accusations about.'

Mac and Cheese stared back at him. But Warlow

wasn't finished. He had his finger out, pointing at the two officers, jabbing it towards them to emphasise his anger. Thank Christ it wasn't a gun. 'I came back to work because I was asked to. So that I can do the job I was trained to do. Now, unless you have any serious questions for me – relevant, sensible questions – I'm going to get on with it and you two jokers can put on your peaky hats and piss off back to Birmingham.'

Someone knocked on the door. Rhys stood there, hands holding two steaming mugs.

Warlow stood up. 'Thanks, Rhys. Unfortunately, our colleagues here will not be staying.'

Mac and Cheese exchanged glances. Denial of tea ranked up there as a major insult. Warlow might as well have taken off a gauntlet and slapped them across the face with it. 'No need to be arsey about this,' Mac grumbled.

'This isn't arsey. You haven't seen me arsey. And you don't want to.' Warlow's eye caught a poster next to a filing cabinet in the office. A September Open Day from last year. *Diwrnod Agored* in Blue – Open Day in red in English. Warlow smiled and let his anger calm to a simmer before he addressed Mac and Cheese once more. 'Next time, make an appointment. But don't rush because I've got a feeling I'll be busy. Or, even better, since we're in Wales, and we have language laws, why don't I request we do the whole interview in Welsh? *Beth am 'ny?*' He threw out the 'How about that?' in Welsh, not bothering to translate. Then, eyes blazing, let his gaze drift over to Rhys, the tallest in the room by a good few inches, who flinched visibly in the glare of it. 'Leave the tea here and see these gentlemen out of my Incident Room, DC Harris.'

Mac and Cheese looked at the tea and then at each other.

Mac said, 'This is out of order.' And without another

word, they stood and left, with Rhys in tow. The DC came back a while later, sporting his usual grin.

'They weren't happy, sir,' Rhys remarked happily.

'No, they were grumpy and dozy.'

'That's a Seven Dwarfs thing, isn't it sir? I know the song, Hi-Ho Silver Lining.'

Warlow thought about correcting him but knew that Catrin had once tried and failed. So instead, he smiled and nodded. 'That's the one, Rhys. Now, see if you can find Gil's biscuit box. Be a shame to waste this tea.'

CHAPTER SEVENTEEN

With Mac and Cheese out of his sight, Warlow sat mulling. He'd expected the investigation into corruption involving the marijuana farm and the Pickerings' murder case to have involved him. Of course he had. But as a collaborator, not a bloody… suspect.

He'd been naïve.

Christ. Is that what people thought? That he pushed Mel Lewis off a cliff to cover up his own involvement?

No one else had ever mentioned such a theory, yet Mac and bloody Cheese clearly did.

They'd come to press his buttons. See how he'd react. Thinking it through, Warlow's anger faded. He'd done the same thing himself enough times to thieves and bullies and violent thugs. Never to a colleague, though.

And perhaps it wasn't Mac and Cheese's theory. Maybe some West Mids' superintendent had sent them on a kamikaze mission. And it had been kamikaze because they'd crashed and burned in terms of Warlow's relationship with them.

Still, it left a sour, vinegary taste in his mouth.

The knock on his door, when it came, seemed a welcome distraction from his tumble dryer thoughts.

Catrin stuck her head around the door. 'Alright, sir?'

'Fine.'

'Mac and Cheese gone, have they?'

'They have. Did they speak to you?'

Catrin shook her head dismissively. 'Some minor thing a text or email could have sorted out in half a minute. I was their doorway to you.'

'Yes, well, I just slammed it in their faces.'

Catrin gave him a lopsided grin. 'They looked well peeved on the way out, sir.'

'Hmm.' Warlow let out a deep growl. 'With a bit of luck, we won't see the buggers again. But somehow I doubt that wish is going to be granted.'

Catrin lifted her chin. 'At least we've made some progress while you were being… interviewed.'

'Good, talk me through it.' Warlow waved Catrin forward and followed her into the Incident Room.

Progress comprised information from two sources. The first came via the ANPR system that had picked up Padrig Randal's Subaru in Oswestry the night before. That tallied with what Elis Prosser had told them of his haunts. The second bit of information, however, came from Gil, who stood at the Gallery writing down a location using a blue felt tip. He wrote with the tip of his tongue protruding from the corner of his mouth, his concentration evident for all to see.

'I know you can do joined-up writing, but try capitals next time to make the damn thing legible.' Warlow peered at the letters.

Gil looked around, annoyed. 'I've done a course in calligraphy, I'll have you know.'

'Then I'd ask for my money back.' Warlow stood closer and tilted his head to make out the words.

Gil continued to write.

'Does that say ladyboy?'

'Lay-by. It says lay-by.' Gil didn't turn this time. 'And the rest is a descriptive address since lay-bys tend not to have post codes.'

Rhys, sitting at his desk, provided the explanation. 'We had a call from Shropshire Uniforms, sir. Some walkers found a coat under a wooden bridge. It looked blood-stained. And the wallet in the pocket belongs to Aeron Randal.'

Warlow's eyebrows shot up.

'Where exactly is this lay-by?'

Catrin had a map up on her screen and Warlow leaned over to look at it. 'It's in the middle of nowhere, sir. Habberley, southwest of Shrewsbury. It's not even a lay-by. It's a pull-in near a wooden bridge over a brook.'

Warlow looked on as Catrin called up the street view on Google maps. The image showed a wooden footbridge guarded by a steel gate and marked by a public footpath post and arrow. Beyond the bridge stood a stile and open fields.

'Let me look at that map again,' Warlow muttered.

Catrin pulled out of street view to a road map. These were country roads leading to Shrewsbury, and beyond that, Telford and the rest of the Midlands. She toggled back. These were the sort of roads you'd get stuck behind a lorry carrying livestock. Maybe even stolen livestock.

'What does the report from whoever found the coat say?' Warlow wondered.

Rhys picked up a sheet of paper and scanned the notes he'd made. 'Found it dangling under the bridge. Like someone threw it in but it got caught underneath. They pulled it up and realised it was bloodstained so they called it in.'

'How far from Oswestry?'

'Three quarters of an hour, sir.'

Gil stood up and Warlow saw that he'd crossed out his curly handwriting and written everything in capitals. With one word thickly underlined.

BLOODSTAINED COAT, WOODEN BRIDGE, LAY-BY, HABBERLEY. AERON RANDAL WALLET.

'Why would someone throw Aeron Randal's coat over a bridge like that?' Warlow realised he was more or less talking out loud as his thoughts spun.

'Hoping no one would find it, sir?' Rhys offered.

Warlow's face crinkled with doubt. 'I can think of better ways to get rid of evidence.'

'Perhaps they were spooked, sir,' Catrin said, and earned a pointed look from Gil.

'That's possible, I suppose. Getting rid of evidence as opposed to destroying it could be a hurried response.' But even as he spoke the words, they didn't quite fit in Warlow's head.

He should have been pleased. These new findings showed demonstrable progress of a sort. Yet, after two days of not really getting anywhere, this sudden flurry of information served only to make the case murkier than ever. But there was more to come.

The Uniform manning the phones got up and leaned over to talk to Lowri, who'd been watching Warlow and the team work. She listened as he whispered something, her eyes widening first in surprise and then in consternation. Warlow didn't take much notice as his brain struggled to fit these new pieces of info into the jigsaw.

'Excuse me, sir?' Lowri's voice, high pitched and nervous, made Warlow pivot. Once again, the residual glower in his expression triggered a rabbit staring-down-the-barrel-of-a-shotgun expression on the young PC's face. 'Just had a message from Hana Prosser, sir. She's responded to a call from Pistyll Rhaeadr, the waterfall. Someone found some clothes and a wallet.'

Warlow stared at her. He didn't need to ask the question.

Lowri nodded. 'It's Joseph Randal's, sir.'

'What?' Rhys's words emerged falsetto and loud. But the shock of Lowri's declaration meant that no one in the team responded to the golden opportunity for the piss take it offered.

Instead, all eyes turned to Warlow. 'Right. Rhys, you're with me. Call Hana and tell her to stay where she is and we'll meet her there. Gil, you and Catrin shoot over to wherever the hell Habberley is and look at where the coat was found. Let Kapil know. Up to him to decide where he wants to go first. Lowri, you're in charge here. Anything else comes in I want to know yesterday.'

Lowri nodded. But Warlow was already reaching for his coat and heading out of the door.

———

GIL AND CATRIN arrived at the little footbridge across Habberley Brook forty minutes after leaving Newtown. The good news was that the rain had stopped. The bad news was that the lanes weren't much wider than Catrin's Focus and several times they had to reverse into farm entrances or muddy pull-ins to let other cars or tractors pass. Luckily, Kapil had dispatched a couple of techs to photograph and retrieve the coat and wallet so they had long gone, leaving Gil and Catrin to contemplate the spot alone.

'Isolated and not overlooked.' Gil stood in the middle of the lane and pirouetted. Behind him on the opposite side, a field ran up to another hedgerow. Beyond that was a line of hills. The bridge itself ran directly off the pull-in with two bends in the road cutting it off from any view from following or oncoming traffic for fifty yards either way.

'If you wanted to get rid of something quickly, this is as good a spot as any.' Catrin opened the little gate guarding the bridge and stood over the brook, before walking to the stile and into the field, tip-toeing to avoid the worst of the mud and cursing quietly as she failed to do so. To her right, a couple of hundred yards away, sat a farmhouse, not visible from the road.

'Any point chatting with the farmers?'

'We could try.'

They did and came up blank. No one on the farm had seen or heard anything unusual over the last few days and certainly not on the night the Randals went missing. The walkers who'd discovered the coat, two local septuagenarians with mad Spaniels, met the police officers at the bridge ten minutes later. Both much more appropriately dressed in waxed coats and wellies than either Gil or Catrin. Though they were helpful and detailed in their descriptions of what they'd found, it proved to be a relatively useless exercise.

The conclusion both sergeants drew was that the bridge had been chosen for convenience and because it could be a quick and unseen way to get rid of the coat.

An idea struck Catrin as they drove through the village, past The Mytton Arms. The brook under the footbridge hadn't looked deep, but at this time of year, it was flowing freely.

'Think they were aiming to get it into the water? I mean, that would make sense. Perhaps they did it in the dark. Couldn't see where it landed,' Catrin suggested.

Gil nodded absently, craning his neck to stare at the pub.

'Fancy a quick half? Chance to write up your notes

while I pump the locals. You never know, we might get wind of a haunted barn or two we could call into.'

Catrin sighed and sent him a daggers look. 'Hilarious. But yeah, why not. Thought you'd never ask.' She pulled the car in.

'Well, well. Wonders never cease. I didn't have you down as a daytime drinker, Sergeant Richards.'

'I'm not. But places like this have toilets and I need one of those more than I need a glass of tepid white wine.'

As they parked, Gil's eyes kept staring at the pub, but it wasn't what he was seeing. When he didn't try to get out, Catrin sighed and folded her arms. 'What now? If this is another horror film charade, I swear I'll—'

'Those were narrow lanes we were on, weren't they?' Gil's voice had dropped to a whisper.

Catrin shut one eye and squinted at the sky with the other, concentrating. 'Uh… Sixth Sense? Saw? Cabin in the Woods?'

Gil shook his head. 'Forget charades. The lanes. Narrow for your little Focus. Way too narrow for a livestock lorry, don't you think?'

That made Catrin pause. Working with Gil was like training a puppy. You had no idea what it was going to do next because it was so easily distracted until, in one special moment, it sat up and gave you a paw. 'Tractors use them, and, I suppose, cattle trucks, too. But narrow. Agreed.'

'Yeah,' Gil mused and refocused on the pub. '*Diawl*. Wonder if I dare mention sheep rustling in here.'

CHAPTER EIGHTEEN

It took Warlow and Rhys an hour to get to the little car park at the bottom of the waterfall at Rhaeadr. Neither of them had ever been there, though Warlow had heard of it. Rhys did the online research as they travelled north.

'What it says here is that the River Disgynfa falls in three stages over a 240-foot cliff face. The tallest bit is about 130 feet. It's the highest in Wales, according to this. There are footpaths to the top.'

'Hmm.' Warlow came back with a grunt. 'But can you walk behind it?'

'What?'

'Can you walk behind the waterfall?'

Rhys frowned. 'I don't think so.' He consulted his phone. 'It says nothing about that.'

'Then you need to visit Sgwd yr Eira in the Brecon Beacons. That one you can walk behind and look through the falling water.'

'Sounds like you know it, sir.'

'I do. Been there a few times. More my neck of the woods.' He'd taken the boys many times over the years. The good news was that you couldn't drive up to it.

Getting there involved a bit of effort and that deterred the worst of the selfie-obsessed tourists in ridiculous shoes. Warlow's mind went back to sharp winter days when Denise was fit enough to get her act together and come with them without falling over. They'd been happy times and he could remember the oohs and ahhhs from the boys the first time they walked hand in hand with him behind the curtain of water. There was indeed something magical about waterfalls. They'd once been there when the water had been semi-frozen, a rare event in temperate West Wales. He still had the framed photo of the four of them from the winter of 2009 in his living room.

But Pistyll Owen Rhaeadr was different because of its accessibility. From the village of Llanrhaeadr, the narrow road, appropriately named Waterfall Street, ran for four miles, passing only a handful of houses and farms, to end in the car park. Warlow could only imagine what this was like in summer given the narrowness of the access and how close this was to the Midlands and tourists.

As they neared the end of the road, the waterfall appeared up ahead, set against the rising hills of the Berwyn Mountains. Even Warlow, not a man overly impressed by views, had to slow down to take a better look.

'That's pretty cool,' Rhys exclaimed.

Warlow considered that enough of an approbation so he didn't add anything.

'And to think this, so far north, is still on our patch.' Rhys shook his head.

Warlow detected wonder in the DC's voice. And it was a remarkable geographic fact. He'd looked it up. Almost 150 miles from Dale on the southwest tip of Pembrokeshire to the waterfall in Powys. A good four hours drive, give or take. You could tootle up the M4 to London from Carmarthen in less time. It meant a vast area to police and though large swathes of Central Wales were empty, such spaces often provided opportunities for all sorts of criminal shenanigans in all kinds of out of the way places.

Take the case in point. But he didn't feel like raining on the DC's parade and he resisted the urge to tell Rhys that the attraction of staying away in a hotel hunting for murderers lost a bit of its sheen with the passage of time. He believed that you often needed separation from the case to be efficient. The kind provided by a home environment and familiar things as a band-aid for dealing with the horrors. You didn't get that living and breathing the case with only a hotel bedroom to escape to and eating every meal with your colleagues. But the DC was still young, and he'd find out for himself given enough time.

They pressed on past a dark barn into what was essentially a courtyard car park and pulled up next to a yellow and blue police issue Ford Explorer in front of a stone building with painted weatherboards.

A uniformed Hana Prosser walked across from where she and Tomo were talking to someone wearing a lanyard around his neck.

'Morning,' she sang out, as Warlow and Rhys exited the Jeep. 'We meet again.'

'We do.' Warlow took in the dozen or so cars parked around the edge of the car park and the few visitors who eyed their arrival with suspicion. A stone-built toilet block on the other side of the parking area had seating and a map. At the car park entrance, they'd passed a green notice board announcing a holiday cottage and the fact that they were "Licensed for Weddings" next to a post with an arrow pointing up some steps.

'They do coffee in the shop?' Rhys asked.

Hana nodded.

Warlow glowered at him. 'For God's sake, man, you and your damn coffee.'

Rhys's face remained impassive, knowing there was more to come.

'It's tea we'll want at this time of day. Besides, that stuff you drink with all the cream on the top is coffee masquerading as a giant bloody dessert.' Warlow handed Rhys a tenner. 'Go ahead. Bring one back for Hana and Tomo as well.'

Grinning, Rhys ambled off, sucking in the air like he'd never smelled it before.

Hana watched him go. 'He seems… enthusiastic.'

'He's one of the good ones. Even if he's easily distracted.'

'Oh? By what?'

Warlow raised one eyebrow. 'Anything that moves quickly: food, shiny things, and the new. But mainly food and the new.'

Hana chuckled. 'You make him sound like a Labrador.'

Warlow nodded. 'Not a bad analogy.' Warlow waved at Tomo, who returned the gesture.

He turned back and fixed the young PCSO with a serious gaze. 'So, Hana, what do we have here?'

'You know about the waterfall. Gets lots of visitors. Hundreds a day, sometimes a thousand or more in the summer,' Hana explained.

'Where were the clothes found?'

'At the bottom. Around the other side of the tearooms. A family with two small children wanted to paddle in their wellies. They found jeans with a wallet in it and one shoe.'

'Shoe, singular?'

'A trainer, sir. A blue Nike, size nine.'

'Has Kapil been?'

Hana nodded with a sanguine smile. 'He wasn't happy. He's taken the clothes, but the kids dragged them out of the water and brought them up to the rooms here. They showed us where they were found, but there was nothing to see. We think they were washed down from above.'

'Have you told the POLSA?'

'We have. He's sending some dogs and a team over. They've reached the edge of the search perimeter around the feed shed, anyway. He was toying with extending it, but after this...' Hana shrugged.

Warlow groaned. 'So they've found nothing at the shed?'

Hana shook her head.

'And here, any CCTV?'

'No need for it out here, sir. There is only one road in and out. It's a fiver for the car park which goes to the upkeep of the facilities here. But security isn't usually a problem.'

Warlow took another glance about him. He could see that.

Rhys returned with four cups in a cardboard holder. Hana took one over to Tomo and they exchanged a few words before she joined the detectives.

'Tomo suggests I give you the tour, show you where things were found and take you up to the top. He'll stay down here and manage the cars and the punters until we're done.'

'Good idea.' Warlow wanted to get a feel for the place. Finding Joseph Randal's clothes here was a bizarre twist, and he needed to get a picture of the geography if nothing else.

They took their tea with them and followed Hana to the fenced-off path that took them directly to the foot of the waterfall and the bridge that spanned it.

'Loud,' Rhys said, as they watched the roiling white water cascading down. To their left, the waterfall became a placid stream. 'That's where they found the clothes.' Hana pointed. She backtracked and clambered down to the stream's bank and a small pool of water between a couple of enormous stones marked with a little yellow flag. 'Tomo reckons they got caught in the eddy. The trainer was further down.'

Warlow looked back up. No doubt that the force and volume of water could have washed clothes down from above.

'Right, let's see the top.'

'The hard or easy walk?'

'Quickest,' Warlow answered.

The route took them up to the waterfall through a woodland to the right of the car park. Warlow wasn't dressed for it. Neither was Rhys, and they both found footing difficult on the slippery sections. On a different day, the DCI might have taken in more of the stunning scenery as they climbed. But some sections were steep. A hand out in front of you grabbing on, steep. It all required a lot of concentration, and the weather wasn't exactly warm. Hana, on the other hand, seemed to dance up. Warlow wondered if she was part mountain goat.

The tea was more a hindrance than a help, needing to be held in one hand which, given the terrain, added an extra degree of difficulty in the balance stakes. When Warlow almost lost his footing for the third time, he tossed the remnants of the liquid into the grass, crushed the cup into a ball, pocketed it and kept going.

After nearly three miles, they reached a summit of sorts with rocky pools and various paths leading off in all directions. Warlow went to the top of the waterfall and looked down into the valley. Partly to catch his breath and partly to wonder how the hell Joseph Randal's jeans and wallet got there. Unfenced, it could be a dangerous spot.

No wonder people came here in their droves, though he also wondered, given the way his heart was pumping, how many stayed at the bottom as opposed to trekking up to the top.

'No roads to here?' he asked Hana, hands on his hips, his heart gradually slowing to a canter.

'No, sir.'

'And if you turn east?'

'The Berwyn Mountains, sir. If you kept on walking, you might eventually come to roads. You might even hit my place in Llangadwaladr.' She grinned. 'And west, cross Bala Lake and you'd be in Snowdonia. But mostly it's empty up here.'

'This is so weird, sir,' Rhys said, joining Warlow to watch the flowing water. 'Why would Joseph Randal's clothes be here?'

'Be good to know, wouldn't it?' Warlow considered the mountains and the water and wondered what they might tell him. 'Bugger all, as usual,' he muttered. Then he turned to the younger officers, already feeling the cold from the sharp wind that had picked up. 'No point us standing here, is there? Let the POLSA see what they can find, though I'm not hopeful. I'll need the name of the family who found the wallet so that Rhys can take a statement.'

The journey down was quicker.

When they got to their cars, Warlow thanked Hana once more. 'I'm a firm believer in threes,' he said. 'So no doubt we'll meet again before this case is over.'

'You superstitious, sir?'

'I'd prefer to call it experienced with a healthy dose of gut feeling.'

Hana's smile was ear to ear.

Warlow drove out, realising he was no wiser than when he drove in. Frustration ate at him. This wasn't new to him. Police work often meant dead ends, or at least road blocks that needed to be surmounted.

As they neared the exit, Warlow pulled in to let a car through. A Land Rover Defender with a steel canopy on the pickup bed. As the driver came through, he held up a hand and waved. Warlow wound down his window, puzzled to see Elis Prosser grinning back at him.

'What are you doing up here?'

'Thought I'd bring Hana and Tomo some food. No need to spend money in the cafe. Tourist rates and all that.' His smile gave way to sudden seriousness. 'Nothing too nasty, is it?'

'No. Nothing nasty at all, in fact.'

Elis nodded, and the smile returned. 'Good. I know she's in the police and everything, but you still worry. You still want to protect them, don't you?'

Another car had pulled up behind Elis. The farmer put his Defender in gear and, with a wave, drove in. Warlow waited for the second car and then made for the gate. They drove out along the narrow lane, stopping at least four times to let other cars and a lorry pass. During one especially long delay, Warlow saw Rhys shuffling and fiddling with his seat belt.

'Where to now, sir?' he asked.

'Back to the office. But first, judging by the way you're shifting in your seat and looking at your watch, I think some lunch is in order, don't you?'

Rhys grinned. 'I do, sir. Most definitely.'

CHAPTER NINETEEN

WARLOW SAT at his desk in the Incident Room, waiting for Gil and Catrin to get back from their away day, looking at online maps trying to make sense of what the hell could link Pistyll Rhaeadr and Habberley. Looking and failing. When the phone on his desk rang, it came as a welcome distraction. At least it did until he answered it and listened to the voice of the sergeant down on the reception desk with growing consternation.

'She's downstairs now, you say?'

'Yes.'

'And you're sure it's me she wants to speak to?'

'Oh, yes. By name. Says she has information relevant to the missing farmers.'

Warlow puffed his cheeks out. 'Right. Tell her I'll be five minutes.'

He stuck his head out of the door and called out to Lowri. 'You will not believe who's in reception claiming to have information.'

Lowri did an impression of a meerkat and peered over the top of her monitor. 'Not Padrig Randal, is it, sir?'

'I wish. No, it's the woman with the megaphone.'

'Julia Lloyd?' At mention of the name, several other people in the office stopped what they were doing and looked up. All with knowing looks on their faces.

Warlow joined Lowri at her desk. 'You know her and the case, I take it?'

Lowri nodded. From the way they exchanged wary glances, the other CID and Uniforms in the room clearly did as well.

'Right. You've got five minutes to bring me up to speed.'

He grabbed a chair and sat next to her as she called up the misper reports for Robert Lloyd.

She found a summary document and, despite his dislike of reading from the screen, Warlow skimmed through the details of what had been found so far.

Robert Lloyd, twenty-two years old, failed to return home from a night out in Wrexham in November 2019. He'd made the thirty-five-mile journey with a group of friends who'd hired a minibus. Sometime towards the end of that evening, Robert told a friend he was going to meet someone 'special' and might stay over. His mother, having heard nothing from him the following day, reported him missing on the Sunday afternoon.

Warlow called up the photo file. Robert looked young for his age. Short hair, five eight, slim. He worked on a poultry farm and still lived with his mother. No siblings, a father who'd left the family home many years before.

The relevant facts were that Robert was gay and looked forward to his visits to the larger towns, such as Wrexham, where there were clubs and pubs to visit. No such scene existed in the rural corner of Powys where he lived.

Julia Lloyd told the police that Robert had not been depressed or anxious. In fact, in the weeks leading up to his disappearance, he'd been happy because he thought he'd met someone 'special' – that word again – though she had not supplied any detailed information. Robert had wanted to keep it a secret until the other person was 'sure'.

Though sexually active, Robert had brought no one home to meet his mother. When someone involved in the investigation suggested that perhaps Robert had chosen to go off to a different life with this 'special' person, Julia Lloyd had vehemently disagreed. Robert and she had been very close. There had been no friction between them over his sex life, nor who he identified as.

Various interviews with the friends who'd been with him that night made up the bulk of the files. Of significance was the fact that his mobile's network provider showed the phone had remained in Wrexham until the small hours when it was turned off. Then, two days later, it got turned back on in Liverpool for three hours. During that period, Julia Lloyd had received a message.

Don't worry, Mum. I have to do this. My chance of a new start. Love you. Robert.

There'd been no contact to or from the number on the SIM since, and using IMEI tracking, the phone itself had never been found.

Quite simply, Robert Lloyd had disappeared along with his phone. Police traced Robert's movements in Wrexham. At around 1.15am CCTV tracked him to an entrance at Bellevue Park. That sighting was the last that anyone had ever seen of him.

'Right.' Warlow's chair squeaked as he pushed it back and stood. 'Let's have a chat.'

Lowri didn't move. Her expression reminded Warlow of one of his kids when they'd eaten something they wished they hadn't.

'What?' Warlow demanded.

'Sir, you ought to know that Mrs Lloyd isn't quite… she has some odd ideas.'

'Good, let's hear them.'

Still, Lowri didn't move. 'They're not… normal ideas.'

Some of the other Uniforms looked up. One or two were smirking. They slid off when Warlow met their eyes.

'Either way, we can't ignore someone volunteering relevant information. Come on.'

'Relevant might be stretching it a bit, sir,' Lowri said, her unhappy expression remaining as she followed Warlow out.

———

'CUP OF TEA, MRS LLOYD?'

'No thank you.' The woman sitting across the table from Warlow sat with her lips clamped shut in what wasn't quite a smile. An odd, default expression she returned to after every time she spoke.

'Right. Okay to call you Julia?' Warlow continued.

'Julia, yes, that's my name.'

He'd adopted an elbow on the table position to ensure she knew he didn't have any time to waste. 'So, Julia. You told the desk sergeant you had information about Aeron and Joseph Randal.'

Julia nodded. She hadn't changed out of her green cagoule and sat impassive, hands clamped together on her lap. 'You are Warlow, aren't you?'

Warlow had his ID card hanging on a lanyard around his neck. He held it up for her to see. 'And this is Constable Lowri Fellows. She's helping me with this case—'

'I googled you,' Julia said, cutting across Warlow's words. 'You've been in the papers.'

'Not through choice,' Warlow said, and added a sheepish grin for good measure.

Julia didn't reciprocate. She kept up her inscrutable expression, her eyes never leaving Warlow's. It was then he noticed her slow blink rate. The net effect was an unremitting and disquieting stare.

'What was it you wanted to tell us, Julia?'

'There's a link.'

Warlow waited. Julia stared.

'Between the missing men and my Robert,' she added after a while.

'Your missing son Robert?' Lowri asked.

Julia turned her gaze on the PC, who returned it for all of ten seconds before wilting and dropping her eyes to her notebook to write something. Warlow glanced at the word LINK.

'How are they linked, Julia?' Warlow asked.

'Robert knew Joseph Randal. They were friends in college. Robert did an HNC there. They got pally.'

'So they know one another. At college, you say?' He threw Lowri a questioning glance.

'We have a campus in Newtown. It's an NPTC college. Weird, really. It stands for Neath Port Talbot. Which is a very long way from Newtown. But they merged resources with Powys some time ago,' she explained.

Warlow slid his eyes back to Julia. 'So, were Robert and Joseph close? Before Robert went missing, I mean?'

'They spent time together. Went out in the same gang for a while. Joseph came to see me after Robert went missing. It upset him a lot. Nice boy.'

'He had no idea where Robert was?' Warlow asked.

'No. But Robert knows where Joe is.' Her delivery was matter of fact. Conversational almost.

Warlow's mouth contorted into a variety of shapes. Most of which were aimed at forming the question he wanted to ask, but somehow failed to enunciate. Eventually, he managed, 'Can you say that again, Julia?'

'I said, Robert knows where Joseph is.'

Warlow's eyelids fluttered. He felt Lowri tense beside

him, her pen hovering an inch above the paper of her notebook.

The DCI leaned forward. 'You mean you've spoken with Robert?'

'He speaks to me.'

Warlow turned to Lowri. 'You know about this?'

The same uncomfortable look had returned to Lowri's face. 'Mrs Lloyd has informed us, sir, yes.'

Warlow frowned. 'Then why—'

'From the other side,' Julia interrupted.

That stopped him in his tracks. 'The other side of where?'

'The veil. I know Robert is dead. He's dead in a dark and horrible place. And now Joe is with him. He wants me to find him and bring him home. Find them both. I've been telling this lot for months.' She nodded at Lowri. 'But they won't listen.'

Warlow nodded because he couldn't think of anything else to do. The pointed looks and smirks on the faces of the Uniforms in the Incident Room suddenly made complete sense. He cleared his throat. 'How often does Robert speak to you?'

'I don't keep a diary.' She seemed put out by his question. 'He speaks to me at night. When he sits on my bed.'

'Right. But he doesn't tell you where he is?'

'As I said. In a dark and horrible place.'

'Yes. That's not much to go on, Julia,' Warlow said.

'I can't help that. Finding him isn't my job. That's your job.'

Warlow felt the urge to tell her that googling dark and horrible places was unlikely to bring up any useful GPS coordinates. But he trod on that thought easily enough. This woman was grieving. Even if they had no evidence that Robert Lloyd was dead, she was still grieving because he'd buggered off and left her all alone.

'What about Robert's father, Julia? He around?'

She blinked then. That must have got to her. 'He lives in Cardiff. I haven't seen him since Robert was two years old.'

A grieving, lonely, bereft single parent then, thought Warlow. 'I see. Well, thanks for coming in and sharing all this with us.'

Julia nodded. 'I've got some photographs of Joe and Robert together. I copied them. I have them here, and extra photographs of Robert because you are new to his case.'

Warlow sat back, hands up. 'I don't think I'll be involved in looking for your son, Julia.'

'But you will. When you find Joe, you'll find Robert.' Her gaze held his. Convinced and unflinching. She reached up under her cagoule. For one millisecond, Warlow wondered if they'd searched her in reception. The space was voluminous. Could be anything up there. A machete, a gun, a hand grenade even. But all that came out was a brown envelope, which she placed on the desk.

'Sure we can't get you a cup of tea?' Warlow asked.

'No, thank you. I need to get to work.'

'What do you do, Julia?'

'Clean. Airbnbs and holiday homes, mainly. Some others. Regulars.'

Warlow nodded. 'Okay. Right. Well, thanks for coming in. Lowri will show you out.'

Lowri scrambled to her feet.

After a few seconds of staring at the DCI with those unblinking eyes, Julia stood up. She reminded him of an emotionless mannequin. He'd seen some Dr Who episode when the kids were young; the first of the new iteration with Billie Piper. He'd watched it with the boys and despite their teenage bravado, they'd been genuinely scared. He doubted Julia Lloyd was scooting off back to attack the

Tardis, but her loss of affect was equally disconcerting. Loss brought on by whatever mental turmoil she'd suffered from her son's disappearance. But suddenly, her face fell and her lips quivered. She leaned forward on the desk, eyes brimming with tears.

'Will you find him for me, Mr Warlow?' Her voice had plummeted into a desperate whisper. 'He wouldn't leave. He would never just go without… We were so close. We'd faced everything together. He…'

Warlow put his hand on her arm. He probably shouldn't have – he knew some scrotes who would have claimed an assault – but it was the right, the compassionate thing to do. Up to five minutes ago, he'd had no link to Robert Lloyd's case whatsoever. Not his brief. But something about the desperation that had surfaced and broken through Julia Lloyd's impassive guise got to him. 'As soon as I know something, I promise I'll give you an update, Julia. But that's the best I can do.'

She nodded, turned, and walked out.

Warlow sat, more than a little shell shocked. He reached for the envelope. Inside were a dozen photographs. He recognised Robert Lloyd in all of them. Some were of him alone, or on a beach bare chested. One, a close-up in a white t-shirt. Warlow noted a necklace in both the bare-chested shot and on the t-shirt. Only one photo had the image of Joseph Randal. A group snap of young men, arm in arm, on a night out. Robert one end, Joe the other. All laughing and smiling. All alive and well.

He slid the prints back into the envelope and headed for the Incident Room.

The noise reached him as he approached from the corridor outside. Snatches of phrases in between raucous laughter. He didn't need to hear much to tune in to the tasteless theme.

'Real mental case…'

'Who you gonna call…'

'Hashtag round the bloody bend…'

Warlow pushed the door open and stood there. He counted half a dozen people in the room besides Lowri, who sat next to Rhys at her desk. Both junior officers had their heads down. Lowri turned her unhappy gaze up at him while Rhys merely looked confused. The other occupants, mostly male officers, uniformed and plain-clothed plus the odd civilian indexers, all wore broad grins that slid off like ice in a thaw on seeing Warlow.

He glared at them all before he spoke. 'I'm going to say this once only. If I hear anyone using derogatory terms towards Julia Lloyd again in this room, I will personally ensure that HR strings them up by a part of the anatomy best used for other functions. Show some respect. That poor woman is troubled and ill. And I'll say it again; if you lot had done your job properly, she wouldn't be. So think on that while you take the piss.'

Dead silence followed his footsteps as he headed for the SIO office. No one glanced at him. No one except Rhys and Lowri, who followed his passage with grateful smiles.

CHAPTER TWENTY

CATRIN INSISTED on calling back at the hotel before they went to the Incident Room.

'I need to change. My shoes and the bottom of my trousers are filthy. Yours must be, too.'

Gil exited the car and stared at the crusty edges of his shoes and the grey spatter over the hems of his trousers. 'It's all dried off, nothing that a stiff brush and a wet flannel won't sort out. '

'Each to his own.' Catrin hurried off. 'Meet you back here in ten.'

Gil found the toilet and spent a few minutes brushing dried mud off his trouser bottoms and scraping the stuff off his shoes by taking them off and beating seven bells out of them; sole to porcelain over the sink. He'd found a company that specialised in comfort footwear without making the damned things look too much like they were for a six-year-old. Days like today spent tramping about did nothing for his rugby-ravaged knees or his feet.

Good shoes helped.

He wandered back towards reception: a hatch off the main corridor guarding an alcove with a folding desk and a computer. He loitered there while he waited for Catrin to come back down, no doubt spruced and smelling nice as she always did. He had daughters of his own, so he knew the deal.

While he waited, Gil studied a few brochures stuck into a wooden leaflet display box on a table. All the usual suspects were there: Pistyll Rhaeadr, Snowdonia, and of course the zipline a bit further north: the fastest in the world over a kilometre and a half. There were galleries, art centres, textile museums, alternative technologies, canoeing on the rivers… Plenty to do if you had the time and the inclination.

'Excuse me.'

Gil pivoted. The voice belonged to the woman who'd taken Gil's registration when he'd booked in. The hotel was not part of a chain and the staff did not wear uniforms as such, but the receptionist had made an effort and wore a dark-navy trouser suit which gave her a business-like appearance. Her hair looked a little bit too dark to be natural and her glasses hung around her neck on a cord, but she was pleasant enough. Gil put her at mid-fifties.

'I know you're with the police team,' the woman said.

Gil nodded, smiling at the word team. He wondered what position she thought he played. Definitely not on the wing. That would be stretching things. 'What can I do for you, uh…?'

'Tamara.'

'Tamara. Right.' He suppressed the urge to ask her if that meant she never accepted invitations as in "Tamara never comes", but wisely quashed the idea before it gathered enough momentum to be voiced. Anwen, his long-suffering wife, had warned him about his constant need to play the fool with dad jokes.

She was probably right, though it helped him get

through the day and had more to do with the way his brain was wired than any need or intention to offend. Gil crossed the narrow gap between the leaflet display table and the reception desk.

'Someone left something for a DCI Warlow.' Tamara reached under the desk and came back with a sealed manila envelope and handed it over.

Gil took it, weighed it up and studied the writing. 'Hand delivered. Was there a message?'

Tamara shook her head. 'Left it on the desk at around eleven this morning. I assumed you might be expecting it.'

'So you didn't see who left it?'

She shook her head.

The envelope was light, but whatever was inside filled the space. 'Tidy. I'll make sure DCI Warlow gets it.'

Catrin appeared on the stairs, freshened up, wearing an identical pair of trousers and shoes to those she'd changed out of. Efficient and organised were the words that sprung to mind when Gil saw her.

'Shall we?' she said and headed for the door with the briefest smile of acknowledgement to Tamara.

Gil tapped the envelope against his open palm and nodded to Tamara. 'Looks like we're off.'

———

WARLOW GAVE Gil and Catrin fifteen minutes to gather their thoughts before he called the team together for a catch up. He sat on the edge of a desk, the one that he'd laid claim to when not in the SIO office, and watched as DS Richards finished pinning information to the Job Centre and the Gallery. He'd kept back the photos from Julia Lloyd. They sat on the desk as he stirred the freshly made tea in his mug and watched Gil lay out a new biscuit display, trying to swallow back the saliva flooding his mouth.

'You're a bad man, Gil.' Warlow reached for a hob-nob.

Gil raised an eyebrow. 'No one's forcing you but a sugar rush while we talk things through has never, in my experience, been a negative experience.' Gil held the plate up to Catrin who shook her head, sighed, and then dived in for a chocolate finger like a heron after a trout. A movement that made Gil shake his head and elicited a delighted, 'Get in,' from Rhys.

Lowri was less reticent and picked out a custard cream while Rhys, when he chose one of his own, eyed the lot left behind longingly.

'Catrin, you start.' Warlow took a bite of the biscuit and a sip of tea, too polite to dunk. Still, the combination was like nectar in his mouth.

Catrin pointed to a posted-up image of the footbridge. 'Our trip to Habberley did not add much. Other than the fact that where the coat was found is a footbridge to a public footpath which goes cross country.'

'Why would anyone dump a coat there?' Rhys, biscuit already consumed, kept one eye on Catrin, one on the plate of biscuits.

Gil went through their thought processes, emphasising the pull-in and the narrowness of the lanes and the fact that the bridge ran over a wide-ish stream.

'So whoever threw it in hoped it would get carried off in the stream.' Rhys nodded.

'But it wasn't,' Catrin explained. 'It snagged under the gubbins of the bridge.'

Warlow ran his palm down the nape of his neck. 'And Habberley is very much across the border and all points east towards the Midlands.'

Catrin nodded.

Warlow let his thoughts emerge. 'So, done on a quiet road where whoever did it could not be observed in the two minutes it might have taken.'

Gil puffed out his cheeks. 'I had a chat with the landlord of the local pub—'

Warlow's raised eyebrows drew a shake of the head from Gil. 'Purely a pit stop. Mine was half a shandy, and Sergeant Richards had a Diet Coke from one of those mixer taps from behind the bar, which I have serious doubts about. Could be anything in there.'

Catrin folded her arms and Warlow got the distinct impression that this might be a continuation of a discussion they'd already had.

'It tasted fine,' Catrin muttered the words through gritted teeth.

'And while Catrin used the facilities,' Gil went on, 'the barman told me that there had been a couple of random checks on livestock vehicles in the area as the Shropshire constabulary considered Habberley a possible trafficking route.'

The DCI wagged a finger at Rhys. 'We ought to liaise.' The DC scribbled something in his notebook. Warlow looked for help from the two sergeants. 'Impressions?'

Catrin wrinkled her nose. 'All points to this being linked to a rustling operation, sir. Let's say it went pear-shaped at the feed shed and there was a confrontation, then the thieves might have taken the Randals, and tried to dispose of clothing or even a body or bodies along the way. Habberley would do for an out of the way spot on their route.'

Warlow nodded and looked at Gil.

'That would be the logical explanation,' Gil said. 'You might ask why only a coat, but then perhaps it isn't. Perhaps all the other clothes have gone into the stream and washed away.'

Warlow waited. 'I sense a but coming.'

Gil shrugged. 'But if they were driving some kind of transporter, it's a bloody awful route. We struggled in the Focus despite Catrin's driving skills, which are a lot better than mine.'

Catrin's eyes tightened, expecting a sarcastic barb. When none came, somewhat surprised, she said, 'Thank you, Gil.'

'Fair do's.' Gil held up a hand.

All kinds of jumbled thoughts were on a spin cycle in Warlow's head. He stirred his tea with a spoon and watched the liquid swirl. The evidence all pointed towards this being exactly as described. A confrontation, a panicked reaction, and a botched attempt to get rid of incriminating evidence. Maybe they'd planned on dumping a body and were disturbed or panicked again. When he looked up, the team hadn't moved, waiting on his next move.

'It does add up in a convoluted kind of way. What doesn't is finding Joseph Randal's jeans, wallet and trainer, singular, at the Falls in Rhaeadr.'

'It's a tidy few miles from Habberley, that's for sure.' Gil did another round with the biscuit plate. No one abstained.

Warlow continued, 'There's no CCTV, no record of visitors other than receipts at the shop for anyone paying by card. We'd be able to trace some people that way.' Yet he knew already that would be a fruitless exercise. Whoever had put Randal's effects at the site had done so either in panic or for some motive that was, at least for the moment, beyond him.

'You think one of the visitors to the waterfall took Joe's clothes with them?' Catrin asked.

It sounded ludicrous, but in the absence of any other explanation, Warlow was willing to consider it, however unlikely it might seem.

'But why?' Lowri spoke from a desk behind Warlow's.

'Maybe they had a thing about water,' Rhys suggested and pushed the last bit of his second hob-nob home.

'Why not set fire to the clothes?' Lowri asked.

No one could answer that one, and so they didn't try.

'And then,' Warlow took a slurp of tea, 'to round off the day, I had a chat with Julia Lloyd.'

'Who's Julia Lloyd,' Gil said between bites of a chocolate digestive.

Warlow stood up and took out the photographs Julia Lloyd had given him, stuck them on the Gallery for all to see, speaking as he did so.

'The consensus in this station is that Julia Lloyd is a borderline lunatic obsessed with the loss of her son.' He pivoted and let his gaze drift over Lowri to the drafted-in occupants of the Incident Room.

No one looked up. Eventually, Warlow's eyes dropped back to the female officer, but his question to her was not an angry one, it was more by way of obtaining confirmation for the others. 'Am I right?'

'Yes, sir. But the image you had from Mrs Lloyd, the one that shows him and Joseph Randal? We have it on file, sir. North Wales police tracked down and spoke to everyone else in that photograph. They were all eliminated from the enquiry.'

Warlow continued, 'That's one good thing at least. But there are several reasons for people believing that Julia Lloyd is unhinged. One being her insistence on reminding everyone in this station on a daily basis, at irritatingly high volume, that they have not found Robert Lloyd, and the second that she believes he visits her at night asking for her help.'

'As in a dream?' Gil asked.

'More some kind of a vision, I'd say.' Warlow saw not one member of his team sniggering or fighting a smile.

They were never short on banter, but murder and death and disappearances seldom made anyone smile, and a grieving parent even less so. They knew where to draw a line and he never had to draw it for them. 'And yes, easy to dismiss this kind of thing as grief or even some kind of psychosis, but stranger things. Julia Lloyd told me that Robert Lloyd knew Joseph Randal.' He pointed to the photograph of the two men in the same picture. 'That at least is true. She said that they were friends and she's convinced, in her own way, that the cases are linked.'

'So it stays in the mix?' Catrin asked, matter of fact as always.

'It does. Who knows. But what we don't do is dismiss it out of hand. Lowri's emailing you a summary of the Robert Lloyd misper case. Have a read, let it all marinate.'

They all turned towards Lowri. 'I've sent it across. Should be with you directly.'

'Good.' Warlow nodded his approval. 'Now, what else—'

He got no further as Gil's mobile burst into life, the ring tone recently altered by one of his granddaughters to *Baby Shark*. The DS sat bolt upright and fumbled in his jacket pocket, shaking his head in apology before standing and walking to the back of the room to take the call. Warlow watched him with barely restrained amusement before turning back to the Job Centre.

'Anything back from Kapil regarding the effects from Habberley?' He looked hopefully at Catrin.

'Not yet, sir. He should have something later today.'

That made Warlow's eyes stray to his watch and note that it was already later today. 'What about—'

His question never got any further as Gil thanked whoever was on the line and turned back to Warlow, his face animated. 'Shropshire Uniforms. They've found Padrig Randal's car on an unfinished housing estate.'

'Where?'

'Oswestry.'

Warlow grabbed his coat, issuing instructions at the same time. 'Rhys, you're with me. Catrin, take Gil.' He turned at the door to look at Lowri. 'Once again PC Fellows, you have the bridge.'

CHAPTER TWENTY-ONE

WARLOW PARKED behind a marked West Mercia Police Astra. The Uniforms had sensibly chosen to meet up a quarter of a mile away from where they'd spotted Padrig Randal's car in a parking lay-by.

Gil and Catrin were out of their vehicle taking directions. To anyone passing it resembled a routine traffic stop. When they'd finished, Catrin hurried over.

'They're going to drive past and park up further on in case we need any help.'

'He's not under arrest,' Warlow reminded her.

Catrin shrugged. 'There's only one way in and out of where he is. But they're happy to wait around.'

Warlow nodded. Gil joined Catrin and leaned into the Jeep's window, his bulk making Catrin pull back. Warlow smiled at the daggered glare she gave her fellow sergeant. 'What's the plan, then?'

'More an approach than a plan, Gil. I go in, tell him we need a chat, we both come out and get back to Newtown.'

Everyone nodded, not believing it for one moment. 'That's why there are four of us then, is it?' Gil asked.

'You and Catrin around the back of the property, me and Rhys in the front.'

'Tidy.' Gil nodded.

They went back to their vehicles and Warlow fired up the Jeep as he gave Rhys his orders. 'When we get there, you stay behind me, understood? Stab vest on?'

Rhys used a couple of fingers to spread his shirt open between buttons and reveal the vest.

Warlow grunted. 'Good. Shame you don't have a hard hat since we're visiting a building site.'

'Sir?'

'Knowing your luck,' Warlow muttered.

Since being a part of Warlow's team, someone had tried to stab Rhys, he'd been run over by a motorbike and twisted his ankle in a supposedly stealthy pursuit of a suspect. In response, Rhys expelled a thin laugh.

Rain had started spitting against the windscreen. Thin drizzly stuff that needed the odd wipe as the marked police car drew away from the kerb and Warlow followed with Gil and Catrin behind.

The 'estate' for want of a better word, was nothing more than four houses in various states of completion in a turn-off to the north of the town itself. One half of the site adjacent to the road had steel fencing, the other had the original hedge and it was behind this that the eagle-eyed Uniforms had spotted Padrig Randal's Subaru. Once past the entrance, the response vehicle flashed its hazard lights and pulled in.

Warlow tucked the Jeep in and Catrin parked the Focus behind it, blocking the exit. Only one house had been finished to any degree of completion. It looked older and Warlow presumed it had been the original build on land a developer was now adding to. The other three all had foundations and walls, one a half-finished roof but no doors or windows, and one only four layers of breeze blocks.

Warlow chose the almost finished property. Scaffolding encased one end of the building and a couple of half-filled yellow skips awaited collection. A blue rubble chute snaked down from the roof where a chimney had been draped in plastic sheets. Warlow waited for Catrin and Gil to disappear from view and then knocked on the door and spoke loudly and clearly through the plastic faux wood.

'Padrig, I'm DCI Warlow, Dyfed Powys Police. We need a word about your brother.'

Rhys walked across to take a look at Randal's car. He touched the bonnet. 'Cold, sir. I think it's been here all—' His eyes flicked towards an upstairs window. 'He's there, sir. I caught a glimpse.'

Warlow took a couple of steps back. 'We can do this the easy way or the hard way, Padrig.'

A face appeared above, pale and scared looking.

'Is the door locked?'

Randal shook his head.

'Are you going to come down?'

Another shake.

'Can I come up?'

Padrig held two fingers up.

Warlow glanced at Rhys. 'Does that look like an invitation to you, Rhys?'

'It would be rude otherwise, sir.'

Warlow stepped forward and put a hand on the door handle but turned to Rhys and, in a low voice, said, 'Text Catrin, tell her we're going in.' The DC's fingers danced over his phone's touchscreen.

Warlow opened the door.

Inside, the rooms had been stripped back to the plaster. A thick layer of dust and debris littered the floor.

'What do you want?' A voice that Warlow presumed was Padrig's drifted down from above.

'We want to talk to you about Aeron and Joe's disappearance.'

'I don't know anything about that. Leave me alone.' The DCIs eyes flitted around the bare rooms as he stepped slowly towards the stairs.

'We can't do that, Padrig. Either you talk to us here or you can come back to Newtown and we can chat over a cup of tea.' Warlow took in the filthy floor and the absence of fixtures and fittings. 'Do you even have electricity here?'

'Sod off.'

'Not the answer I was hoping for, Padrig.' Warlow put a foot on the stairs and then paused. 'Are you armed?'

No response.

'We're coming up. A chat, that's all we need. Clear up a few things. Sooner we do that the better, yes?'

Warlow took two steps but felt a tug on his sleeve. Behind him, Rhys's face looked animated. He mimed holding a shotgun. Warlow shook his head. Though he had nothing to base that reassuring shake on other than his experience and that much maligned policing method, instinct.

'Where are you, Padrig?'

'Bedroom on the right.' Padrig's voice sounded subdued.

'Fine. We're almost there.' Warlow continued his ascent, the stripped wooden stairs creaking and squeaking as the officers' weight shifted.

The landing walls had channels cut for new electric cabling. Whoever had done that hadn't bothered clearing up after them and chunks of chalky material crunched underfoot. A ladder led to the attic space above and the plastic covering slapped and flapped in the wind on the roof.

Warlow paused. 'Come on, Padrig. Come out.'

Nothing.

The bedroom door stood ajar. Warlow walked around the ladder and put a hand out behind him to keep Rhys at arm's length before taking three quick steps. He pushed the door open. It moved obligingly enough, but with a creaking groan straight out of a horror film suspense moment. Warlow stood side on to look in at a camp bed with a rumpled sleeping bag draped over it, a little stove, empty takeaway trays, but no Padrig Randal.

Warlow stepped in and motioned for Rhys to follow. The DC shimmied around the loft ladder to join the DCI to stand on the threshold of the room.

'Padrig,' Warlow said aloud. 'We've got no time for hide and bloody see—'

An almighty rumble from the landing ended in a roaring crash that shook the floor and sent plumes of dust following through the rooms.

Warlow slumped against the bedroom wall, head tucked in. Rhys went sprawling. Surrounded by a cloud of smut, the space under the ladder was now a pile of broken slate and rubble.

'What did I say about a hard bloody hat,' Warlow growled.

Rhys got to his feet, coughing and waving particles away from his face as he got to the doorway first. 'He's done a runner, sir.'

Eyes running, Warlow clambered over the debris, his feet slipping and sliding as he manoeuvred around the ladder. He ran back down the stairs, through the door, looking left and then right and choosing a direction. The correct direction as it turned out. He reached the corner and saw Catrin and Gil standing near a skip looking not at all bothered.

'See him?'

Gil rapped the outside of the blue rubble chute. 'Still there, Padrig?'

A wailing, muffled voice emerged. 'Let me out.'

Rhys, face chalky with dust, skidded to a halt beside Warlow.

'Goth doesn't sit you, Rhys. Though I've got some blusher if you want to soften that look,' Catrin said, her delivery desert-dry.

Rhys rubbed his face and stared at his grey-coated fingers, then spent the next twenty seconds clearing his throat and spitting.

'The rubble chute? Seriously?' Warlow shook his head before taking in the upended wheelbarrow blocking the chute's exit into the skip. 'That your idea, Gil?'

'Catrin clocked the chute straight away.' Gil nodded. 'And I must have watched Home Alone at least a dozen times since it's my middle granddaughter's favourite. You come away with certain skills.'

More muffled shouts. 'Let me out. I hate small spaces. Please—'

Warlow stepped forward and thumped the plastic barrel to shut him up. 'For the last time, are you armed?'

'No. No, I'm not armed.'

Satisfied, Warlow nodded at Gil. 'Sergeant Jones, if you will.'

Gil pulled the wedged wheelbarrow away and Padrig Randal's legs emerged from the bottom barrel. Several wriggles and shoves later – all accompanied by grunts of effort and the odd whimper – the man followed.

The four officers stood by while he extricated himself from the skip, none of them felt inclined to help. Warlow looked around at his surroundings. He seemed doomed to end up on building sites chasing suspects. At least this time he'd come away unscathed.

Randal leaned against the side of the skip, breath heaving, filthy from the rubble chute, gaze shifting from one face to the other and lingering for a couple of seconds on the space in between.

'Don't even think about it,' Warlow warned him. 'We've played enough silly buggers for one morning. Besides, Rhys here plays flanker and is known in certain rugby circles as the Police Interceptor. You've already rendered his suit virtually unwearable. I suggest you do not test his patience with another run for it. I'm going to ask you nicely one more time. Are you happy to come down to the station and answer some questions?'

Padrig looked at the red-eyed DC glaring at him and, head down, nodded.

'Your car or mine, sir?' Catrin asked.

'You take him. He can sit in the back with Gil and learn all about the dangers of accidents in the home. I'll let the Uniforms know we got our man and I'll see you back at the station where Padrig and I are going to have a little chat.'

———

BACK IN NEWTOWN, Warlow let Randal stew while he let Rhys freshen up, or at least get the Halloween makeup off his face. Just half an hour after returning, he and the DC sat opposite Randal in an interview room. They'd given him a chance to use the toilet and wash his face, but so far only a glass of water, not a cup of tea.

Then Rhys did the necessary so that Randal knew this was an interview under caution. That it was voluntary and that he could have a solicitor present if he so wished.

He did not.

'Right,' Warlow said, 'How much easier would it have been to come in of your own accord, eh?'

Randal had his head down, eyes fixed on the table in front of him. 'I haven't done anything.'

'Great, then all this shouldn't take long.' Warlow smiled. It took some effort. 'You're not under arrest, don't forget. This is all of your own free will. Let's start with the night of—'

'I was at home.'

'You're not married, Padrig?'

Randal shook his head.

'Girlfriend?'

'Another shake.'

'So no one to corroborate your story.'

Silence.

Warlow had some papers in a file on the table. He took one out. 'You and Joseph get on, Padrig?'

'He's a good kid.'

'What about your brother Aeron?' Warlow asked.

No reply.

'Look, we know about you and Aeron falling out. We know about the bit of land you were supposed to get in your father's will. We know all that. You can see how someone might feel a little bit suspicious of the circumstances.' Warlow let that sink in. Not that he needed to. Randal had the look of a dog caught stealing the Sunday roast off a countertop. 'What do you think happened that night?'

'All I know is that it has nothing to do with me,' Randal muttered the denial.

'Good. So if I ask you to let us search your flat, you'd have no objection.'

Randal looked up. 'Why would you want to do that?'

'A show of good faith?'

Randal shook his head.

'See, good faith is what's missing when it comes to you, Padrig. I mean, your brother and nephew go missing under the worst circumstances imaginable. And then you, for reasons best known to yourself, disappear and make yourself completely unavailable by hiding out in the world's worst Airbnb, knowing full well that we'd want a word.' Warlow leaned on the table. 'That doesn't show you in a very good light, does it, DC Harries?' Warlow didn't bother looking around, but Randal's eyes swivelled towards Rhys who sat, arms folded, slowly shaking his head, his eyes never leaving the interviewee's face.

'Not even to a rookie like young Rhys here,' Warlow added. 'It implies you've got something to hide.'

Padrig shook his head. 'I don't like coppers. I was upset, I needed to get away.'

Warlow sat back, considering. 'Fair enough. Upset might work. I'll have a think about that. When was the last time you ate anything?'

'What?' The question took Randal by surprise.

'Fancy a sandwich and a cup of tea?'

He hesitated, clearly wondering if this was a trick question. 'Wouldn't say no.'

'Right.' Warlow smiled. 'We'll see what we can rustle up.'

Randal nodded. 'Thanks.'

Warlow chose his words carefully. The lack of any response to the word 'rustle' from Randal, neither suspicious nor cringing, was the most useful thing he'd learned so far.

'Okay, fifteen minutes. Rhys, sort out a sandwich for Padrig here, will you? You allergic to anything?'

Padrig smirked. 'Only coppers.'

Warlow grinned. Or at least showed his teeth in an approximation. 'I love a comedian me.'

CHAPTER TWENTY-TWO

WARLOW LINGERED in the observation room watching Padrig Randal devour an egg and bacon sarnie, some crisps and a full-fat Coke from the Costcutter in the nearby Texaco service station.

'Messy eater, isn't he?' Gil waited next to Warlow.

A veritable snowstorm of crisp crumbs dotted the surface of the table. Warlow nodded. 'Hunger will do that for you. I'll put money on him clearing up the debris with a wet finger, too.'

'From that table?' Gil made a face. '*Arglwydd*, the stuff they wipe it down with is industrial strength. Half a cup would sterilise a swimming pool after a coach-load of four-year-olds have been in, bladders akimbo. Not the best mix of flavours: bleach, salt and vinegar.'

Obligingly, Padrig Randal wet his right middle finger with a crumbed tongue and started picking up the crisp remnants.

'Nice,' Gil said, grimacing.

'I think we ought to charge him. Get a warrant for his flat.' Warlow let his thoughts shape the words.

'I think we ought to get the bugger to ITU,' Gil

muttered, but then gave Warlow's words some time to percolate and came back with, 'Why do I get the feeling that charging him isn't what you want to do?'

Warlow shrugged. 'There's something missing. This business with the land and the fight with his brother? That's old hat.'

'True, but grumbling resentment is like a slow poison. He doesn't have any land of his own. Maybe he's taking his revenge out by throwing in with sheep thieves.'

'You think he might be the rustler's link to the area?'

Gil explained his thinking. 'One way of getting even. He knows the other side of the border, too. Habberley isn't that far from Oswestry.'

Warlow turned to the big sergeant. 'Why don't you and Catrin have a chat with him. See if you can get him to tell us something useful. It doesn't add up, him hiding out in that unfinished house.'

Gil nodded. 'Tidy. What are you going to do?'

'Change my shirt for one thing and see if Kapil has found anything useful in Joseph Randal's clothing from the Falls. Something we can tie all this together with.' He nodded towards Randal, who was now searching for salt and vinegar remnants in the folds of his trousers on his lap.

'That would be good,' Gil agreed.

Warlow turned and left the room, but not before adding, 'Yes, well, I'm not going to hold my breath.'

He walked out and through the Incident Room, nodding to Lowri, who looked up from her desk.

'We should have something back from the service provider for Joseph Randal's phone by this afternoon, sir.'

'Good. Keep at it.' Warlow sent her a smile. He liked diligence in an officer, even if what they were working on seemed unlikely to be of much help. Police work was often like this, fishing in a murky canal until you got a bite. And when you pulled it out, it might be a rusty old bike or a big old pike who'd swallowed the knife that'd killed the victim. Not a common scenario, but sometimes the tiniest bit of evidence appeared that clicked into place and made it all worthwhile.

In the SIO's room, Warlow jiggled the mouse on his desk to get the computer to come on and logged in to his inbox. Kapil had been as good as his word and sent his report on both items of clothing from the waterfall and Habberley. Yet the small moment of triumph Warlow experienced on seeing the email evaporated as soon as he started reading. In effect, Kapil confirmed that the items of clothing had been identified, via photographs, as belonging to the missing Randals and whereas there might be enough blood staining on the Habberley coat to allow for further forensics, the stuff found at the Falls had been in the water too long.

'Bugger.'

Warlow sighed and sat back, both hands on the desk, arching his neck so that his face pointed up towards a cobweb on the ceiling. He had no idea why the clothes were at separate sites. It made no sense. Had they been discarded by the same person, or different people working in tandem?

He sat forward, his gaze drifting over the small pile of files and reports on his desk he had yet to sign off on, some case notes he'd asked for and, finally and curiously, on a plain manila envelope with his name written in capitals on the front. He picked it up. It felt solid and too thick for paper. He looked again at the handwritten address. It didn't look like anything Geoghan related and then remember Gil mentioning something about a message left for him at the hotel.

Reassured, he slid a finger under the flap and slit the paper open.

Inside was a single photograph. An eight-by-five colour

snap that someone had blown up. The process made it look grainy and out of focus. But not so that you wouldn't recognise the two figures standing close together against a grey wall behind a car. Warlow recognised the arched window in that wall and immediately knew he was looking at the gable end, the one not facing the road, of Hermon Chapel. But that backdrop paled into insignificance as he peered more closely and recognised the two people in the photograph. They stood close, hands on each other, not in a clinch but intimately enough. The snap looked as if it might have been taken either at the moment before or immediately after they'd kissed. The smile on the woman's face told him that.

The look on the man's face told him a lot more.

He pushed back from the desk and found Lowri. 'Get hold of the FLO at the Randal's farm. Tell her there's been a development and that I'd like to see Mari Randal as soon as she can get here.'

'What is it you've found, sir?'

Warlow grinned. 'Motive. Here,' he handed over the snap, 'see if you can get me a photocopy of this.'

———

GIL ENTERED the interview room to join Catrin after having been summoned to a little pow-wow with Warlow. He held a folded piece of A4 copy paper in his hand which he placed, still folded, on the desk.

Randal watched warily.

'Right, Padrig.' Gil settled himself. A movement that made the chair beneath him groan in protest. 'Where were we?'

Catrin answered, 'Padrig was saying nothing in response to all our questions.'

'Ah, yes. The strong silent approach. We were chatting

about stealing sheep, weren't we?' Gil glanced at Catrin, who nodded in reply.

'I've told you, I don't know anything about stealing sheep,' Padrig said.

'Devastating for the farmers, I hear. All those years of careful stewardship, nurturing a flock and all that.' Gil said all of this in a neutral, conversational tone. 'But I suppose if you wanted to target someone, make their life a bit of a misery, it would be a good way to go about it. Especially if you were not the person doing the stealing. The actual dirty work. It must be difficult herding sheep. Must be a bit of a night-meh.'

He smiled at Padrig, encouraging him to respond, if only to complain about his lousy puns. To his right, DS Richards simply shook her head.

Gil sighed. 'What I'm saying is, in my scenario, it's possible to be the one with the local knowledge, pointing the thieves in the right direction without needing to involve yourself directly.'

'I don't know what you're talking about.' Padrig looked up, a defiant expression hardening his features.

'No,' Gil said. 'I'm thinking you don't. So let's up the ante.' He slid the folded paper across to Catrin, who opened it and looked at what was printed on the inside. A look that sent her eyebrows up to meet her hairline. Gil acknowledged her response. She folded the paper and slid it back towards him.

'But it's an avenue of interest we've had to stroll down,' Gil went on with his speech. 'We're big on motive in detection work. Looking for reasons.' Gil sat back. 'Because there's always a reason. No matter how bloody daft it might seem. There's greed. That's a common one. Even psychosis. You know, believing that some red bugger with horns sitting on your shoulder told you to do it.'

'Or self-preservation, for example getting rid of a blackmailer,' Catrin added.

Gil nodded. 'And then there's emotion. Often the most dangerous one because it can be unplanned. Rage, jealousy, passion…'

They waited. Randal said nothing, but the side of his jaw kept tensing.

Gil unfolded the sheet of paper, rotated it and slid it over so that Randal could see it. He didn't move, but his eyes widened as he took in the image. Photographed from a distance on a long lens it looked like. A candid shot of a man and a woman in an embrace of some sort, in as out of the way a place as you could imagine, behind Hermon Chapel.

And there was something about the embrace and the couple's expressions that implied lovers rather than acquaintances, even though they were fully clothed.

'Care to say something about that photograph, Padrig?' Catrin broke the silence that had grown like a fungus in the room.

A series of lines appeared on Randal's brow and the hand holding the sheet of paper started trembling. 'Where did you get this?' he whispered.

'Know what the D in DS Richards and DS Jones stand for, Padrig?'

The fierce glare painted on Randal's face bored into Gil's eyes as his head came up.

'That's right. D for Detective, in case you were in any doubt,' Gil said, answering his own question. 'And the woman in this photograph is on her way here now to offer an explanation, I have no doubt.'

Randal's breath shuddered out of him. 'Leave her out of it. For God's sake.'

Catrin shook her head as if to say she'd had enough of this nonsense. 'We can't. She's a victim as much as your brother and nephew are. The last thing we want to do is make her a suspect. So, Padrig, before she arrives, do yourself a great big favour and tell us how long you and your sister-in-law Mari had been having a fling.' She stabbed her index finger down on the photocopy so that it fell right in between the faces of the man opposite and Mari Randal smiling like teenagers in the photo.

The movement, serpent swift, finally broke through Randal's shell. 'Okay, okay.' He brought his hands forward and his head fell into them. The words he spoke next came through his quivering, splayed fingers. 'Christ Almighty, what a bloody mess. What a bloody mess.'

Catrin and Gil exchanged looks. Catrin sat back, nodding. Gil pulled his chair forward to get closer to Randal and slid the A4 print a little closer. 'Right, Padrig, in your own time.'

CHAPTER TWENTY-THREE

THEY PUT Mari Randal in a different room. Much to Rhys's chagrin, Warlow asked Lowri to sit in. He wanted a female presence, half wondering if he was breaking a 'woke' law by even saying it. Not that he cared much for that stuff. The dynamics of an interview were complicated and anything that would oil the wheels was worth using in his book. Especially when it was a grieving woman.

Mari Randal appeared as if she had not been sleeping very well, judging by the dark half circles under her eyes. She'd used a band to push the hair back from her face. It looked lank and stringy.

'Thanks for coming in, Mrs—'

'Mari will do, please.'

'Thanks for coming in, Mari.'

She sat hunched on the chair, legs crossed, body folded in. 'Have you found them?'

'No. That's not why I asked you here,' Warlow explained.

Mari took several ragged breaths as relief vied with frustration. Warlow recognised the horror of the missing person's loved one in every movement and gesture. Not knowing was torture, but the absence of an actual corpse still offered a smidgen of hope.

She took a sip of water from the plastic cup in front of her. 'So, what is it?'

'We have Padrig Randal in another interview room. He's been helping us, answering a few questions.' He waited, observing. Her response, when it came, looked exaggerated.

'So you found him, then?' Her surprise looked painted on.

'We did. And as soon as we got him in, someone left me an envelope with a photograph in it.' Warlow didn't see the point of wasting any time. He had the original and took it out of the envelope and pushed it across.

She didn't flinch. Instead, she closed her eyes and dropped her chin and Warlow couldn't help but wonder if there was a tiny speck of relief in that movement.

'Can I ask who gave you that?' she said after a moment.

'You can ask, but I have no answer. Does it matter?'

Mari shook her head and seemed to decide. She uncrossed her legs, smoothed down a little fold on the thigh of her jeans, took a deep breath and said, 'What do you want to know?'

'Everything.' Warlow nodded to Lowri, who put her phone on the desk and started recording. 'In your own time.'

It had started not long after Padrig's father died, she explained. She'd sided with Padrig when it came to the dispute over the tract of land that should have been in the will. Everyone had witnessed what had been promised, and yet Aeron decided not to do the decent thing. It drove a wedge between the couple. She'd felt sorry for her brother-in-law. He would come over to talk while Aeron and Joseph were out, or they'd meet in a cafe on the pretext of her weekly shopping. To begin with, she'd wanted only to lend an ear. One thing led to another and before she knew it, they were having a full-blown affair.

'Was it only about the land, though?' Warlow asked. She'd been candid, but he sensed something had been left unsaid. 'The rift between you and Aeron?'

She hesitated as if they had caught her out, but then shook her head. 'No. It wasn't only the land. Aeron and Joe… theirs was not a straightforward relationship. We'd fall out over that. Padrig has been good to Joe. A good uncle.'

'What was the source of the friction between Joseph and his father?'

More hesitation. Mari clasped her hands together. With fingers entwined, she rubbed one palm up over the other. 'Aeron could be very stubborn. The way he treated Padrig tells you that. He had fixed views on things. Being Chapel didn't help.'

Warlow frowned. 'In what way?'

'Lots of ways. The modern world held challenges for a traditionalist like Aeron. And Joseph… Joseph had a life outside of the farm. He'd go off on a Friday and a Saturday night. Go out, I mean, though sometimes he wouldn't come home.'

'Is that unusual? I mean Joseph is what, twenty-four?'

Mari shrugged. 'Not that unusual, I agree. Though Aeron hadn't done it in his youth and so he disapproved. But what he couldn't stomach was that Joseph had come out to us.'

A few gears shifted and locked in Warlow's head and brought to mind Julia Lloyd's photographs of Robert and Joseph and a group of lads on a night out. He knew Robert Lloyd was gay. But he hadn't realised the same applied to Joe. 'Aeron disapproved of Joseph's sexuality?'

'More than disapproved. He'd always say that his, and

the Bible's, understanding of a Christian marriage was a union between a man and a woman. Anything else was a perversion.'

Warlow's awareness of nonconformism was sketchy, but, like all religions in secular Wales, he suspected it to be in decline. And rigid attitudes like the one Mari described now could only accelerate that.

'How did that sit with Joe?'

'It didn't. It didn't sit at all. But it meant that Joseph brought none of his friends back. He went to bars and clubs. Gay bars and clubs. I don't think he had a steady relationship ever. Partly because he wanted no more disapproval from his father. So Joe never talked about his life outside the farm.'

'Not even to you?' Warlow pressed for more.

Mari gave a resigned little shrug. 'Rarely. The farm is so busy, we'd never get time alone together.'

Warlow waited and saw something flicker behind her lids. 'And yes, of course, I regret that. Now more than ever.' She squeezed her eyes shut.

'Whoever printed this photograph of you knew full well you were having an affair. No one has tried to tell you to end it?'

'No… I mean, there's always emphasis on fidelity and living the pious life whenever there's a Chapel service. But nothing ever aimed directly at me.'

'Still, someone had that knowledge. And someone might not have put pressure on you, but there's a chance they put pressure on Padrig, isn't there?'

A flicker of anxiety darted across the woman's face. 'What does that mean? What are you trying to say?'

Warlow decided it was time to light the blue touch paper. 'I'm saying that I may not have been the only person they showed this photograph to. What if someone threatened to show it to Aeron? How would Padrig react?'

'Padrig?' A shrill little mirthless laugh escaped Mari Randal's lips, but then realisation of what the DCI implied slotted home. 'You don't think... you can't believe that Padrig...'

'I'm just about ready to believe anything in this case, Mari. You and Padrig were having an affair, and as soon as your husband and son go missing, he buggers off and plays ostrich. How do you think that looks?'

Panic seized Mari and her voice went up an octave. 'But he did that to spare me. To avoid having to explain.'

'Explain what?'

'All this.' She shook her head. 'This mess.'

'Well, he hasn't done a very good bloody job of it so far because here we all are, mess and all. And from where I'm sitting, Padrig is very much in the frame for whatever happened that night.'

'No,' Mari said and a slow tear trickled down her cheek.

'Much as you'd like us not to consider it, I'm afraid—'

'You don't understand,' Mari broke in. 'It has nothing to do with what I want to believe. I know Padrig wasn't involved.'

'Are you going to tell my why you're so convinced?'

Mari sniffed, fetched a tissue from her sleeve and wiped first her cheek and then her nose. She looked up into Warlow's unforgiving eyes. 'I know because Padrig was with me when Aeron and Joseph went missing.'

———

'IT'S NOT HIM.' Warlow stood in front of the Gallery to address the team.

Gil and Catrin had just joined from the interview room and stood, wearing puzzled expressions, as the DCI fumed in front of them. He told them what he'd learned from

Mari Randal. That Padrig had been in his car and on the way home from some job when Aeron and Joseph left to look at the feed shed field that Saturday night. On a whim, like a naughty schoolgirl, and finding herself alone, Mari had texted him to learn that he was only a few miles away. She jumped in the car and they met for an assignation.

'Is that what they're calling it these days?' Gil muttered.

'Wow,' Rhys said, grinning. 'You'd think they'd be too old for that sort of thing, right?'

That earned him an amused look from Warlow. 'So what's the official age limit for rumpy pumpy then, DC Harries?'

Rhys opened his mouth, shut it, opened it again and then stuttered, 'I-I-I...'

'Best you keep your powder dry on matters of a delicate nature, Rhys,' Gil whispered. 'In case you hadn't noticed, we are all older than you.'

'Yes, Sarge.' Rhys nodded, busying himself with a pad and pencil and trying his best to hide the horror on his face at the prospect of contemplating each member of the team in terms of their sexual proclivity.

'What did Randal say when you showed him the photo?' Warlow asked.

'Randal admits it's him, obviously,' Catrin answered. 'But he's concocted some story about visiting his father's grave that day and bumping into his sister-in-law.'

'Sounds like he was bumping into her on a regular basis,' Gil muttered.

Rhys grinned but froze it before it could morph into a chortle when Catrin sent him a daggers look.

'Do we accept her story, sir?' She turned back to Warlow and asked what they were all wanting to ask.

'Reasons not to?' Warlow responded.

Catrin perched on the edge of a desk. 'They might be in it together.'

'Fair point and one I'd buy into if it didn't involve Joseph. Hatching something to get rid of Aeron, who, according to his wife, is a bigot of the first water, could be something she and Padrig might do together. But Joseph as well?' He shook his head.

Lowri stood next to her desk, frowning. 'I'm still confused, sir. Why's he been hiding? What was he trying to achieve?'

Another good question from the PC. 'My guess is he's been protecting Mari Randal. And if it hadn't been for the whistle blower who left the photograph, it was working pretty well. If it hadn't been for our mysterious posty,' he tapped the posted-up copy of Mari and Padrig outside the chapel, 'we'd have been none the wiser, would we?'

Catrin hadn't moved. 'Back to Padrig, sir. Do we let him go?'

Warlow nodded. 'But we'll need a statement about his movements on the night the others went missing. Tell him Mari Randal has spilled all. There's no need for him to keep on denying it. We need to see if their stories tally. Tell him we'll be holding her, too, until he puts something down on paper. That should get him scribbling.'

'What next then, sir?' Rhys asked, just about recovered from his gaffe of earlier.

'Next is a cup of tea and a rethink. We're back to bloody square one. So, here's your chance to redeem yourself. Milk and one as per.'

CHAPTER TWENTY-FOUR

SQUARE ONE WAS a place Warlow had visited many times, and he hated being there with a vengeance. But, in situations like this, you ignored things at your peril.

Even the little things that might seem inconsequential.

Everyone had a list of actions and an angle from which to view the case. And the easiest way to appreciate these angles was to give everyone a chance to talk. They were on their second cup of tea, but the HUMAN TISSUE FOR TRANSPLANT box had been put away, though admittedly in a depleted state. Gil and Catrin were back from securing a signed statement from Padrig Randal. Rhys and Lowri had done the same for Mari Randal so that Warlow could have time to think.

It hadn't helped. But this might.

'Right, Rhys, you first.'

The DC stood up, notebook in hand. 'No luck with Joseph Randal's clothing at the Falls. We traced as many people as we could from credit card usage in the tearoom in the hours before the finding. So far, those we've contacted have come up blank. No one saw anyone dumping anything in the water.'

'What about the family that actually found the clothing?' Warlow asked.

'Same, sir. They're from Wolverhampton and it was their first visit. No links with the area or the Randals.'

'Hmm.' Warlow growled. He'd chosen to sit in a chair with his feet straight out in front of him and his arms folded. 'Kapil's report on the jeans and trainer, singular, doesn't help much either. You've all seen it?'

Nods all around.

'Anything else?' Warlow eyed the DC.

'Aeron Randal's phone records, sir. Again, nothing remarkable going back over the week before his disappearance. No contact with his brother during that time.' He finished up with one of his trademark apologetic toothless smiles. Warlow nodded a thanks and let the DC sit down before turning to Gil. 'Thoughts?'

The big sergeant walked over to the Gallery and let his eyes drift down first to the image of the clothing at the Falls, then the blood-spattered feed-shed door, and ending up at the Habberley footbridge. 'All this... *Mae'n drewi.*'

Everyone in the room knew what he meant. It did indeed stink.

'But,' Gil continued, 'The most telling bit of evidence now is Aeron Randal's coat snagged on a footbridge off a country road across the border. And, reluctant as I am to admit it, we come right back around to the rustling angle. That's our best bet, I think. We still haven't liaised with West Mercia, so we ought to. See if there's anything they might be able to contribute.'

Warlow nodded his appreciation again and watched as Catrin pushed her hip off a desk and took Gil's place. 'I agree with Gil. On the face of it, and though I don't like it, a sheep theft gone wrong still looks the most likely. Having said that, the Mari-Padrig angle intrigues me still.' Her gaze scanned the posted photo of the couple outside the chapel. 'I think they're telling the truth, but someone wanted to implicate them. Whoever sent you this photograph may know a lot more.'

'Agreed,' Warlow said.

Catrin didn't turn around. Instead she kept talking, it appeared, to herself. 'I think a visit to the hotel is in order. Someone must have seen something. Envelopes don't appear out of thin air.'

The DCI turned his head towards the only Uniformed officer on the team. 'Lowri?'

She strode to the front, obviously terrified.

'We got hold of Joseph Randal's phone records. He has lots of friends. It looked like he was planning a big night out the following weekend. Talk of a club in Liverpool and a couple of pubs in Wrexham. I've checked them out, sir and they are gay haunts.'

'Was he in a relationship?'

Lowri grimaced. 'Difficult to say. One number appears more frequently of late, but there aren't many messages. It may be that they were using apps to communicate, in which case none of that would show up.'

Warlow nodded. Privacy and encryption again. Great for the user, pain in the arse for the police.

'But it looks as if there was some conflict. I've copied one text exchange as an example.' She handed out some sheets.

I want to see you.

Not a good idea. I'm working until eight.

When can we meet up?

Not tonight. I could make it to the crossroads at three tomorrow.

I want to. I can't wait until we're official.

WhatsApp me lunchtime.

———

'Whose number is that?' Catrin asked.

'It's a prepaid SIM,' Lowri answered. 'No address.'

'Anyone rung it?' Gil asked.

Lowri nodded. 'No longer available, sarge.'

'So we know Joseph was seeing someone but not who,' Warlow mused.

'I've gone back through, sir, and found links to Robert Lloyd as well. They were in communication. It doesn't sound intimate. But they were friends, definitely.'

'Robert Lloyd?' Catrin asked.

'That's a different story—' Warlow began to explain but was cut off by the sound of Rick Astley singing *Never Gonna Give You Up*, which Rhys had chosen for his mobile ring tone. Catrin had quizzed him about it, expecting him to reply with a kind of post-modern ironic response. He hadn't. He used the tune because he liked it. The good thing was he answered calls pretty sharpish, as it irritated the hell out of everyone else.

Rhys listened, then put his hand over the mouthpiece and said with exaggerated mouth movements, 'Hana Prosser, sir.' He listened some more, spoke a few words, and put the phone down. When he turned to face the team, he looked befuddled.

'Well?' Warlow asked.

'She says there's been another rustling incident, sir. Thought you ought to be made aware.'

Warlow sat up.

'How come Hana Prosser has your number?' Catrin asked, eyes narrowed in suspicion.

'We've been liaising over the Falls.'

'Really?'

'Yes, Sarge.' Rhys let the appellation end with an upward inflection that implied he resented her tone.

Warlow sat up. 'Okay. Catrin, Gil, chase up the hotel, see if we can find who has it in for Padrig and Mari.

Meanwhile, Rhys, get back on to Prosser, get an address and tell her we'll meet her there, wherever the hell there is.'

'You're still keen on the sheep theft angle then, Evan?' Gil asked.

'It's not baa'd as theories go, but let's just say I'm not counting on it.'

Gil responded with a broad smile. Catrin groaned. Lowri looked confused and Rhys... felt the urge to explain to her what just happened.

'That was the boss making a little joke,' he whispered. 'He does that now and again.' He nodded at the DCI. 'Good one, sir.'

'I don't know why I bother.' Warlow sighed before adding, 'But right now, I'd take anything that gave us a bit of direction.'

———

GIL MADE a beeline for reception once he and Catrin got to the Angler's Lodge. The miserable drizzle cloaking the day had finally abated, but wary residents still wore anoraks and coats mindful of the damp's return. The officers stood in line behind some tourists enquiring about the times of trains to Snowdonia.

There was one, the receptionist explained – or rather droned – but it took four hours and went through Shrews-bury and Bangor. The tourists, French by the sound of it, moved away, bemused.

Gil stepped up to be met, not by Tamara, but by a bespectacled youth with an almost monobrow and lank hair held back in a top-knot bun, who'd somehow missed the lecture on welcoming smiles. Probably because he'd been busy practising his miserable git look in the mirror. He did not wear a badge, nor did he introduce himself.

Instead, he looked primed and keen to fend off the next inane question. Gil smiled and held up his warrant card.

'Afternoon.'

'Help you?' A mumble.

'I hope so. Do you have a name?'

For a moment, the boy, who Gil put at about seventeen, hesitated, but realised that not giving it would probably cause more hassle than it was worth. 'Damien.'

Gil, straight faced, glanced pointedly at Catrin.

He didn't need to say anything. They'd both seen The Omen.

'Right, Damian.' Gil found a smile from somewhere for the kid. 'I spoke to a woman sitting in that chair a few hours ago. She handed me an envelope that someone had left here. Her name was Tamara. Is she around?'

'No. She's eating. I do this shift so that she can eat lunch.' Damian's expression oozed defiant indifference.

Gil glanced at his watch. It must be a very late lunch. 'Will she be back?'

'Yeah, in a couple of hours.'

'Right, then maybe you can help. We're trying to find out who might have left the envelope.'

'Tamara didn't know?'

'She did not. It wasn't handed to her, it was left on the counter, here.' Gil pointed an index finger.

'Tamara does the day shift. Eight to four. But we have an office behind. She might have been in there, sorting out bookings. We're understaffed.' The deadpan delivery must have done wonders for the hotel's Yelp score.

'Is there a chance someone else might have been around? Cleaners? Concierge?'

Damian's lids dropped a millimetre or two. 'We don't have a concierge. Cleaners do this area first thing before seven.'

'Damn,' muttered Gil.

Catrin stepped forward, all smiles. 'You know Tamara, Damian?'

'She's my mother.'

Catrin nodded. 'Isn't she the lucky one? And she has you doing these shifts after school? That must be a pain.'

'She pays me to do it.'

'Of course she does. Not enough, obviously. And you can't think of anyone who might have seen our delivery man?'

'You could ask the guests.'

'How?' Gil wondered.

Damian shrugged. Not his problem.

Catrin's smile widened as she stared beyond Damian into the dark interior of the reception area and noted two things. Damian's laptop bag, trailing charging wires, sat on a shelf behind him. Amongst the many stickers covering the surface, she read 'Kill The Bill' and 'Defund The Police'. That said it all. She also followed a cable running from a black box up to the ceiling and out along the edge of the coving to a blinking light in the corner of the corridor.

She leaned in. 'Or, you could run through the CCTV that you have of this corridor and find him for us.'

'Oh yeah, there is that.' Damian smiled for the first time. A sly thing that dripped cynicism. 'I forgot. I might have time to look later.'

'How about you take a look now?' Catrin's smile mirrored Damian's in its insincerity.

Damian didn't flinch. 'As you can see, I'm busy working.' He had his laptop open at an angle. A bouncing image of an RPG character in armour wielding an enormous sword in an imagined landscape oozed blue light over Damian's face.

'Obviously,' Gil said. 'So we can do this two ways. Either my colleague and I can take a seat in the lounge and wait for you to bring the information to us in the next fifteen minutes. Or, I make a call and get a warrant and confiscate all this equipment, including your laptop, as it may contain material evidence in a very serious case.'

'My laptop is personal property.' Damian's objection contained the merest hint of panic.

'And yet here you are, an employee of the hotel, clearly using it as a part of your work,' Catrin said. 'By your own admission.'

For the first time, Damian's expression betrayed a range of emotions. His mouth puckered as if preparing to deliver a devastating rejoinder. But his eyes strayed to the laptop and his lips slackened as the implication of Gil's threat thudded home.

'We'll be in the lounge,' Catrin said, as she and Gill walked away.

'What's it like to be fascist pawns?' Damian blurted out to their departing backs.

Catrin stopped and turned. This time Damian did flinch and flushed bright pink when she spoke. 'No idea, but if we find any, we'll be sure to ask them. We'll give you fifteen minutes before my colleague Sergeant Jones makes the call. And don't think about disappearing. He has a very special set of skills. And if you attempt to corrupt the evidence, or obstruct us in our work in any way, he will track you down and he will find you. And when he does…'

The whites of Damian's eyes told her he'd got the message.

She caught up with Gil as they entered the lounge.

'Nice Liam Neeson reference there,' Gil said, grinning.

'Blame Netflix. But sometimes, Hollywood speak is the only language little Antifa shits like Damian understand.'

CHAPTER TWENTY-FIVE

THEY TRAVELLED north in a grey Focus. Warlow wanted to think. The car smelled of food and cheap air freshener, but Rhys drove steadily and Warlow let him have his choice of music, so long as it was Radio Six. He wasn't averse to a bit of innovative Indie. What he could not bloody stand was all the poppy autotuned crap that made people sound like they were either singing in a tunnel or whooping like a family of gibbons.

They'd driven for twenty minutes and were roughly halfway to the pin location Hana had dropped on Google maps when the DCI's phone rang. Gil Jones's name appeared in the screen window.

'Gil, any joy?'

'Joy would be putting it a little strongly, but we've got some news. I'm putting you on speaker so that Catrin can put her oar in, I mean uh… talk.'

'I'm listening.' Warlow let a smile flick the corner of his mouth.

'Sir,' Catrin's voice came on, 'they have CCTV in the hotel corridor recording comings and goings. At 11.05 this morning a man appeared carrying an envelope which he placed on the reception desk and left.'

'And?'

'And,' Gil said, spinning things out. 'We'd already met him. Yesterday, as it turns out.'

The line went quiet until Warlow growled. 'If either of you are going to ask me to guess, I'll—'

'It's Hari Gregory, sir,' Catrin said.

'Gregory? The farmer?'

'He's also a deacon at the chapel. That's where we met him yesterday.'

'Where Sergeant Richards thought he was a ghoul or some such,' Gil added.

Catrin sighed.

'Right, get copies of the footage,' Warlow ordered. 'We'll need to talk to him. Meanwhile, chase up West Mercia over the rustling side of things.'

Gil answered, 'We'll head back to the station and get on with that now. See you both back here for supper later, then?'

Warlow glanced at his watch. 'Hopefully.'

'Don't eat all the bread,' Rhys shouted.

'Hari Gregory,' Warlow said when they'd rung off.

'That's not what I expected at all, sir.'

'No? What were you expecting?'

'I don't know. A nosy journalist or something?'

'It would have been neater. This muddies the waters even more.' Warlow sat back and let his brain sift through this new knowledge. Gregory must have his reasons.

The nice Google lady told them to take a left at the next junction. A few lines appeared on Rhys's brow. 'Can I see the pin again, sir?'

Warlow used his fingers to make the map a little smaller and held it up. Rhys squinted at it. 'It looks to be not far from where the Randals disappeared.'

'How can you tell?' Warlow peered at the screen. Few, if any, landmarks were obvious. Only the curves of the roads and thin blue lines of river gave any indication of where Prosser wanted them to go.

'If you look a little more to the left with the map this small, you'll see where the Falls are, sir. It's definitely in the same area.'

Rhys was right. Warlow recognised some buildings and the odd garage that they'd passed that morning. But instead of sending them left to where Hermon Chapel and the feed shed would be, they continued for another five miles before curving back on themselves in a big loop.

A uniformed Hana Prosser leaned against the bonnet of her car as they pulled up.

She stooped when Rhys lowered his window, red cheeked from the brisk wind that always seemed to blow up here. 'You found us then?'

'Google did,' Rhys answered. 'What's the story.'

'Thirty sheep missing from a flock. The farmer's out looking.' She flicked her gaze to Warlow. 'But since you wanted to know, I thought…'

Warlow held up a hand in appreciation. 'You thought correctly. We'll follow you.'

The entrance to the farm meandered for half a mile along a track off the road. An old milk churn hung from a tree with the farm's name painted on it. The letters were faded and Warlow only caught a glimpse but he picked out a D and an I. Then they were pulling into a well-kept yard with an array of old-fashioned tractors, the kind without cabs, parked in a barn. A big blue New Holland stood guard in front of its predecessors. The farmer must be a collector. A woman in wellingtons and a weather-beaten coat stood waiting.

Hana got out first, Warlow and Rhys followed. The PCSO made the introductions.

'Detective Chief Inspector Warlow and Detective Constable Harries, this is Sian Gregory.'

Warlow saw Rhys's eyebrows shoot up and a glance jerk his way. The DCI held out his hand to the woman in front of him. 'The farm name on your churn needs touching up.'

Mrs Gregory nodded, a faltering smile touching her lips.

'Mr Gregory not here?'

'He's out looking. Gone to the high field. There's a road that runs past it, you see.' Anxiety dragged down the corner of her eyes. 'He knew something was wrong this morning. But it's only this afternoon that the numbers didn't add up.'

'How far to the high field?' Warlow asked.

'Not too far. Couple of miles,' Hana answered. She knew the farm. Knew the Gregorys. 'We can go in mine. It's four-wheel-drive.'

'Good idea.'

In the car, Warlow told Hana about the photograph of Mari and Padrig and of who made sure it reached him, anonymously.

'Not that anonymously, sir,' Rhys said.

'Exactly. And before you say it, yes, I agree. I don't like coincidences either.'

They travelled farm tracks and Rhys had to get out to open and shut gates four times before they climbed along a sunken lane towards the horizon. 'That's Gregory's vehicle up ahead.'

A Land Cruiser sat in the field. They pulled up on a ridge, but there was no sign of Gregory.

'Where's the road from here?'

Hana pointed down to where a copse of trees broke up the rolling fields. The hedges earmarked the direction of a narrow road that disappeared behind the hilly ground in front of them. But Gregory was nowhere to be seen. From this high point, the field rolled away over a series of humps that limited their view.

'Which direction?' Rhys asked.

'Easiest if we split up.'

It would be. But then something about this place had Warlow's skin prickling. Another abandoned vehicle in an isolated spot. He shook his head. 'No, we stay together.'

They stood, listening and looking for any clue for which direction Gregory might have taken.

The shot decided it for them. It ruptured the silence and all three officers turned to the right.

'For Christ's sake,' Warlow protested. 'Does everyone up here have a bloody gun?'

He set off at a brisk half jog. Down and then up again until he crested a rise and came to a halt. The field fell away towards the road and a little access lane guarded by a metal gate.

'What's that at the gate? Rhys asked. He pointed towards a cluster of what looked like pale bags. 'Are they feed sacks?'

'No,' Hana replied, and something in her voice made Warlow look closer. When one sack jerked convulsively, the answer became terrifyingly clear.

'They're sheep,' Hana said.

'Why are they all lying down?'

A figure appeared from within the cluster of animals. It stood up and pointed at something.

'Is that Greg—' Hana began.

The second shot made even Warlow flinch. The figure slumped and dropped to its knees amidst the slaughter.

'Christ,' Warlow said. 'Stay behind me. The both of you, do you hear?'

Rhys nodded. Hana, her face drawn, muttered, 'Sir.'

He barely heard her because he was already moving, his brain fizzing with likely scenarios, none of which were pleasant. It didn't help that they were running towards an armed man. Images of the gore on the feed-shed door exploded into his head. When they were within sixty yards, he called a halt and hunched down. He waved to the others to do the same, and all three officers fell into a bent knee squat. Not that it helped a great deal as there was no cover. But they made smaller targets than if they were upright.

'Mr Gregory? Is that you?' Warlow shouted.

The figure stood up and stared towards the huddled group, a desperate, vacant expression on his face. He held up a wavering hand. 'Yes, it's me.'

Rhys exhaled loudly.

'Put the gun down, Mr Gregory,' Warlow ordered.

The farmer glanced at the weapon and placed it on the ground.

Warlow stood up and trudged forward. With every step, the charnel house scene in front of him got worse. Gregory didn't move. He stood, rooted to the spot, staring from one dead animal to the other.

'I had to,' he mumbled. 'I couldn't let them suffer.'

Thirty sheep lay at his feet, their dead legs sticking out from their immobile bodies. Gregory had blood all over him, but it was nothing compared to the amount on and around the animals. Starkly red against the white wool of the fleeces, blacker where it had pooled on the grass.

Warlow picked up the shotgun by the barrel end and used as little contact as possible before placing it out of harm's way behind Rhys. The metal felt warm under his touch. 'What happened here?'

'I found them. Up against the gate like this. I had to

finish five of them off. Couldn't let them suffer. Couldn't do that.' Gregory's eyes were empty voids.

'Did you see anyone?' Warlow asked.

Gregory shook his head. 'They'd long gone.'

Hana's radio crackled and she turned away to answer.

'Are they all dead now?' Rhys's voice cracked a little.

'All dead.' Gregory nodded. He wiped his eyes roughly with his sleeve. 'Herded here and butchered.'

'Why weren't they taken?' Rhys's gaze swept over the devastation.

'Who knows.' Gregory made a noise in his throat that might have been a curse, or just as easily a sob. Then he turned his face up and let go a plaintive utterance, '*Arglwydd Mawr.*'

Eventually, Tomo arrived. There'd be no difficulty protecting the crime scene out here. Warlow spoke to Kapil who volunteered sending someone up to look at tyre tracks near the access to the gate and anything else that might be helpful. Then Hana called someone to take the sheep away. But not before Warlow had inspected a couple. All had been killed with a knife cut to the throat, except for the five who'd been shot because that knife cut had left them injured but not dead.

By the time they got Gregory back to the farmhouse he'd become monosyllabic. Warlow recognised shock when he saw it and decided now was not the time to ask him questions about the photograph. Instead, he instructed Hana to bring him to Newtown first thing so that they could take a proper statement. He'd use that as a springboard for other discussions. A technique he often deployed when he wanted to sideswipe a witness.

Mrs Gregory insisted on seeing him and Rhys to their car when they finally left.

'Will you catch these monsters?' she asked, her lip trembling.

'We will. Please tell your husband that for us.'

She nodded. 'Hana says you're good.'

He wanted to twist that into something suitably disparaging and self-deprecating but for the life of him found nothing to say. Instead, he offered her a worthless smile and turned away, leaving the Gregorys to cope with the disaster.

CHAPTER TWENTY-SIX

WARLOW SAT on the bed in his room at the hotel feeling a distinct sense of deja vu over what he was about to do. And then did it anyway.

'She's fine,' Jess answered before even saying hello. 'Cadi is on top form.'

'Good. Glad to hear it.'

'Molly's taken her out for an evening toilet walk.'

'Christ, don't spoil her or she'll expect that from me, too. And you?'

'I don't think I need an evening toilet walk.'

Warlow huffed out a laugh. 'Sorry, it's been a long day spent mostly in the company of DC Harries. So you'll excuse me for not being able to string more than three words together.'

'How's it going up there?'

'Don't ask. It's going precisely nowhere at a rate of knots.'

'Want to talk about it?'

'Not yet. I need a night's sleep to let things percolate.'

'Well, I got to have a chat with two officers from West Mids this afternoon.'

'Mac and Cheese? I'd almost forgotten them. Your thoughts?'

'Not brimming with personality, either of them. They wanted to know what my working relationship with Mel Lewis was like. And what kind of interactions I'd witnessed between you and him.'

Warlow had almost forgotten this morning's charmless interview. 'So you told them about me and Mel?'

'I told them you were the one who worked out how he'd been stringing us all along, yes.'

'I bet they loved that.'

'You'd think they would. Praise where praise is due and all that. But they were strangely subdued when I told them.'

'I'm not surprised. They're trying desperately to make me Mel's silent organised-crime partner.'

'What?' Jess's voice skyrocketed to soprano.

'They're fishing, that's all,' Warlow explained, with a lot more nonchalance than he actually felt. 'I'm sure they're both very nice people under the shit stains.'

'If I'd have known, I'd—'

'Just as well you didn't, then. On another point, Gil is enjoying being out and about. He and Catrin look on the verge of a cat-fight most of the time.'

'I bet they spark off each other. Oh, and on that note, my cast comes off next week. I'll be back in as soon as.'

'Great. Don't you need physio?'

'No. I get plenty of exercise batting away Molly's sarcasm.'

Warlow fell back on the bed and let out an involuntary groan as taut back muscles relaxed, but he kept the phone to his ear. 'You'll have to excuse me. Had to stretch out there for a minute.'

'Glad you qualified it. I thought you were having a stroke.'

'I haven't eaten yet, either. Best I get downstairs before Rhys empties the kitchen of everything edible, or I fall asleep where I lie.'

'How are you holding up?'

As always, her question took him by surprise. She knew he was on Anti-Retroviral Therapy for HIV. Had been since diagnosis. He didn't talk about it to anyone. He merely lived with it. And the medications kept his CD4 levels high and the viral load very low. But he'd shied away from telling his family, and so discussing it openly always made him uncomfortable. 'Me? I'm fine.'

'Good.' Jess was chirpy. 'I've been reading up. They say that people who start treatment with CD4 levels above 500 may never have an HIV related illness. What was yours?'

She had been doing her homework. 'Mine were good, around 850. Pure luck the virus was picked up when I went to give blood.'

'What's your level now?'

'A thousand.'

'Normal, then.'

'For now, yes.'

'Great. That is good.' She sounded genuinely pleased. And she was right. He'd been lucky so far. As regards treatment anyway. And ART didn't sound so bad when you pronounced the letters singly. Certainly more palatable than the ridiculous descriptive terms they gave the actual drugs. Nucleoside reverse transcriptase inhibitors, protease inhibitors, integrase inhibitors – a wonder he didn't rattle. And he'd be on this stuff for the rest of his life thanks to a vindictive junky who laced her hair with used needles to deliberately infect anyone who 'messed' with her.

'Thanks, Doctor Allanby.' The little sarky comment was all he could muster as a comeback.

But it did the job, triggering a throaty laugh from the

DI. 'Sorry, I realise you don't enjoy talking about this and it's none of my business, really.'

'No, you're alright. I'm grateful you're taking an interest. After all, us invalids need to stick together. Support groups and all that.'

'Hilarious.' Jess had broken her wrist on the job. They were both victims of circumstance. That circumstance being mixing with society's dregs, killers, chancers, junkies. That was the trouble. You were never sure who or what was around the corner in this game.

Warlow steered things back to the case in hand. 'We're interviewing a neighbour of the mispers tomorrow who just had thirty sheep butchered on his land.'

'Ugh. Why?'

'Why indeed? Botched thievery again, we assume. I won't be eating lamb this evening, that's for certain. Once I have a theory to run past you, I'll be in touch.'

'I'll give Cadi a hug for you.'

'You do that. And thank Molly for her care.'

Warlow ended the call. He took off his shoes and trousers, trying not to worry too much about Mac and Cheese and their opinion of him.

He was hungry and thirsty, but the events of the day had turned his brain to mush. Too much had happened. Too many threads unravelling. Threads that had nothing on the end of them when they were pulled. He needed some fuel. He needed to recharge. But not yet. Supper could wait a few more minutes.

Sighing, he flopped back on the bed and let the day play out like a film in his head. In case something might jump out at him.

Nothing did.

When he opened his eyes, light was streaming in through the open curtains over the window and he was lying in the exact same position across the bed, his legs drawn up, his shirt still on.

Christ. He'd slept right through. Something he hadn't done for months.

At breakfast, a sheepish Warlow walked in, ready for a roasting, only to find all three of his fellow officers already there. But none of them were at the buffet. Instead, they all stood in front of the TV on the wall, staring up at a BBC local news piece.

Gil, mug in hand, beckoned to the DCI. 'Hurry up, or you'll miss it.'

'Miss what?'

The piece to camera involved a reporter holding a microphone up to his guest's ruddy face.

'Is this live?' Warlow asked.

'It is, sir,' Catrin answered.

Warlow caught the tail end of the reporter's set up, something about the peace of this quiet area having been shattered by two serious incidents, the latest involving the slaughter of a herd of sheep. But then he tuned in.

'With me is Elis Prosser, a neighbouring farmer and spokesman for the local breeders here. What do you make of this most recent incident?'

'It wasn't the whole herd. Thirty sheep were killed. But thirty is bad enough.'

'What motivates this kind of behaviour, you reckon?'

Elis looked stern. 'Money. These are people out to sell the carcasses. Cheap meat into the black market. But of course there are great dangers in that. Risk of food poisoning because the meat will not have been handled properly. Some of these animals that are taken from our farms are being treated for worms or fleas.'

'Do the police have any leads?'

'I'm sure they're doing what they can.'

'Do you think this incident is linked to the disappearance of Joseph and Aeron Randal?'

Elis refused to rise to the bait. 'I'm not a police officer. You'll have to ask them.'

'This is a shocking crime. You've been to the scene. Can you describe it to us?'

Elis shook his head. 'It was a gruesome sight. These animals were fit and healthy only days ago. I can't begin to explain the cruelty I saw. I know that some were being raised for the abattoir, but this is different, and my thoughts go out to my colleague and his family. He is distraught as you can imagine.'

'But this is an isolated area. It must be difficult to watch over the flocks?'

'It is, and so we depend on the public to help. Any odd behaviour, any strange vehicles, please report them immediately to the police. That's what we as a farming community depend upon. Report everything suspicious. It might mean nothing, but then it might mean everything. And the police have units set up specifically to deal with crimes such as these.'

'Mr Prosser, thank you for your time.'

The camera swung away from Elis and focused in on the reporter. 'Statistics show that there has been a sharp rise in rural crime, and in particular animal theft over the last few years. Unfortunately, last night's incident shows that not even this quiet part of Wales is immune from this wave.'

'Hmm,' Warlow muttered.

They drifted across to a table where Catrin and Rhys already had empty bowls and Gil had two rounds of buttered toast as yet uneaten on his plate. Warlow fetched some coffee, scrambled eggs and bacon and joined them.

'He did well there, did Hana's dad, don't you think?' Gil commented.

'He probably knows more than he's letting on. I mean Hana probably tells him bits and pieces,' Rhys argued.

'If she does, he has enough sense not to let the hyenas in on it.' Warlow forked some food into his mouth and nicked one of Gil's toasts.

'That's theft,' Gil warned.

'That's me looking after your coronaries,' Warlow countered. 'Anything come through this morning from Kapil?'

Catrin shook her head. 'Nothing yet, sir.'

'Okay. Hana Prosser is on the way in with Gregory. I'd like a crack at him myself. This time with Rhys. You up for it?'

Rhys blinked like a dog shown his favourite lead. 'I'm your man, sir.'

Catrin, sitting next to him, rolled her eyes and sighed. 'I think I'm going to be sick.'

'And by the way, what happened to you last night?' Gil squinted at Warlow over his toast.

'You know the score, Gil. A DCI's work is never done. I had phone calls to make, colleagues to talk to, reports to write up—'

'You fell asleep in your clothes then did you?'

Warlow shook his head. 'Why is it that I've been lumbered with such a bunch of cynics?'

'Takes one to know one, sir,' Rhys said, and got a stern look for his troubles.

But Gil had his back. 'Well said, that man. Thing is you're getting old. Plus, you didn't have your usual afternoon nap yesterday.'

'Right, for that, you,' he pointed at Rhys, 'refill my cup with the hotel's terrible but strong coffee. You,' his finger swung towards Gil, 'get more toast. And you,' his eyes settled on Catrin, 'stay here and have a sensible conversation with me. I need confirmation I'm not still asleep and having a very bad dream. I've always been able to rely on you, Detective Sergeant.'

'Pleasure, sir.' Catrin beamed smugly at the other officers before re-engaging Warlow. 'By the way, your face has a crease with the shape of a button in the middle of it. Happens when you sleep heavily on the collar of your shirt.'

Warlow exhaled. 'You are all going into my little black book. Be aware that I have a page for who will be first for the firing squad after the revolution.'

CHAPTER TWENTY-SEVEN

It made for a curiously formal set up. Warlow didn't want to use an interview room, so he arranged to chat with Gregory in the SIO room. The same sort of set up for when he'd spoken to Elis Prosser. Which meant he sat in one chair and Gregory in another on the other side of the desk. Rhys pulled in a spare chair and found one for Hana Prosser, whom Warlow wanted in on things. He'd instructed them to take notes so that they didn't look so much like a pair of sodding bookends.

Warlow gave them time to take a written statement from Gregory of how events had panned out yesterday before joining them. He sat at the desk and made a show of reading through it.

Gregory, for want of a better word or two, looked a broken man. They'd provided him with tea and a couple of half-coated digestives from Gil's stash, though they'd wisely kept the HUMAN TISSUE FOR TRANSPLANT box well out of sight.

'I will not insult you by asking how you're feeling this morning, Mr Gregory.' Warlow used his own mug of tea as a prop.

'It's Hari,' Gregory said.

Warlow acknowledged that. 'There seems little point in me asking this, but do you have any idea who might have done that to your livestock, Hari?'

Gregory kept his head down. 'They must have been disturbed. They'd butchered a couple, and by that, I mean cut them up, removed the guts. Strung them all over the ground.' He gave a little shake of his head.

Warlow nodded. 'The road that runs nearby, is it well travelled?'

Gregory exhaled a puff of air, as if he regretted the answer he was about to give. 'It's a tiny road. That's why someone must have had local knowledge, to know that the road is there and how close it comes to my fields.'

'That's a common theme, isn't it?' Warlow threw Hana a questioning glance. Even if she might not have been expecting it, she responded as if she had.

'It is, sir. We think that reconnaissance must have been a part of the planning in almost all cases. It's unlikely they would have driven up on spec. They planned where they were going.'

'How many did you lose? Thirty was it?' Warlow asked.

'Twenty-nine,' Gregory replied. 'We found an ewe injured but still alive. The vet thinks she'll be okay.' He tilted his head and glanced at Hana. 'I saw Elis on the TV. They're saying that what happened to my sheep might be tied up with Aeron and Joseph.'

Hana looked uncomfortable, wavering on how to answer. Warlow stepped in. 'I saw it too. But then that's exactly the sort of thing the press would say. More often than not, without a shred of any actual evidence. They're not very good at maths the press. Two and two makes think of a number, so long as that number causes doubts and wondering in people's minds.'

'So there isn't a link?' Gregory asked.

Warlow saw no point in being anything but honest. 'If there is, we've yet to find it. I'm not discounting the possibility, but the press specialises in innuendo. Which brings me on to something else you can help us with, Hari.'

A fresh set of deeper lines appeared on the farmer's already wrinkled brow.

Warlow opened the thin file on his desk and slid over the image of Padrig and Mari Randal that had been delivered to him yesterday.

'Can you tell me something about this photograph, Hari?'

For a moment, Hari Gregory's eyes widened. It looked like he might default to denial, but then they narrowed defiantly before looking back at the DCI's face. 'It was the simplest way I could think of to give you the information.'

'And what information is that exactly, Hari?' In his peripheral vision, Warlow saw Hana Prosser's big eyes become even bigger.

Gregory's back straightened. 'That Aeron Randal's wife is a fornicator and an adulterer.' He spoke the words as if their obviousness needed no more clarification.

'And why do you suppose it's important that we're aware of that?'

Gregory let out a tiny expulsion of air, implying surprise at the idea that anyone needed to ask such a thing.

Warlow sat forward, one elbow on the desk. The movement made Gregory shift back an inch in his chair. 'Did Aeron know about the photograph? Had you shown it to him?'

Gregory shook his head. 'I showed it to our minister. He promised to talk to Mari Randal. He assures me he has. It seems it has made no difference.' His eyes drifted back to the image.

'It's the twenty-first century, Hari. Things like this happen all the time.'

'God has given us Commandments. A way to live a Christian life. Aeron believes that. He believes in the sanctity of the family.'

'So why hold this information back from him?'

Gregory bristled. 'Mari needed an opportunity to mend her ways. If she did, I was prepared to let a sin go unpunished. Aeron would do the same for me.'

'How can you possibly know that?'

'There speaks a man of little Faith,' Gregory said.

'I am not a religious man, I admit. My truths need to be backed up by facts and evidence I can see or touch or smell. And, right now, the aroma in my nostrils is an unpleasant one. Did you show me this photograph to implicate Mari and Padrig Randal in what's happened to Aeron and Joseph?' Warlow observed his reaction. Watched him blink as he processed what he'd just been asked and not liking it much.

'No. I...' His reaction was one of genuine surprise.

Warlow pressed him. 'Oh, come on. According to you, they're sinners. If they can flout God's will, and she is a member of the Chapel, they could be capable of all manner of sins, right?'

The dawning implication of Warlow's words finally sank home and Gregory's expression gave way to a dull horror. 'You think Mari—'

'The way this works, Hari, is that I ask the questions. Tell me about Aeron. Does he share your views about marriage?'

'They are not just my views. They are the views of the Christian Church.'

'What about the gay community? Where does all that sit with the Church?'

Gregory's face hardened. 'The Church is clear in its guidance. Alliances that are not traditional are unbiblical. Marriage is an institution created by God in which one man and one woman enter into an exclusive relationship for life. Marriage is the only form of partnership approved by God for sexual relations. Anything else is incompatible with His will, as revealed in Scripture. We do not accept that holding these theological and ethical views on biblical grounds is wrong.'

'Right. So how about Joseph?'

'What about Joseph?'

'Oh, come on. Joseph is gay. How did that fit into the scheme of things?'

Gregory's eyes dropped. 'Joseph no longer comes to services.' It didn't answer Warlow's question directly. Yet, in a way, it surely did.

'Did Aeron ever discuss Joseph with you?'

'No. He determined to bear that cross alone.'

'Christ.' Warlow shook his head, paused at the irony of his oath, and then shook his head again. He looked at his two young officers. 'Rhys, check the calendar. It is 2022, isn't it?'

'It is, sir.' Rhys's response was terse.

'Right, Mr Gregory—'

'It's Hari.'

'No, it's Mr Gregory,' Warlow told him. 'Thanks for coming in. I'm going to arrange for someone to take you back. But I doubt it'll be PCSO Prosser because from the look on her face, she might not be able to control herself. Stay here and someone will be in to fetch you.'

'What about my sheep?'

'I'm sorry for what happened to them. We have numerous people trying to find out who did this. As soon as we find out anything meaningful, we'll let you know.'

Warlow was out of his chair and motioned for the others to join him.

Gregory followed the DCI's progress but had to add one more thing. 'We encourage all gay people into the

Church. But we do so in the expectation that they live outside God's purpose. And that they will come to see the need for transformation so that they can live in accordance with biblical revelation and teaching. Once they understand the Church's love, renunciation will surely be inevitable.'

'Is that what you told Joseph? No wonder he never attended.'

'We were willing to offer him counsel and pastoral support.'

Warlow could feel his anger building. 'How about simple acceptance instead?'

'Is that truly God's will?'

'I have no idea. Why don't you ask him? Oh, yes, I forgot. All lines are down, right? Bloody convenient that, isn't it?'

———

WARLOW WALKED through the Incident Room and kept on walking.

'Should we come, sir?' Rhys asked.

Warlow didn't stop or turn around. 'Feel free. I need a breath of fresh air.'

They stood outside, none of them in coats. The wind had freshened, but morning sunlight warmed the day enough. Warlow put his hands on his hips and sucked in some lungfuls of air before turning back to the junior officers who stood watching him.

'Nothing like the reek of hypocrisy, is there? Gets trapped in your sinuses, I find.'

'Difficult to believe I just heard all that, sir,' Rhys said.

'You better. There'll be worse to come in this job.'

'Did you ever go to that Chapel, Hana?'

'I did when I was very little. My mum used to take me,

I think. But after she died, my father never took me. He never went himself either.'

'I don't blame him,' Warlow said. 'And I presume Gregory has an alibi for the night of Joseph and Aeron going missing?'

'I'll recheck that timeline, sir,' Hana said. 'From what I recall his wife said he was at home.'

'But it was Gregory who alerted the others about seeing lights that night, wasn't it?' Rhys said.

Hana nodded. 'It was.'

Warlow turned as a couple of vehicles pulled in from the street. He frowned. 'Did I miss our serial protestor this morning?'

'No, sir. Someone else commented on the fact that she wasn't yelling through her megaphone for once.'

'Hmm.' The tiniest of niggles pulled at Warlow's consciousness. He took a deep breath but nothing tangible came and so he filed it away. He turned to Hana. 'Your dad did a good job handling the press this morning. He ought to come and do some of my releases. At least he doesn't end up screaming at the bastards.'

Hana beamed. 'He's good in front of a camera. He takes pride in his presentation.'

'Right. When we get back inside, let's get Gregory a lift back up the road. And Rhys—' Warlow's phone interrupted him. He looked at the caller and said to the others, 'I need to take this. I'll be up in a minute.'

He took a few steps away and, still outside in the spring sunshine, answered the call.

'Tom, how are you?'

'It's Mum, Dad. Have you got a minute?'

CHAPTER TWENTY-EIGHT

'ALL OKAY, TOM?' The old paternal alarm bell was on its lowest setting, yet a call at ten in the morning always set it off.

'Yes, I'm fine. Did you get a call last night about Mam?'

'No.'

'Ah, Martin says he tried to call you.'

Warlow remembered having the phone on silent as he collapsed on his bed. He hadn't looked at his missed messages yet today.

'What's up? I spoke to your mother a couple of days ago.'

'She's had a relapse, Dad. She's in ITU.'

'What? But she sounded fine. Sounded better than she had in a while, in fact.'

'It's definitely pancreatitis. Notorious for doing this sort of thing.'

'But—'

Tom cut him off. 'I'll have a better idea when I catch up with the consultant later. I thought you ought to know.'

'Yes, of course. And I'm stuck up here on this bloody case, otherwise I'd go and see her.'

'Probably no point if she's in ITU. Martin says she's not really well enough for visitors.'

Warlow's pulse beat a rapid tattoo in his ears. 'Have you spoken to your brother?'

'Yeah, Al knows. It's already tonight with them.'

'Of course.' It would be 6pm on an autumn evening in Western Australia. 'Okay, keep me informed if you learn anything. And I'll see you on the weekend, right?'

'Yeah. We'll be down on Saturday. I've got to go, Dad. I'm in clinic.'

Tom ended the call, leaving Warlow staring at his phone. Pancreatitis? He knew bugger all about pancreatitis except that it sounded bloody awful. For a moment he toyed with trying Denise's phone again, just as he had the other day. But that would be hopeless if she was in Intensive Care.

Instead, he pocketed it, took some deep breaths and went back inside the building.

———

THE TEAM WAS WAITING for him. Rhys had made a fresh cuppa and handed one to Warlow as he took his place in front of the Gallery and the Job Centre. But Gil peered at the DCI and stepped in close.

'You alright, Evan? You look a bit… upset.'

'I'm fine. Some family issues.'

'You need to go back south? We can hold the fort here.' Gil's unusual earnestness, in stark contrast to the jokey facetiousness that was his usual stock in trade, struck home with Warlow. He'd considered it and he knew Gil could run through this with his eyes closed. But what would he do in the hospital? He probably wouldn't even be allowed to see Denise. Intensive Care Units tended not to have open visiting. And the idea of hanging around in a waiting room for hours did not sit easily with him. Better he keep himself busy and hope for the best.

'Thanks Gil, but I'm okay. Besides, I want to walk through everything we have here because I'm getting more and more certain we're missing a trick or two.' Warlow stepped forward. 'Okay, we've done this more than once already, but it doesn't do any harm to go through everything again. At the very least, it'll bring everyone back up to speed.' He nodded towards Hana. 'I've asked PCSO Prosser to sit in on this one since she's turning up at almost every bloody turn. You're sure you're not stalking us?' He grinned at her.

She kept her cool with an impassive expression tempered by the slightest of smiles.

They set themselves in a semi-circle of chairs around the boards. Gil kicked things off with a run through of the missing Randals' clothing. Identification and confirmation of DNA belonging to Aeron Randal in the blood staining on the coat found in Habberley left that in no doubt. But the mystery of what Joseph Randal's jeans, one trainer and wallet were doing at Rhaeadr Falls remained. They'd drawn a complete blank in getting anything useful from contacting the limited list of visitors to the Falls they'd traced.

'So what do we think?' Warlow asked the team. 'What explanation is there for Joseph Randal's clothes to be there?'

'I see only two possibilities,' Gil ventured. 'The first is that they've been washed down in the river from higher up. The second that they've been placed there for us to find.'

They were intriguing theories that Warlow was happy to explore. 'You say washed down from the river above. There isn't much up there from what I can remember.

Only open moorland and a lot of bugger all. How did Joseph Randal's clothes get there?'

'Could he have tried to get away?' Catrin asked. 'How far is it cross country from the feed shed to the Falls?'

Warlow looked to Hana for an answer. 'Seven or eight miles,' said the PCSO. 'And there's no path. Only sheep tracks.'

Rhys looked unhappy. 'I don't buy that. Why would he run across open moorland and then take off his clothes?'

'Injury? Confusion?' Gil suggested. 'Exposure can make you hallucinate and it's bloody cold out there at that elevation, especially at night. It could mean the poor bugger might be up there still.'

Warlow mulled this over with a frown. They were stretching things, but it was just about plausible. They'd found brain matter on the feed-shed door, suggesting a severe head wound. Just how anyone could survive with bits of their brain missing, he had no idea, though it might add credence to the dazed and confused theory. People sometimes survived the most horrific injuries. Which left Gil's other theory to consider. 'And what reason could anyone have for leaving his clothes for us to find?'

'Obfuscation?' Rhys asked.

'Christ, that's a big word, DC Harries. Nutella dictionary spread for breakfast, was it?' Gil lifted an eyebrow.

'Go on, Rhys. I'm listening,' Warlow said, sending Gil a dirty look.

Rhys sat up. 'It doesn't make much sense to believe that Joseph Randal got away and wandered over the hills and shed his clothing. But letting us find his clothes makes sense if you consider it from a different angle. I mean, here we all are, spending time and resources trying to find an answer when perhaps there isn't one. When the reason someone put the clothes there was to confuse us.'

'They've achieved that alright.' Warlow nodded.

Gil shook his head. 'Does that mean that Aeron Randal's coat is a plant, too?'

Rhys threw up his hands.

'So that leaves us with a few possibilities.' Warlow summarised his thoughts. 'The first is that Joseph and Aeron disturbed thieves, were shot, then Joseph somehow got away and headed into the night, but Aeron did not and has been abducted. The thieves then try to get rid of evidence by throwing Aeron's coat and perhaps other clothing into a stream in Habberley as they drive through and mess that up by his coat getting snagged under the bridge. Meanwhile, Joseph, injured, gets confused on the mountain, strips off and his clothes wash down into the river.'

'If that happened, it would be the first-time livestock theft has ever led to a crime against the person,' Hana said. 'I can't remember a case. These thieves are cowards. They'd run a mile from any altercation.'

And who in their right mind would want an altercation with a farmer? Every one of them seemed to have a bloody shotgun.

'Or,' Rhys countered, reverting to his theory. 'Someone wants us to believe all that.'

Warlow moved on to Padrig and Mari Randal's affair. 'The question is, did Aeron Randal know about it? Hari Gregory did and disapproved. He's made that clear enough.'

'But Padrig has an alibi,' Rhys muttered. 'Mari Randal.'

Warlow nodded. 'And I accept that alibi because though she might lie for him when it came to Aeron, she wouldn't when it came to Joseph.'

They all stared at the Gallery and the Job Centre, all tied up with their own thoughts, until Catrin asked, 'And

Gregory, sir. He'd have no reason to shoot the Randals, would he?'

The straightforward answer would be no. But Warlow paused before giving it up because the question, now that he'd been exposed to Gregory's mind-set, didn't seem quite so obvious.

'I would have said no. And he has his wife as an alibi. But from our little chat this morning, if I had to describe Gregory to you, the words religious bigot would make top of the list.'

'Surely he's just a deacon in the Chapel?' Catrin asked.

'He is,' Rhys answered her. 'But whatever denomination it is, they don't seem to like anyone who has affairs, or gay people, very much, if at all. They're unbiblical, and I quote.'

'Which brings us back to Aeron and Joseph,' Warlow said, tapping the desk with his middle finger, trying to shift his thoughts into some kind of order. 'We know that there was friction between father and son because of Joseph's sexual orientation. And we now know that the friction had to do with the Chapel and a set of rigid beliefs.'

'Are you saying that Gregory, or someone from the Chapel, might have been ridding the world of adulterers and gays at that feed shed?' Gil asked. 'This sounds more and more like the Spanish Inquisition sketch.'

'That doesn't work anyway because Aeron wasn't an adulterer, it was his wife,' Rhys pointed out.

'But perhaps he put up with it,' Catrin shrugged. 'Could be that's seen as a worse sin?'

Sin. How many people had died over the centuries because of that word? Something, a vague stirring, shifted in Warlow's head. 'Anyone hear the protests this morning?'

The change of tack took people a few moments to tune in to.

'The megaphone lady?' Catrin asked.

'Julia Lloyd, yes,' Warlow confirmed. 'Anyone seen or heard?'

'We were spared this morning. Why? Is she a suspect?' Gil threw Warlow a quizzical look.

'No, but we're not so overburdened with leads here that we shouldn't take what she's given us seriously. Lowri, remind us about the link between Joseph Randal and Robert Lloyd.'

Lowri, who'd been doing a grand impression of a church mouse until now, cleared her throat. 'Mrs Lloyd provided us with some photographs of Robert Lloyd and one where Robert Lloyd and Joseph Randal are seen together as part of a bigger group. They knew one another from college and were both gay.'

'Both part of the same scene,' Warlow added. 'And by scene, I mean something pretty clandestine, given the attitudes of the communities they both found themselves a part of. They had to keep their private lives under wraps. Lowri, have you looked through the misper reports on Lloyd? Anything there?'

'There may be. You'll remember I showed you a transcript of communication from Joseph Randal's phone?'

'Remind me,' Gil said.

'He was texting someone. A pay as you go number that isn't registered.'

'The secret meeting?' Gil asked.

Lowri nodded. 'That's the one. I looked back through Robert Lloyd's records and that number is one he contacted too. Oddly enough, along the same lines. Arranging meetings. Can't wait to hook up, that sort of thing.'

Warlow frowned. A small but definite link in the chain had formed here. He sat forward, index finger moving back and forth across the little patch of stubble he somehow always missed in his daily shave. Lowri had moved on to running through the rest of their interview with Julia Lloyd, adding a little of the background to her blacklisted status at the station. The one that meant no one took her seriously anymore.

Except DCI Warlow.

'Good work,' he said when she'd finished. 'But there's more to be done. Catrin, I want you to help Lowri dig into this misper case. I have no idea why it might be important, but we've found two things to link Joseph Randal and Robert Lloyd together. There may be more. And yes, it may have nothing to do with anything, but you never know.'

Catrin sent Lowri a smile and nodded.

'Hana, I realise you've got work to do up north, so we'll let you get on with that. Thanks for bringing Gregory down. I hope that wasn't too painful for you?'

She smiled thinly. 'No, sir. If anything, it reminded me of how glad I am my father didn't make us go to Chapel like the rest of the kids.'

'Keep us in the loop regarding the Gregory farm. Any leads on the sheep killings and I want to know. Either me or Gil or Rhys.'

Hana nodded.

'Rhys, get an address for Julia Lloyd and grab your coat. I have a few more questions for our megaphone lady, but I think I can spare her the ignominy of coming back into the station. We'll pay her a visit at home.' Warlow added a little volume to his last couple of sentences. If anyone in the Incident Room outside of the main investigating team heard – and he made sure they would – they all had enough sense to keep their heads down and keep their mocking thoughts to themselves.

They had been warned.

CHAPTER TWENTY-NINE

THE ADDRESS they had for Julia Lloyd was in a residential park called Crossfields out on the edge of farmland to the east of the town. They drove in past a row of prefabricated single-storey boxes in a row. All had identical vinyl cladding made to look like wood. Something they spectacularly failed at since they were all of an identical, regimented, apple green colour. One or two of the boxes had tiny front lawns and the odd shrub in a bucket. Three, at least, had fake grass instead. They were so closely packed together you could probably reach through the window from inside one kitchen and put the kettle on in the one next door.

At least Rhys, with his arm span, could.

'Who actually lives here?' The DC asked.

'Retired people, maybe? No doubt some are holiday homes,' Warlow ventured.

'They call these trailer parks in the states, don't they?'

'I think they do, Rhys.' Warlow drove slowly. They were looking for Barnside.

'There.' Rhys pointed to a scuffed black sign that had seen better days. Warlow took the turning through a gap in a hedge and came to a halt next to a much older and poorly maintained area where three older single-storey prefab cabins stood around a tarmac courtyard.

Breeze-block pillars held two of the buildings off the ground. These same two had chipboard over the windows.

The third, however, did not. This one had a warped wooden fascia around its base to hide the pillars. But the rendering on the walls looked stained as if some kind of black fungus had taken hold, blotching the whitewash a murky grey. A length of guttering hung free of its attachment to the roof, and the TV aerial leaned at an improbable angle. It struck Warlow that this might have been the spot where the farmer first had the bright idea of diversifying. He'd got better at it, obviously. But this spot would be the cheapest lot on the site by a long way. And careful screening and planting hid it from the better kept area they'd come in through.

Better being a relative term.

Warlow parked up. A dirty, off-white Fiat 500 stood off to one side. 'Does Julia Lloyd have a car?'

'Don't know, sir.'

Warlow exited and walked up some wooden steps scattered with resin gravel. Rhys followed, and they stood on an elevated section next to the front door. The DCI knocked but got no reply.

The windows looked clean, but net curtains obscured any view.

Warlow knocked again. 'Mrs Lloyd, it's DCI Warlow. We spoke at the station.'

Some crows from the nearby fields took exception to his voice and launched themselves with a raucous chorus of cawing.

'Take a walk back through to the main park, Rhys. See if you can find someone who might have a key. A caretaker maybe.'

Rhys jogged away and Warlow took a walk around the property. It didn't take long. To the rear, a small gap between the house and dilapidated wooden panelling had space for some refuse bags and two tall LPG gas canisters. Several old placards stapled to some two by one piece of wood lay discarded. Warlow leaned in to read what was written on one.

'Bring Robert Lloyd HOME.'

He walked across to the next building. This one had nothing behind it. Nor did the third. Both were in a much worse state than Julia's home, which was saying something.

Warlow took stock. Clearly, she lived in the cheapest home in the worst part of this less than salubrious residential park. He'd read that she'd sold her house in Welshpool in order to finance her campaign. There'd even been talk of a private detective in one report Lowri had given him.

As he stood in that forlorn plot of land listening to the crows, something tugged at his awareness. Warlow walked back to the rear of the cabin and looked again. On the ground next to where the two LPG cylinders stood, he'd noticed a round space. A footprint of a third cylinder.

Julia Lloyd would be off grid here. For gas anyway. Electricity and water, she'd have, but a gas cooker needed power supplied from the cylinders. Two cylinders. So where was the third?

The bare bones of the property's construction were evident at the rear, too. The breeze-block pillars over the foundations had not been covered over here and revealed dark gaps leading to a dead space under the floor. Warlow got down on his haunches and used a torch. Three feet in sat another LPG bottle on its side, a rubber tube running up from it through a jagged gap.

Confused, Warlow stood up.

The building had two doors. The rear one was close to him, screened off from the rest of the plot by a rickety reed panel. Warlow stepped up, knocked once more and got no answer again.

The door had glass in the upper panel, solid UPVC on the lower. But the hanging curtain behind the glass did not obscure the view completely. Something flickered to the edge of Warlow's vision as he peered in. Something bright to his left. He cupped his hands around the glass and stared in. The view was hazy.

Bloody net curtains.

He stood back. The curtain came down and then angled in near the level of the handle. There, at the corner of the pane, a small triangle of glass remained unobscured. Warlow got down on his knees and repeated the cupping of his hands over the glass. He had to turn his face and squint to look in. He saw a utility area with coats and shoes and then, beyond and through an open door, he glimpsed a sink, the corner of a counter top where a kitchen roll had spilled its sheets from the counter to the floor and the flickering light… was that a candle?

On his knees, his face was about level with an aluminium letter slot. He lifted the spring-loaded cover and saw nylon draught-proof brushes. He poked his fingers through to make a gap and shouted. 'Julia? Julia Lloyd? Are you in there?'

No reply. He heard nothing. But he smelled something.

A chemical mixture of sulphur and petrol.

Warlow let the flap fall and reared up. He turned and jumped off the step, ran around the reed panel and back towards where the car was parked just as Rhys and a short, balding man in a padded jacket appeared.

'Get DOWN,' Warlow yelled. He grabbed Rhys and the man he was with, turned them and yanked them forward and down behind the Jeep.

Rhys had time only to ask, 'What's going—' Before his words were cut off by a clattering explosion followed by a roar as the cabin went up in a ball of flame. The noise took all hearing away from Warlow and replaced it with a dull ringing, like listening to a note played underwater.

Rhys, too, had his hands over his ears. Warlow half stood and looked through the windows of the Jeep at the inferno that had been Julia Lloyd's home just moments before.

All he could think of were the two other LPG canisters at the rear that were now being engulfed in flames.

He grabbed Rhys's arm and snarled out an order. 'Get back. Take him away and wait for me.'

Rhys nodded and ran in a half crouch back towards the park, dragging the balding man at his side. Warlow felt for his keys and opened the car door. Heat from the inferno was fierce even at this distance. He got in, gunned the engine and reversed at speed after Rhys until he got to forty yards away.

Then he got his phone out and called it in.

———

THOUGH NOT A BIG FIRE, it took them an hour to get things under control by cooling down the gas bottles and dousing the flames. It then took another ten minutes to find the body. Or rather, the charred remains of one.

There wasn't enough left of her to know if it was Julia Lloyd or not. That would need dental or DNA analysis. But Warlow would assume it was until proven otherwise.

He spoke to the fire investigator and filled him in on what he'd seen.

The man, named Chalmers, a veteran of the fire service, listened and nodded. 'Petrol as an accelerant more than likely,' he said on hearing Warlow's description. Both men stood at the side of the Jeep as the investigator delivered his take. 'You say you saw kitchen paper in a cascade?'

'I did.'

Chalmers nodded. 'The candle burns down until it reaches the petrol-soaked paper and ignites it. Meanwhile, the whole building is filling up with gas. Only one outcome in that situation.'

Warlow nodded grimly.

'You okay?'

'I'm fine,' Warlow said. His hearing had almost returned to normal. 'Pissed off that someone is one step ahead of us, but otherwise hunky-dory. Unlike the victim inside that tinder box. You'll brief Kapil when he arrives?'

'Will do. Kapil and I have worked on more than one arson case, unfortunately.'

Warlow drove Rhys back to Newtown station. It wasn't yet one-thirty, but he didn't follow the DC inside. 'Need a bit of me time. Let the juices stew.' Warlow tapped his head. 'Brief the others, will you?'

Rhys nodded. Warlow had lost his appetite, but he picked up a drive-through coffee from McDonalds, and drove to a parking lot in town where he sat, sipped the coffee and dialled a number on his phone.

'Decided against end of day calls then, have you?' Jess said by way of a greeting.

'Today, most definitely.'

She picked up on the tension in his voice right away. 'Oh dear, eventful morning?'

He told her all about it. And in the telling realised just how close he'd come to not telling anyone anything ever again.

'God, Evan. That sounds awful.'

'I can't help thinking that it's my fault,' he growled. 'Julia Lloyd had been in everyone's face here for months. But she'd been ignored. The minute I start taking an interest, this happens.' The coffee cup in his hand shook a little.

He put it back in its holder and squeezed the steering wheel to steady himself.

'It means you've rattled someone's cage, alright. But you didn't do this to her, Evan. Some other sod did.' Jess switched into DI mode. 'Is there CCTV at the park site?'

'Yes. But there are other ways in to the farm. A delivery entrance. A lane the milk lorry uses.'

'Shit. I wish I could be there.'

'You are, in spirit,' Warlow told her. 'Trouble is I think I'm off my game. I just found out my ex is in Intensive Care with pancreatitis.'

'That can't be easy.'

'She's been sick for a few days and we thought she was getting better, but she relapsed. Tom says it can turn nasty really quickly. Funny thing, I'm supposed to not care. And on one level I don't. But she's still the boys' mother, you know?'

'I do know. Rock and hard place is never a good spot to be in.'

Warlow sighed. She understood. More so than most.

'And you're stuck up there. Shit,' Jess added when Warlow's silence left a void.

'*Plus de merde*, as Gil would say.'

'Look, it can't be easy with all these distractions and the frustration of no real leads. But whenever this happens to me, I channel it into something hard and sharp I can pierce the sod who did this with.'

Jess was right.

'Yeah, I'm working on that. Thanks for the listen.'

'Any time. God, I wish I could be there with you lot. Bloody plaster cast. And before you ask, Cadi's fine. She's sitting here with me while Molly does some coursework.'

'Say hello and I'll put the phone near her.'

'Hello, Cadi.'

Some rustling noises followed before Jess said, 'her tail is wagging.'

He smiled, seeing it in his head. It made him feel a lot better. 'Good to know.'

He ended the call, finished his coffee, and went back to work.

CHAPTER THIRTY

WARLOW WALKED BACK into the Incident Room bearing gifts. He'd stopped off at a cake shop on Broad Street and got a selection of stickies. Eccles, almond, cinnamon, eclairs. None of your cupcake nonsense. When he put the box on the desk and revealed the contents, Rhys almost did a backflip.

'I'll get the teas on, sir.'

'No. I'll make the tea. You're alright,' Warlow said.

The sound of eyebrows climbing up foreheads was almost audible.

'You okay, Evan?' Gil asked, looking at him askance. 'I read that sometime strokes can masquerade as excess shows of generosity and bonhomie.'

'Are you suggesting that being almost blown up has addled my brain, Sergeant?'

'Along those lines, yes.'

Warlow swept his hands down his body. 'I am unscathed, as you see. Besides, now and again it doesn't do any harm to be at the coal face.'

'Of tea-making you mean, sir,' Rhys asked, after a momentary flicker of confusion washed over his face.

'Exactly that, Detective Constable Harries. No flies on you. Besides, I want everyone eyeballing those boards again. A fresh look.'

He had to ask where the tea-making facilities were, but made sure he did it out of earshot of the team and their bemused stares. He texted Rhys for confirmation of how they all took it and came back in with a tray. Gil had deployed the cakes in a display. Warlow handed round the mugs and got them all, once more, in a semicircle.

'Okay,' he addressed the team. 'Lock and load with the pastries. Someone has died since we did this last and that makes me furious. I'm dealing with it through baked goods therapy. If anyone has a problem with that, they can leave now.'

Everyone held a bun in their hands. No one got up.

Warlow nodded and continued, 'We won't have crime scene photos yet. Probably best you finish eating anyway before they come through. But I saw what happened in Julia Lloyd's house this morning. This was arson. This was murder. Let's be crystal clear about that. Someone did not want me talking to her. I want to know who that was and why.'

Nods all around.

'That means we need to look again at Robert Lloyd and his links to Aeron and Joseph Randal. Joseph in partic-ular. Agreed?'

Catrin cut a cinnamon roll into six pieces on her plate. She dabbed her mouth with a tissue before speaking. 'Lowri's brought the whole file up from the basement, sir. Julia Lloyd provided us with stacks of photographs.'

'There's also his Facebook page,' Lowri added. She'd gone the Eccles cake route and brushed a crumb away from her bottom lip. 'It doesn't appear that Julia told them he'd passed. You can do that, apparently. Make it a remembrance page.'

'And there'll be Joseph Randal's social media stuff, too,' Rhys added.

'It can't have been a coincidence that this happens once we took an interest.' Warlow voiced again his niggling disquiet over this aspect of things.

'You suggesting someone inside this building is involved?' Gil asked.

'We did—' Rhys began, but had to stop to swallow a chunk of eclair before he could continue. 'We stopped to talk to her in the car the other day, sir.'

Warlow nodded. He'd forgotten. And anyone could have seen that.

'We did. And if that was the signal for someone to murder her, I'm even angrier.' He stopped mid-chew, looked down for a couple of beats, but then continued eating and looked back up. 'Enough to do then. Anything else happened while we were away?'

Catrin side-eyed Gil. 'Sergeant Jones has a message from a fan.'

Gil shook his head.

'Padrig Randal's neighbour. A Mrs Nowacki.' Catrin licked her fingers clean of sugar before flicking through a few pages in her notebook. 'She's rung more than once. I took her last call. She said, and I quote, "I have information for Sergeant Geel. The big poleecemen with round belly. He told me to reeng him if I have news. I have reenged twice, but he does not return my calls. Can you please tell him I have information on bins."' Catrin delivered all of this in a stagey Eastern European accent, all rolling 'r's and elongated vowels.

'Is she Japanese?' Rhys asked.

Catrin sent him her trademark glare. The one that often made criminals feel like they might turn to stone.

Gil sighed. 'She is on my list. But since we've lost interest in Padrig, I didn't prioritise it.'

Warlow shrugged. 'Fair enough. But as things stand now, I don't think we should lose interest in anyone we've interviewed.'

'We could send Rhys out there.' Gil sent the DC a pointed glance.

'No. We need the kids here to go through Robert Lloyd and Joseph Randal's social media stuff. Not your strong point, we can agree on that.'

Rhys pointed a finger at Catrin, Lowri, and then himself, grinned and mouthed, 'kids'.

'Fine.' Gil nodded. 'I'll head over there and have a chat.' He got up, drained his tea and reached for his coat.

'You could finish your sticky bun first,' Warlow said.

Gil shook his head. 'Thanks for the cakes, but, as a purist, I prefer *les biscuits* with my tea.' He turned away from the team and headed for the door. 'If there is even a hint of anything useful, I will let you know pronto. If I am not back in three hours, assume I've been eaten by cats.'

Catrin watched him leave, not even attempting to hide her schadenfreude smile. As the door closed behind him, she said, 'So nice to see he hasn't lost his edge.' Then she turned back to her notes. 'Okay. Regarding Julia Lloyd...'

———

HARI GREGORY STOOD and watched as men from the fallen stock company loaded the sheep carcasses into a lorry. They wore full protective gear and used shovels and bags for the scattered organs and entrails. He'd lost animals before. In the harsher winters, it wasn't that uncommon. Foxes were an ever present danger for lambs, especially injured ones. But dead and frozen sheep were not the same as animals that had been ripped apart. And never had there been so many at once.

Usually, when one or two passed, he'd ring up the local

hunt. They were happy to take fresh meat and their pack dogs often preferred goat and sheep to horse and cow flesh. But with thirty, there'd be no chance. He'd been forced into using DEFRA's field services. These carcasses would end up being burned in an appropriate crematorium.

He stood next to the gate, saying nothing, grim faced. His wife had offered to come up and supervise, but he'd wanted to be there himself. Watch over them. Their shepherd even in death. He was glad – though somehow that was not the right word – of something to do after his meeting with the police.

He'd revealed his soul and his inner self to the DCI, Warlow. And the man forced him into a theological corner. He'd seen how Hana Prosser winced when he'd answered the questions about his and the Chapel's attitude towards… relationships. He knew they'd be treated with scorn. They weren't modern. Weren't fashionable. But since when had modern or fashionable been a true alternative to faith?

He'd discussed it with the minister and his fellow deacons many times. What if a couple of the same sex asked to marry at Hermon? Not that any of the minuscule congregation they had would ever dream of doing so. Thankfully, the guidance from the Church leaders seemed clear. On the one hand, it was only right to affirm God's love for all human beings, whatever their sexuality. But a service of blessing for civil partnerships or same-sex marriage remained unbiblical, and it was up to the minister and the deacons of the Chapel to parry any moves to allow any such request.

It was an uphill struggle, this battle for constancy. He'd seen the way young people had become brazen. His wife told him that Joseph Randal had been that way. Conflicted. Though Aeron never discussed it with him, the other deacons remained hopeful that perhaps Joseph would find a way to live a chaste life and eventually seek experiences that might change the direction of his same-sex attractions.

Others within the movement were less understanding. They sought more direct ways to educate, or even punish, such behaviour. Lessons needed to be learned, they said. Examples needed to be made of transgressors. But Hari believed in God's purpose. Live a good life, do unto others, resist change when it brought chaos.

And chaos had visited his farm. One harrowing glance at his dead sheep being thrown like sacks into the lorry was proof enough of that. A sudden unaccustomed tightness closed his throat, and he swallowed back a threatened sob loudly.

Whoever had done this deserved God's wrath. Hari promised himself that if the opportunity ever arose, he would be happy to wield the sword of vengeance and woe betide the devil's disciples that stood in his way.

CHAPTER THIRTY-ONE

LIVESEY HOUSE in Welshpool looked just as nondescript as when Gil had been the last time. He thought about knocking on Padrig Randal's door as he stood once again on the first-floor landing. If he was at home, he could maybe get some info on the lady in number four. But Mrs Nowacki was who he was there to see and so, of course, it was her door he approached.

He knocked, stood back, and spoke through the closed door. 'Mrs Nowacki. It's me, Detective Sergeant Jones.'

Bolts slid back, locks clicked free and the door, as before, opened to reveal a one-inch crack through which a bespectacled Mrs Nowacki peered out. She took her time, staring, her face moving up and down, eyeing the police officer like some kind of robot scanner.

'Are you alone?'

'I am an army of one,' Gil replied. 'How are you?'

'I am well. Thank you for asking. I am pleased you come.'

'No trouble. So, what information do you have that you think will help us?'

The door opened a couple of inches more. 'You receive my message about bins?'

'I did. Though, being completely honest, we have little or no influence on refuse collection. That's Powys County Council's territory.'

'I have no complaint about refuse collection.'

'Great, glad to hear that.'

Mrs Nowacki dropped her voice. 'But I watch the bins. Padrig takes mine out. I leave black bag outside door. Black wheelie bins every three weeks for items we cannot recycle. Red box and net for plastic and cans. Bottles and jars in blue box. Paper and card in blue box with lid. Green caddy for food waste. Red box, blue boxes and food go every week. Black wheelie bin every three weeks.'

The sinking feeling inside Gil, present since he'd received notification that Mrs Nowacki had wanted to see him with "news", dragged him ever lower as she delivered this litany of rules. He couldn't help but be at the same time impressed and mortified by her memory. Christ, all it took was a bank holiday to throw his refuse organisation into chaos. Many's the time he'd resorted to a cheeky peep at the neighbours' bins for confirmation of what sort of collection day it was. No one could deny that Mrs N's grasp was impressive. Still, the thought of coming all this way for a lecture on refuse collection, no matter how accurate and thorough it might be, left him flat. But if the job had taught him anything, it had taught him that patience was indeed a virtue. Time flies like an arrow, he thought, and – still on the refuse angle – fruit flies like a banana.

'Right. Got that,' he replied, sensibly deciding not to voice said thoughts.

'We are in week two of black wheelie bin cycle. Ten more days before it is collected again.'

'So glad we've got that detail nailed down. I'll jot that down, shall I?' Gil took out his notebook.

Mrs Nowacki paused, stiffening her gaze behind the thick glasses.

Gil sensed she might be picking up on his sarcasm. But he was not a vindictive man and this woman was convinced she was trying to help. 'I will write it down because I will forget,' he reassured her.

She nodded once and went on. 'Bins are left down in alcove to left of main entrance. All have numbers painted on them in white. Mine is number four, Padrig is seven. Alcove is under my flat. I hear everything. Three days ago I hear noise in night. Early hours. 3.27am. Someone is in bin. I sleep very little. I hear car. At 5am I go down to look and find new black bag in number seven bin.' Mrs Nowacki turned away and came back a few moments later. The safety chain rattled and the door to number four finally opened. Mrs Nowacki stood there. She held herself straight, dressed in a long, padded coat, dark tights and fur boots, with a knitted hat on her head. She looked Gil up and down.

'You are big policeman.'

'That I can't deny, though I would point out that my family are well known for the density of our bones,' Gil replied, a little bemused by her candidness.

Mrs Nowacki held a black plastic bag in her hands. 'You have gun?'

'No, I don't have gun.'

'Pity.' She stepped out, turned and closed the door, tested it to make certain it was shut tight and then walked towards the stairs. 'Come, I will show you.'

Gil saw no point in arguing. He followed the woman down the stairs. She took them carefully, one hand on the banister anchored to the wall.

'Mrs Nowacki, how old are you?'

'I am eighty-six.'

Only then did Gil notice she wore blue nitrile gloves, as

favoured by all people who dealt in forensic work. She walked through the communal area under the stairs containing the post boxes and out through the door. She took a right and stood next to a covered area that would double for a bike shelter were it not for the ten black wheelie bins inside.

'Noise here,' she pointed, 'car there,' she turned, walked forward and pointed to the street where it joined another road at a T junction. 'I have car licence number. Five out of seven letters and numbers.'

'Of course you do,' Gil said, becoming increasingly nonplussed by this little charade.

'Here is bag that was left.' She held up the black refuse bag. 'I know because it was one week after last collection. All bins empty.'

Gil looked at the bag, which also looked almost empty. 'How do you know Padrig didn't put this in his own bin?'

'I ask. He says no.'

'Fair enough.'

She held out the crumpled bag. Gil took it and immediately knew it wasn't empty. Something, not too heavy, lay inside. Gil looked again at Mrs Nowacki eyeing him through her glasses. He fished a pair of plastic gloves out of his pocket. Then he opened the bag. Something nestled right at the bottom. He reached in and felt around and pulled out a running shoe.

'You're sure this isn't Padrig's?' He looked up at the woman.

Mrs Nowacki shook her head.

'And there isn't another one rattling around loose in the wheelie bin?'

'Look.'

He did. Numbers four and seven were empty. As were a random selection of others.

'Well, this is all very interesting, but—'

Mrs Nowacki put an emphatic finger up into the air. It succeeded in both attracting Gil's attention and in stopping him talking. She stepped into the sudden silence with a rhetorical question that had a slightly encouraging, almost goading edge to it. The kind of edge a schoolteacher might use when a student needed a bit of prodding to get the right answer. 'Who would put one running shoe in wheelie bin in the middle of the night, I ask myself?'

'Who knows? Kids messing about. I mean, one trainer is—' The light, when it came on in Gil's head, was almost blinding. He looked at the shoe in his hand and pulled the tongue back to check the size. There it was. A blue Nike, size nine.

'Mrs Nowacki,' Gil began, blinking rapidly. 'Do you have a first name? And if you do, can I call you by it?'

'Antonia.'

Gil held out his gloved hand. 'I'm Gil.'

They shook. The frail, upright woman and the big police officer.

Gil still had the trainer in his other hand, half a grin on his face. 'Tidy. This is... were you ever a police officer, Antonia?'

Antonia Nowacki shook her head. 'I am from Poland. When I was nine, I and my brother joined the Armia Krajowa. The AK. You call it Resistance. I learn to be careful, to watch. To take note.'

Those Nazis didn't stand a bloody chance, he thought. 'Good to see you're still fighting,' Gil said, his grin widening. 'Did you say you had a partial licence number for the car you saw?'

CHAPTER THIRTY-TWO

By the time they'd finished sorting through what needed to be done regarding Julia Lloyd, Robert Lloyd and Joseph Randal, Warlow felt a deep weariness descending. He took himself off to the SIO's office to write up his report on what had taken place at Crossfields that morning. It didn't take long, but even when he'd finished, he stayed in there nursing a dull headache.

He'd been lucky to escape any direct injury. Lucky to have got away from that door before the bloody thing blew up in his face. Lucky Rhys hadn't been with him, because the DC's track record in the accident stakes was not a good one.

He'd need to inspect the Jeep properly, having noticed several marks where some bits of Julia Lloyd's house collided with the metalwork. But better the Jeep than him or Rhys, that was certain.

He'd left the others trawling through files and social media. Until they'd done all that, he'd stay in a holding pattern. It wasn't unusual in an investigation to experience twinges of despair. You rode with them, hopeful that when you reached the bottom, there'd be a bounce and you'd start coming back up again. But he recognised this sensation now. If he'd been the captain of a submarine in a war film, the sonar would have been beeping off the scale with the sea bed feet away.

Funny thing, the old brain. You think you're in charge, but really you're at its mercy. Where the hell had it dredged a submarine analogy up from, for instance? It was a good one he had to admit. Because in a submarine, yes there was the sea bed below, but there were also the yards of ocean above. And he felt the weight of the conviction he'd somehow been responsible for Julia Lloyd's death like a billion gallons of sea water pressing down on his head. Yes, okay, it hadn't been him who'd set the crude petrol fuse and lit the candle. But he'd been the one who'd showed an interest in a dormant case. The one who'd alerted someone to that interest. And added to all that self-flagellating guilt was the baggage of his personal problems.

Correction, family problems.

By right, they shouldn't exist because his family was no more. But just because they no longer lived together as a unit, the Warlows were still attached by invisible strings pulling in all kinds of directions. And they'd been pulling hard for several days now.

He took the opportunity of the lull to phone Martin Foley, Jeez Denise's new partner. Though new was a relative term. Martin was a few years older than Denise for a start, and their relationship had been trundling along for a good few years now. Still, compared with the decades Warlow spent as Denise's significant other, new would probably still apply to good old Martin.

'Hello?' Martin's voice, almost as cigarette ravaged as Denise's, answered after several rings.

'Martin, it's Evan. How's the patient?'

'Good question, Evan. I'm only allowed visits a couple

of times a day and then for only fifteen minutes at a time. She's full of tubes and drips. I don't think she knew it was me that last time.'

'Christ. I'm sorry to hear that.'

'Yeah. Still, one way to avoid going to court, right?'

'Was that due this week?'

'Tomorrow actually.' A few weeks before, Denise was arrested for being drunk in charge of a vehicle and refused to give a sample. There'd been a strong chance she'd end up in prison for a catalogue of offences, including driving without a licence and insurance on top of the sample issue.

Warlow didn't know Martin well, but he'd always struck him as someone not too troubled by the details of daily living. Martin had always been a big picture kind of guy. And it'll all work out, trust in fate, let's have another one for the road, kind of bloke.

Warlow tried again. 'Acute pancreatitis is what I've heard. Do you know anything different?'

'Pancreatitis, that's the word. Someone else asked me about it on the golf course today and you think I could remember the bloody name? I came up with Pancake-it is.' He chortled. An inappropriate response for many reasons. Jesus. The bloke was bloody hopeless. 'It sounds serious, doesn't it?' Martin added, and for once, an undercurrent of genuine fear trickled through the bravado. Warlow wondered how many shandy's Martin had already sunk at the nineteenth hole.

'Yes, it does. But they're bloody good these days. They're doing wonders, these doctors, and, you know, she's in expert hands.' Warlow squeezed his eyes shut. Denial or ignorance, it didn't matter. Denise had found an enabler in Martin. Someone who turned a blind eye to her drinking and moods, happy to join her at the bar whenever they got the chance. 'When you see her, tell her I called, okay?'

'I will, Evan. I will.'

'I'll try to get across to the hospital this weekend.'

'You do that. I'm sure she'd appreciate it.'

Warlow doubted that sincerely. But he detected no sardonic edge in Martin's reply. The bloke was plain vanilla. A retiree golfer drifting through his sixties on a cloud of vodka and tobacco.

'You take care, Martin,' Warlow said.

He felt no better having spoken to the one man who should know the detail of Denise's illness but didn't. Warlow shut his eyes. His headache swelled and then abated like a spring tide. He reached for his wallet and found a couple of paracetamol he kept for emergencies and dry swallowed them, regretting it immediately as one got stuck in his throat. But he forced it down and sat, elbows on the desk, head in his hands, thoughts whirling randomly like a plastic bag in a gale. The phone's strident ring came as a welcome intrusion. He pushed back, groggy and disoriented, took in a big lungful of air and picked up the phone.

'Evan, it's Kapil Rani.'

'Kapil. What have you got for me?'

'You're certainly keeping me busy up here. I was hoping to have gone back south by now. I should have known with you in the picture things are never straight-forward.'

'None taken, Kapil.'

Warlow heard a low chuckle before Kapil explained. 'Right, the explosion. I can confirm the body is that of Julia Lloyd. Once again, I was able to call in some help from my colleagues in West Mercia. We used their portable rapid DNA kit.'

'You need to get one of those.'

'On my Christmas list,' Kapil said. 'I've also done a prelim assessment on the remains. No obvious fractures or signs of injury, though she's badly charred. Of significance is that it looks like she'd been restrained. I found some melted plastic around her left wrist. The remains of a cable tie would be my guess.'

Warlow breathed out. The exhalation made a noise he hadn't meant to make.

'It'll go to Cardiff for the post-mortem, now,' Kapil added.

'She,' said Warlow. 'Not it.'

'Sorry, of course, I meant she.'

'I'm not going to be able to spare anyone. The HOP will have to keep him or herself amused for once. But thanks for being so prompt. I appreciate it.'

Kapil sounded tired and regretful for his error. 'Dare I ask how things are going? Everyone I've asked has no idea how this poor woman fits in.'

'We're working on it,' Warlow told him, but he didn't elaborate.

Correction. At that precise moment, he couldn't elaborate. All he really knew was someone, somewhere, had become desperate enough to ensure Warlow did not get any closer to Julia Lloyd.

The question was, why?

What could trigger such a desperate act?

His gut rolled over at the thought that he might now never find out.

But he was a senior officer in the job with years of experience. It didn't take a genius to work out how Julia Lloyd was the key to this whole sorry mess all along. And though someone somewhere was hoping Warlow had not had enough time to interrogate her and get to whatever truth lay hidden, what if he already had?

Somewhere in the depths of his subconscious, a feeling was growing. All he needed to do was nurture it and let it bloom.

Or for someone to give it that one tiny little boost to

make it erupt like a triffid and scare the daylights out of whoever hoped the seed would never come to fruition.

CHAPTER THIRTY-THREE

While Warlow brooded, Lowri, Catrin, and Rhys sat at their desk, doing the glamorous work of sifting through words and images left by two young men as their legacy to those they'd left behind.

'And what exactly is it we're looking for?' Rhys asked for probably the fifth time.

Catrin sighed. 'You'll know it when you see it. That's what the boss said. Any complaints, take it up with him.' She'd allocated herself Robert Lloyd's Facebook timeline and images to wade through. The site remained active, though little or no activity had taken place since he'd gone missing. Rhys was doing the same for Joseph Randal. While Lowri had hard copies of photographs from the Lloyd files and more recently provided images from Mari Randal of Joseph. Though, with his phone missing, these were few and far between.

'Wouldn't it be great if there was a robot who could do this sort of thing,' Rhys muttered.

'There's already facial recognition software. Stands to reason they'll have something someday.' Catrin scribbled some dates down on her notes.

'What do you think, Lowri?' Rhys stuck his head above his monitor and grinned at his colleague. Lowri had two piles of photographs and clippings on her desk. One she'd labelled with a post-it note 'Useful', the other 'Not'. The 'Not' was bigger by a very large margin. She paused, scrunching her nose, and blinking her eyes a few times at Rhys.

'Do I think some jobs could be automated? Yes, I do. As Sarge says, facial recognition is one thing, and finger-print ID is all software, isn't it?'

'I suppose. But those are comparison engines. No one has taught a computer WKIWWSI.'

Lowri raised her eyebrows.

'We'll know it when we see it,' Catrin explained.

'Well, I'm still waiting for a light to go on in my head or a bell to ring. I mean, are we looking for a pattern? Links? What?' Rhys asked.

'The good news is that Robert wasn't on Insta. At least we won't have to wade through that,' Catrin said.

'So far, the only thing I've seen that links these two together is the odd photo of them out with mates and Hana Prosser.' Rhys sat back and stretched.

'She's on Robert's timeline, too,' Catrin told him.

Rhys sat forward, his face lighting up. 'My God, of course. Hana. It's so obvious. She should be here doing this. Or, she should be here talking to us so that we don't have to do this.'

Lowri sent Catrin a pained look.

'Welcome to my world,' Catrin said. 'He'll get to the point, eventually. We just need to be patient.'

'Hana,' Rhys said again, expecting the other two to understand simply by dint of him repeating her name. When all Lowri did was shake her head, Rhys finally explained. 'Hana knew Joseph Randal because they were neighbours. She's what, four years older than him? But still neighbours. She also knew Robert Lloyd because they were the same age and, what did you say, Sarge? They were in the same club?'

'Young Farmers. It's all over his Facebook page when he was younger.'

'Right. So Hana is our expert on these two missing persons. We should ask her if she knows of any links between them instead of playing WIKIWAWOO, or whatever, with blindfolds on.'

Catrin grinned. 'Rhys, sometimes you astonish even me. Where is she?'

'Could be anywhere, Sarge,' Lowri said. 'She's up north, I know that.'

Catrin nodded. 'Doesn't matter. We'll FaceTime her. Rhys, you have her number, don't you?'

'I do.'

'No surprise there,' Catrin muttered under her breath, suddenly pretending to be completely preoccupied by a blank piece of paper on her desk.

Rhys looked hurt. 'We've been liaising, okay?'

'I'm sure you have. Let's hope that's all you've been doing, too.'

'That would be unprofessional. Besides, I'm with Gina.' Rhys shook his head. But he walked to Catrin's desk and set up his phone in silence so that both he and Catrin could view it.

They got through to Hana as she sat in her car. Not while it was moving, thankfully. Not the most complimentary of angles from below, either. At least it would not have been for anyone other than Hana who looked pretty amazing from any angle to Rhys, though he said nothing. The image wavered drunkenly until it came to a stop.

'Hi there,' Hana sang out.

'Hi Hana,' Catrin replied. 'Where are you?'

'Following up with a farmer just north of Machynlleth.

He had two sheepdogs stolen three months ago, and we found them both last week.'

'Sheepdogs? I didn't realise that was a thing,' Rhys said.

'It's become a big thing. Some of these dogs are worth thousands and, because they're trained with simple commands, it's easy to sell them on.'

'But you found these two?' Catrin said.

'We did. In Bristol, of all places. Along with some other dogs. One happy farmer and his family.'

'Stealing dogs, killing sheep, it's like the Wild West up here,' Rhys commented.

'I can't imagine having your dog stolen. It must be devastating.' Catrin spoke with feeling.

'I didn't know you were a dog person, Sarge.' Rhys, stuck next to her at the desk, sent her a sideways glance.

Catrin shrugged and got down to business. 'Hana, you must have heard about Julia Lloyd?'

Hana closed her eyes and shook her head. 'So it definitely was Julia?'

'Yes,' Catrin said.

'My God, what's going on?'

'DCI Warlow has asked us to take a fresh look at any links between what's happened to the Randals and Robert Lloyd.'

Hana's brow crumpled in consternation. 'He thinks they're linked?'

'He thinks it's worth us looking. And Rhys rightly pointed out that you knew them both.'

Hana nodded quickly. 'I did, I do. I mean Julia… you saw how this affected her. She sold her house in Welshpool so that she could dedicate all of her time looking for Rob. She was a teacher once, were you aware of that?'

Catrin and Rhys exchanged glances. 'No, we weren't.'

'Primary school. Brought Rob up alone, mostly. When he disappeared, it hit her really hard.'

'We're looking through Robert Lloyd's Facebook account. Saw your face there.'

Hana's smile was tinged with sadness. 'You would. Robert did an NVQ in agriculture. It was what he wanted to do. He did some work experience at Caemawr, our farm. That's where I first met him. Then we'd come across each other in Young Farmers' dos for years. I'd text him, post on his timeline.'

'You knew he was gay?'

'God, yes. We were mates, nothing else. Even after I went to uni, we'd see each other over holidays. Christmas especially. But in the six months or so before he went missing, he seemed to drop off the radar. My radar at least.'

'Why?' Catrin asked.

Hana frowned. 'I have no idea. Julia said the same. Something changed in his life, I guess.'

'Was he in a relationship?' Rhys asked.

Hana shook her head. 'He struggled a bit with that. He looked forward to his nights out in Wrexham and Liverpool. I don't pretend to know much about the gay lifestyle, but Rob didn't struggle for partners.' She hesitated, picking up on Rhys's question. 'Why do you ask about him being in a relationship?'

'We've found a number that both Joseph and Robert were contacting. It's not traceable, but it's another common thread.'

'Drugs?' Hana suggested.

It would be the obvious conclusion to draw from an untraceable number. A dealer's phone was hardly ever on a contract.

'Could be.' Catrin turned over a sheet on the desk. 'What about Joseph Randal?'

Hana sighed. 'I've known Joe since he was a baby. I'm almost his big sister.'

'But we've found images of him and Robert Lloyd from a couple of years ago,' Rhys said. 'Out together in a group. At parties. In the same social circle at least.'

Hana nodded. 'I don't know when Joe realised he was gay, but it's not a big scene up here. Hardly surprising that they found each other.'

'So, they weren't in a relationship?' Rhys pressed her.

'Robert and Joe? I don't think so. That I'm sure I would have heard about.' Hana's expression clouded. 'Not that it's any of my business, but isn't this a bit of a reach? I mean, the circumstances of their disappearances are totally different. And how would it tie in with Aeron Randal?'

'No idea,' Catrin said. 'But DCI Warlow likes to look at every possibility.'

'How is he? I heard he was injured in the explosion.'

Rhys shook his head. 'He's fine.'

'Rhys was there, too,' Catrin explained. 'He saw the building go up.'

Rhys nodded. 'Close thing. The Wolf had been at the back door a minute before. We'd both be toast if he hadn't run back and thrown us behind his Jeep.'

'Poor Julia,' Hana said.

No one spoke for a long beat. But Catrin broke the impasse, eventually. 'Right. Hana, you've been a great help.'

'Have I?'

'Yeah, you have,' Rhys added with an over-egged smile that earned him a side-eyed glance from Catrin.

'If anything else comes up we need clarifying, we'll give you another call. That okay?' she said.

'Sure. I'll be on my mobile. But if not, I'm staying at my dad's tonight. Have been for the last few nights since

Iestyn, my partner, is away on a course. You can get me there, if not on the mobile.'

They rang off, and the detectives drifted back to their monitors and the joys of social media.

'She's great, isn't she?' Rhys said, largely to himself but still grinning.

Catrin sent Lowri a glance. 'You do have showers in the station?'

Lowri blinked. 'Yes, Sarge.'

'Good.' Catrin nodded. 'I think DC Harries is going to need a cold one.'

———

GIL WALKED Mrs Nowacki back to her apartment, stood on the landing outside and waited until she let herself in.

'Thanks for your help. Much appreciated.' He beamed at her.

'I do it for Padrig. He is not bad man.' She walked in, put the door back on its safety chain and stood regarding him through the crack.

'Understood.' Gil nodded.

And in one of those little quirks of fate that arrive unbidden, as he exited the building, who should pull up on the opposite side of the road in his Subaru but the 'not a bad man' himself. Gil stood on the pavement and waited for Padrig to get out of his car.

'Mr Randal,' Gil said.

'What is it now?' Padrig demanded, but his expression showed more concern than anger. 'You switching careers?'

Gil glanced at the bag. 'I've been clearing up people's crap for the last twenty years. So, no change there. But since you ask, I've been up visiting your neighbour, Mrs Nowacki.'

'Antonia? Is she okay?'

'She's fine. And a highly trained member of the Polish Resistance by all accounts.'

'She's an interesting character.' Padrig remained wary. His eyes drifted to the black plastic bag in Gil's hands. 'What's that?'

'A piece of the jigsaw. Someone has been putting rubbish in your bins, Padrig.'

'What?' Padrig pulled a face.

'I take it this isn't yours?'

'It's a black plastic bag. How do I know?'

'Let me rephrase,' Gil's delivery remained calm and collected. 'Have you put anything in your wheelie bin since it was last emptied?'

Padrig shook his head, thinking. 'No. There's a bag slowly filling up in my kitchen. I'll take it out when it's full.'

Gil nodded. 'Exactly what I do, too. Unless Mrs Jones has put the Friday fish wrapping in there, in which case out it goes, full or not full. So you have not discarded any trainers, singular, of late?'

'Trainers, no.'

'And Long John Silver doesn't live in one of the other flats, does he?'

'Who?'

'Parrot, crutch, wooden leg?'

Padrig looked even more confused.

'Pieces of eight? Black spot? Pirate with a disability?'

A blank shake of the head.

Gil sighed, disappointed at the world's ignorance once again. 'Robert Louis Stevenson will be turning in his shallow grave, probably on an island somewhere. Never mind. This,' he held up the bag afresh, 'means that someone else wants us to think it was you.'

'Why? What's in—'

Neither man had taken much notice of the big Land Cruiser coming up the street. But Gil was the one facing the road. And it was Gil who picked up on the big diesel's change of tone as the driver floored the accelerator. Gil who looked up and saw the pickup swerve towards them. In the end, the kerb saved both men. If Padrig had turned, his inclination would have been to step away, off the kerb. But Gil did the opposite. He pulled back and grabbed onto Padrig as he did so, yanking him forward to stagger and fall just as Gil lost his footing and fell back towards the building's entrance.

The truck hit the kerb and jumped. But the jolt threw the vehicle left, where the men had gone right.

Gil's backside met the hard ground, making him grunt in pain. Padrig yelled and tumbled onto the sergeant's legs. Feet away, the Land Cruiser reversed with a squeal of tyres. Gil looked up and saw a masked face in the window, the eyes blazing with emotion, before it accelerated away.

Gil scrambled to his feet while Padrig got to his knees.

'You okay?' Gil yelled.

'Yes, I… what the fuck just happened?'

But Gil barely heard Padrig's confused voice in his wake as he ran to his car, got in, and set off in pursuit.

CHAPTER THIRTY-FOUR

WARLOW EMERGED from the SIO room, ever hopeful that one of the team had come up with something. Anything that might give them some direction. No one spoke as he sat at Gil's desk and called up the CCTV video from Robert Lloyd's misper file. Those last ever late-at-night images of him walking through Wrexham towards Bellevue Park.

'Who were you on the way to meet, Robert?' Warlow muttered.

'Sorry, sir?' Rhys asked, hearing only an unintelligible series of words.

'Unanswerable question. Anything new?' Warlow turned to the DC.

'Not much. We've been chatting with Hana Prosser who happens to know both Robert Lloyd and Joseph Randal.'

'She come up with anything?'

'Nothing we didn't already know, sir.'

Catrin turned to add, 'Once a month, Robert organised a trip to Stanley Street in Liverpool. Sometimes half a dozen of them would go up there and book into the

Premier Inn overnight. Once Joe got to nineteen, he went as well. The last time, a month ago. But not with Robert, obviously.'

'Stanley Street?' Warlow asked.

'The gay quarter, sir,' Catrin explained.

'But there was some overlap between Joseph and Robert?' Warlow asked.

'Yes. For about eight months before Robert Lloyd disappeared.'

Warlow sighed. 'Not much to go on, is it?'

The room fell quiet until a voice spoke. 'I think I may have something, sir.'

Warlow looked around to see Lowri doing an impression of the innocent victim from any teen horror movie of choice. The scene where dawning awareness as to the true nature of her dire predicament thuds home. Only here, the horror emanated not from a vampire or a ghoul, but from the glare of a frustrated senior detective desperate for a lead to follow.

'Let's hear it,' Warlow ordered.

The PC got up and walked to the Gallery. She posted two photographs. One of Robert, the other of Joe. 'These are hard copy photographs of the two men. They're separated by four years from what I can gather, but if you look closely, they seem to be wearing the same pendant on a thin chain necklace.'

Warlow got up and peered at the photographs. He'd seen one of them before. Given to them by Julia Lloyd, depicting her son grinning at the camera in an open-necked shirt. Lowri had scanned and enlarged the photograph to show the pendant. Not large; Warlow guessed about half an inch in diameter. A flat but textured padlock shape with loops dividing it into three sections, silver in the middle, darker at the edges, with the clasp of the padlock shaped like a silver rainbow in different shades of grey. His gaze drifted across to the photograph of Joseph Randal. This one a more candid shot in a t-shirt and again, underneath it, Lowri had enlarged the pendant hanging around his neck. Not as clear, but no doubt that it looked identical.

'It's an unusual design. And not something I've seen on any of the bigger retailer sites I've visited,' Lowri told the team.

'Definitely a link,' Warlow said, and tried to temper his disappointment by injecting a little enthusiasm into his reply by way of encouragement.

Lowri nodded. But they both know this was no smoking gun.

'Good work.' Warlow flashed her a smile and turned to include the others in what he said next. 'Kapil told me that Julia Lloyd had plastic ties around her wrist. Make room on the board for her because if there was any doubt before, there isn't now. She was murdered.'

Catrin dropped her head. Rhys winced.

'But we're going to find whoever did this by concentrating here.' He swept a hand across the board. 'Anyone heard from Gil?'

Rhys shook his head.

'Okay. Then let's keep working.'

They talked about next steps and Warlow wrote up the actions before everyone got back to their desks and attacked their individual tasks. There was a mountain of work to get through. In the end, Lowri reported back first.

'I think I've found it on Etsy, sir.'

'What?' Warlow got up and joined her at her desk.

'The pendant, sir. It's handmade to order. An artisan jeweller from,' Lowri clicked her mouse twice, 'Norfolk.'

'So not mass produced, then?' Rhys commented.

'No,' Lowri agreed.

'Follow it through. Give the designer a ring,' Warlow ordered. Part of him wanted to tell her to stop wasting her time, but it remained a thread that needed pulling. 'And while we wait for inspiration, I'll try to find Sergeant Jones.'

Back in his SIO cupboard, Warlow dialled Gil's number. When he got through, the sound of a vehicle travelling at speed provided a background rumble.

'You on the way?' Warlow asked.

'On the way?' Gil's voice sounded shouty with excitement. 'I'm in pursuit of a *cachgu* that tried to mow me and Padrig Randal down, I'll have you know.'

Warlow pushed up from the desk. 'Christ, man. It isn't safe to let you out on your own.' The sound of a siren passing at high speed came through Warlow's phone.

'That's the cavalry arriving,' Gil said and Warlow heard the glee in his voice. 'They're pulling him in. Let me get back to you, Evan. Five minutes. Starsky out.'

Warlow stared at the phone in his hand, fighting a smile, shaking his head and wondering if he'd just hallucinated the last forty seconds. He wandered back out to tell the team, but when he saw the look on everyone's faces, all he managed was a 'What?'

'Lowri got through to the jeweller, sir,' Rhys answered.

'And?'

Rhys nodded at the PC. This was her lead.

'She keeps good records, sir,' Lowri explained. 'She doesn't sell many of these, and so when I asked if she'd sold any to mid Wales, she looked it up right away and… she's sold two over the last four years, sir. Both to the same buyer at the same address.'

Warlow's insides fluttered and his breath seemed to stall in his throat. 'Who?' He barked.

'The address they have was Caemawr Farm near Hermon. And the name… Hana Prosser, sir.'

The air around Warlow seemed to hum.

Hana Prosser?

Wait, thought Warlow. So what? She'd known both. Perhaps she'd given both the same birthday present. That didn't mean much of anything. But a dreadful sinking feeling had overtaken the fluttering. The whole team was staring at him. Every one of them waiting for his direction, searching for the reasonable explanation that would explain all of this.

The phone's shrill ring shook him out of his paralysis. Gil's number.

'Gil, what the hell is going on?'

'Good question,' Gil's voice sounded animated.

'I'm putting you on speaker for the team to hear.'

'Yeah, do that. While you're all sitting there raiding the HUMAN TISSUE FOR TRANSPLANT box, I've been out here doing real policing. Our colleagues in traffic have responded to my request to pull over a Toyota Land Cruiser that, not fifteen minutes ago, attempted to lay waste to me and Padrig Randal outside his flat. The vehicle mounted the pavement and almost mounted me.'

Catrin's mouth turned down in disgust.

'I am about to find out who the driver is.' Gil's out of breath voice mingled with the sound of movement. 'Get him out!' he yelled.

A car door opened. Mumbled orders followed from an unknown voice, and then Gil again.

'Well, well. If it isn't our old friend Hari Gregory.'

'It wasn't you… I wasn't trying to harm you.' Gregory's voice sounded petulant.

'Then what the hell were you trying to do?'

'Padrig Randal. This is all his fault.' Gregory preached the words. Loudly and proudly.

'*Arglwydd mawr*, Padrig Randal didn't kill your sheep, man.'

'The sheep are retribution for sins unpunished. Can't you see that? The sheep were a sign. I had to punish the adulterer. God's hammer will fall.' Pulpit words bellowed for all to hear.

'Take him away before I do something I will seriously regret,' Gil said. No one needed to see the sergeant to realise he was seething.

Scuffling sounds followed, threats, yells and then a car door shutting.

'Right, that's him in the back of a secure vehicle,' Gil said.

'Hari Gregory?' Warlow asked, unable to hide the scepticism in his tone.

'Yes. Hari bloody Gregory finding a scapegoat for his dead sheep by the sound of it.'

'Think he might be our man for the other missing Randals?'

There wasn't even a second's pause before Gil's reply. 'Not a chance.'

Warlow frowned. 'Why so definite?'

'Because I have in my car Joseph Randal's other trainer. Placed in Padrig Randal's refuse for us to find. Had we obtained a search warrant, that is. Planted there by person or persons unknown.'

'Mrs Nowacki gave you that?' Catrin laughed.

'The same. I'm thinking of asking her to join the team. There are one or two people I can think of she might stand in for.'

He let that one sink in and Warlow turned a chuckle into a cough to avoid incurring the wrath of either Catrin or Rhys.

'She heard someone messing about with the bins and found a fresh black bag with one trainer in it. It looks identical to the one found in your waterfall,' Gil finished explaining.

'Did she see who it was?' Rhys asked.

'No, but she got almost the whole of the licence plate.

I'm sending that to you now. I'll follow the Uniforms and Gregory back in. Shouldn't be too long.'

'As I say, it isn't safe to let you go out on your own.' Warlow watched Catrin shake her head. But the grin on his face belied the words he spoke.

Rhys's phone buzzed. 'That's the licence plate, sir. I'll check it now.' He turned to his computer.

'Why the other trainer?' Catrin asked.

'A breadcrumb trail,' Warlow replied. 'A link from Padrig Randal to the waterfall, and therefore Joseph Randal.'

'It's bewildering,' Catrin muttered.

'Perhaps that's the whole idea here. Misdirection.' Warlow walked back to the Gallery. The little flutter in his gut had disappeared on hearing Gil's collar, but now it came back again afresh. They were close, really close. He could feel it like static electricity in the air.

Rhys called over, 'We have seven vehicles in the local postcode areas that would match the licence plate, allowing for one substitu—' His words petered out.

Warlow scalp contracted. 'What?' He blurted.

'There's a black Yaris here, sir.'

'And?'

'It's registered to…' Rhys turned his face up, confusion fighting with outright disbelief. 'It's registered to Hana Prosser, sir.'

Warlow sucked in air. The pendant might be a coincidence, but the car… the car was now the game changer. And, when he allowed himself to think it through, the whole thing clicked into place like the last rotation of a Rubik's cube.

Who'd been present at almost every crime scene?

Who'd been privy to the investigation intelligence?

Who knew the geography and the people involved intimately?

'Where is she now?' Warlow asked, his voice a low rumble. No one needed to ask who he was talking about.

But no one answered for a couple of seconds.

'Where is she?' Warlow repeated the question.

Catrin answered, but the look on her face told Warlow she'd rather have been chewing broken glass. 'Out in the sticks near Machynlleth.'

'And we have her home address?'

'Uh, she said she was staying at the farm with her dad for a few days, sir.' Rhys said.

'Okay. We know nothing for definite. Not yet. But I don't want to spook anyone, either. So this is how we're going to play it.'

CHAPTER THIRTY-FIVE

WARLOW DROVE with Rhys next to him in the Jeep's passenger seat. They'd left Catrin and Lowri in the Incident Room to brief Gil when he got back. They needed to forge the links in the chain, because when it came to prosecuting one of their own, everything needed to be squeaky clean.

Gil would be good at that. Though he did not give that impression; the amiable clown persona he cultivated was nothing but a front for a copper with an eye for detail. Combined with Catrin's terrier-like relentlessness, Warlow felt sure they'd be able to piece all of it together.

The DCI preferred the direct approach. And, as SIO, he'd want to be the one that confronted Hana.

Rhys hadn't said much for the first fifteen minutes of the journey. Even when Warlow had stopped for fuel, the DC had declined the offer of refreshments. 'Crisps? Nuts? A drink?'

'No thanks, sir.'

Warlow filled up, paid and got back into the car to find a glum-faced DC waiting for him.

'What's the matter with you? I know you've lost your appetite, but this impression of a sick dog is getting to me.'

'I don't understand it, sir,' Rhys said, with a little shake of his head. 'Hana, of all people?'

'Clarify that statement for me, Detective Constable. What do you mean by "of all people?"'

Rhys shifted in his seat. 'You've met her sir, she is… she's great. Enthusiastic, good at her job. It doesn't add up.'

He sensed the DC's anger. Totally understandable when a colleague might be involved in such a heinous crime. But naivety and police work did not sit well together. You did better to believe the 'best' people capable of the 'worst' acts. That way, you might avoid too much disappointment, even if you ended up being unable to take anyone at face value.

'Add up? Since when did murder make any sense?' Warlow spat.

Rhys flinched. 'My bad, sir. But I still don't see what plausible reason she could have had.'

'Ah. So now we're talking motivation again.' Warlow overtook a lorry and flashed a thanks at an oncoming driver who'd had to slow down. In response to his acknowledgement, Warlow got an extended middle finger by reply. He probably would have done exactly the same thing had the roles been reversed.

He sent Rhys a sideways glance. 'I don't pretend to know what that motivation might be. But we can postulate.'

'Postulate?'

'Look, I don't like this any more than you do. But the evidence, such that we have, points to Hana now. We can't ignore that just because she's someone you know and like. It's time to put on your big boy trousers and be a copper. So, postulate.'

Rhys's beetling brows eased a smidgen. 'The five P's, sir.'

'Exactly. So?' Warlow waited. All he wanted to do was get to Caemawr Farm and find Hana Prosser. But every situation in this job provided a learning opportunity. And as much as he didn't feel like teaching, he needed to keep Rhys on point. 'Come on, why do people commit the ultimate crime?'

Rhys sighed. 'Passion, sir. Often carried out in a moment of rage or jealousy and usually unplanned.'

'Good.' Warlow nodded.

'Then there's profit, generated by greed.'

'And I'd lump organised crime in there, and in fact, most if not all, drug-related killings. Either for product or money. But always for perceived gain anyway, if you're depraved enough to class the next "fix" as gain. What else?'

Rhys pondered before answering, but when he did, he looked pleased with having come up with another P. 'Psychoses. The mad, not the bad. Paranoid schizophrenics who think they're ridding the world of devils. Or lashing out at strangers. Some people would put hate crime in the same bracket too, sir.'

'Number four?'

'Protection. Of oneself or others. Blackmailers or perhaps someone who gets to breaking point in a violent or abusive relationship.'

'Good, Rhys. There's one left. And who knows if this one might be what drove Hana Prosser to do what she's done.'

'Panic, sir?'

'Panic. Precisely. Another unplanned act. Not so easy to cover your tracks, either. Though in this case someone has had a bloody good go at it.'

'Someone with a bit of inside knowledge, sir.'

Warlow didn't answer because he would only be stating the barn-door obvious. He risked coming across as hard-nosed here; dehumanising the fellow officer, making Rhys think of her in terms of her criminal activity, not as the bubbly blonde PCSO that had cooperated to the maximum.

Cooperated perhaps a bit too quickly and too enthusiastically, maybe?

Warlow could have called Hana in to the station. Confronted her there in the presence of her fellow officers. And whatever the outcome, she'd have been stigmatised by that. Better this took place away from that hot house. Rhys might not appreciate it, but Catrin had looked grateful when Warlow had outlined his plan.

Hana Prosser would face enough hate and scrutiny in the days and weeks and months to come. No need to ladle it on with a trowel.

'Okay, so panic then.' Rhys's words brought Warlow back to the moment. When he glanced across, the DC had a pained look back on his face. 'How do you see it, sir?'

'Hypothetically, it could be that despite the evidence of their sexual orientation, Hana might have been involved with Robert and or Joseph. Maybe she has a thing for young gay men.'

Rhys frowned at this.

'No point looking at me like that. Stranger things, as you well know.'

'Where does Aeron Randal fit in with that, sir?'

'He doesn't. But there is such a thing as collateral damage.'

Rhys simply shook his head. He'd been in scrapes with Warlow a dozen times already, but Hana's involvement had got to him.

A sudden thought struck Warlow. 'You're not upset because you and Hana…?'

'No, sir.' Rhys shook his head. 'Sergeant Richards has already tried stirring that pot. Every time there's a young woman involved in the case, I'm fair game for a ribbing. As for Hana, I like her. Of course I do. She's great. But she has a partner. And I'm in a relationship with Gina.'

'Ah yes, the delightful Officer Mellings.' Warlow recalled the attractive FLO he'd worked with on a couple of occasions. He recalled, too, that she resembled Hana Prosser quite a bit: age, looks, personality. Perhaps it went some way to explaining Rhys's pain and disappointment.

'Hana seems so normal, sir. That's all.'

Warlow nodded. 'I hear what you're saying, Rhys. But if this little shit show teaches you one thing, it'll be that there is no such thing as normal in this job.'

———

GIL GOT BACK to the Incident Room carrying the plastic bag like a hunter returning with enough food to feed the tribe for a month. He held it up for all to see. Though, as it was material evidence, he left the trainer in the bag, which meant no one could see anything but an uninspiring, crumpled, roughly oval-shaped blob of black plastic. Besides, the 'all to see' consisted only of Catrin, Lowri, and half a dozen typists and indexers.

'Behold, the head of the Hydroid.'

'It's Hydra,' Catrin said.

'Whatevoid, as my granddaughter would say.' Gil stood with his prize held up in triumph until the lack of any response made him drop his arm. The grin on his face melted into a disappointed scowl. 'Where is our Lord and King?'

'On the way to meet Hana Prosser.'

'Bloody Nora, don't tell me she's found something else? That girl is a trouble magnet.'

Catrin sighed. 'You'd better log that in as evidence and then sit down. I'm even going to make you a cup of tea. There is a lot to tell.'

'I smell bad news in the air,' Gil said. 'Or is that yesterday's bean casserole escaping through a partially closed torpedo hatch?'

Catrin winced.

Lowri giggled.

'Do not encourage him or you'll regret it.' Catrin pointed towards the back of the room and then to Gil's desk. 'Evidence. Then tea.'

'Yes, ma'am,' Gil said. But, as he walked past Lowri, he put his hand up to the side of his face and mouthed, 'Power mad and anger issues.'

Lowri clamped her mouth shut and squeezed her eyes closed in an attempt at preventing the laugh that threatened.

Catrin shook her head and walked out to put the kettle on, muttering to herself all the way out of the room.

CHAPTER THIRTY-SIX

Caemawr Farm was the third that Warlow had visited in as many days. But unlike the Randal's Wern Ddu that exuded an air of desolation, and Deri Isaf, Gregory's place with its nod to the old ways, the Prosser's farm looked clean and modern. Yes, there were old stone walls and steel gates and dark barns that hinted at history and longevity, but the yard itself had no dumped bales or feed bags, no forgotten bits of rusting equipment abandoned against the walls. And the cobbled close looked neat and swept clean. An old water pump in the middle gleamed a recently painted glossy black. This was a working farm, but Elis Prosser clearly liked to keep the workings under a neat and welcoming facade.

They'd turned up unannounced towards the end of the working day. All appeared quiet. No sign of Hana's Yaris and just the one Land Rover parked neatly in front of the farmhouse.

'Right, she can't be here yet. Probably still at work,' Warlow muttered, as he parked up.

'What do we do, sir? Sit and wait?' Rhys looked anxious and unhappy.

Before Warlow could answer, the front door of the farmhouse opened, spilling warm yellow light out into the afternoon gloom and outlining Elis Prosser who raised a hand in greeting.

'Let me do the talking.' Warlow got out.

'Ah, Evan. I wondered who it might be. Good to see you.' Prosser grinned as he walked out and shook Warlow's hand.

'Sorry to intrude. We're here to see Hana.'

'I'll try to contain my disappointment.' Elis's grin didn't fade. 'Who is that with you?'

'Rhys Harries, one of our DCs,' Warlow explained.

'Oh, your strapping rugby player. Extra muscle is he?'

Warlow snorted. Though playing along like this left him a tad uncomfortable, he was here to do a job. Once it was done, he doubted Elis Prosser would be quite as jovial and welcoming, but for now, the charade ought to continue until his daughter arrived and could be questioned. 'Nice place you have here.'

'We like it. Try to keep it busy and effective. Times are difficult in farming, as you know. Would you like to come in? I'll get the kettle on.'

Warlow would not have minded, but given Rhys's unhappy state of mind, he decided it might not be the best of moves. Trying to get the DC to remain neutral in a situation like this would not be easy. A poker player Rhys was not. Then he hit on a plan. 'Hana keeps telling us what a wonderful set up you have, here. Mind if we look around?'

'Good God, no. I'll give you the tour. Milking's done. All is quiet. Let me get a coat.'

Warlow beckoned Rhys out of the car. 'We're getting a tour of the farm.'

'What?'

'It's fine. It'll pass the time. Stay quiet and follow my lead. And try not to look as if the world is about to end.'

For the first time since leaving the Incident Room, Rhys smiled. 'I always fancied driving a tractor. Ever since I was a kid.'

'If you play your cards right, maybe Mr Prosser will let you ride a pony, or even pet one of the lambs.'

'Really?'

'No, not really. How old are you? This isn't a day out at the bloody petting zoo. Come on, with a bit of luck, we can pass some time here and gain some intelligence. Text Catrin and ask her to ring Welshpool and find out if Hana's clocked off yet.'

———

Gil listened as Catrin and Lowri filled him in on what had happened while he'd been out getting almost run over.

'Hana Prosser? Are you serious?'

'It all adds up if you do the maths. It's all here, including the licence plate you sent us. I know that's not a hundred per cent conclusive but as the Wolf said, there's no room in this world for the C word.'

'C word?' Lowri asked.

'Coincidence,' Catrin replied.

Lowri looked suitably relieved that it wasn't a different C word as Catrin printed off the report she'd compiled, highlighting the timelines and Hana's known movements.

Gil sipped his tea and slid on his reading glasses.

'Want me to get the HUMAN TISSUE FOR TRANS-PLANT box?' Catrin asked.

'Not yet. I don't think I can stomach even a fig roll until I've digested all this.' He looked up into his colleagues' faces. 'Fig rolls settle the stomach. At least until the fig gets down into the lower intestine to do its magic. But can you believe this? I mean Hana...'

Catrin dropped her chin and gave him the same exasperated expression she saved for Rhys, usually. 'I know, she's a blonde-haired, blue-eyed bundle of loveliness. But she lost her mother at a young age. That can do all sorts of weird things to a person.'

Gil nodded slowly, but added a dubious, 'I suppose.'

Catrin shrugged. 'Ours not to reason why, Gil.' Her phone buzzed and she glanced at the screen. 'Oh, that's Rhys. They're at the farm and want to know if Hana's left Welshpool.' She picked up the desk phone and sent Gil a final glance. 'We'll leave you to it. Let me know if you have any questions.'

———

ELIS PROSSER LOVED HIS FARM. That was obvious. And Warlow couldn't help being impressed by the set up and the statistics. 132 dairy cattle milked twice a day, 768 sheep bred for lambs, a sixty-two-hectare holding. They were shown the lambing sheds, the milking parlour – which looked more like a high-tech laboratory than an agricultural building – and the giant barns with open sides where the cattle overwintered.

'Don't they freeze?' Rhys asked.

'Cows are hot. They generate a great deal of heat. They'd roast if you enclosed them in here,' Prosser explained as he led the police officers through the labyrinthine walkways between the buildings.

'Hana showed no interest in running the farm?' Warlow asked.

Elis smiled. 'No. She is destined for greater things. She's good, mind. Turn her hand at anything she can. Very useful to have around when we're grass cutting. But she always wanted to go off to university, so who was I to stand in her way. And then that six months abroad. She's been all over has our Hana. Australia, South America and New

Zealand she's visited. And I was glad to support her. Not easy growing up on a farm with no mother.'

Something pulled at Warlow then. Something that tugged at a memory in the back of his head. He strained, wondering if it would break through the surface of his recollection, but it stayed stubbornly buried.

'What is that smell?' Rhys asked with disgust.

Elis smiled. 'That's our slurry storage. Been a very wet winter, so our lagoons are pretty full. Luckily, you can only smell them when the wind is easterly. Mostly they are westerly, so we're spared the stench.'

'Lagoons?' Rhys asked.

'Lakes where we keep all the stuff that comes out of the back end. And a hundred and thirty-two cows make a lot of slurry,' Elis said, indulgently.

Rhys's expression said it all. The breeze shifted and Warlow received a whiff of what had already bothered Rhys. Pungent and concentrated, it caught in his throat.

'Hardly glamorous,' Elis grinned, 'but you might as well see the back end of this enterprise, too.'

———

Gil read through everything twice, his tea, for once, growing cold on the desk. He had to admit everything pointed towards the police officer. And now with Antonia Nowacki having seen Hana's car at Padrig Randal's place and with Lowri's dogged detective work on the necklace, the evidence seemed overwhelming.

He sat back, his brain whirling like a paper windmill in a storm.

'Well, what do you think?' Catrin asked.

'I don't want to think. I want to lie down and pretend this will all go away.' He narrowed his eyes as if he was in pain. 'And Evan's gone up there with Rhys?'

Catrin nodded. 'He wanted to do it face to face and away from colleagues.'

'Fair enough. Good of him to do that. I want to say she deserves that little bit of respect, but of course she doesn't. Not if this is all true.' He exhaled a deep draught of air. 'She seems such a nice kid. She was even in Patagonia the same month one of my girls was out there a couple of years ago. Missed each other by a week, would you believe? Probably not a bad thing when you think about it now.'

'2019?' Lowri's voice broke in on the sergeants' conversation.

'What?'

'Was that when your daughter was in South America?'

'Yes,' Gil replied, growing more confused by the second.

'Do you have actual dates?' Lowri asked.

'Not off the top of my head, but I have photos on my phone which is how Hana noticed the dates when I showed her.'

Lowri blinked. As close as she ever came to insisting on anything.

Gil picked up his phone and began scrolling.

Catrin watched the exchange with interest. 'Care to share with us why this is so important, Lowri? It is important I take it?'

'I think it might be, Sarge,' Lowri said.

Gil looked up from his phone. 'Here we are. Betsan was in Patagonia in October 2019.'

Lowri looked at her screen. 'The first pendant was bought in October 2019.'

Catrin reached for the report she'd given Gil to read, her eyes widening as she scanned the pages. 'Date of sale, October 18th, 2019.'

They all looked at one another. 'Are you going to text the DCI, or will I?' Catrin said.

'Text the both of them, him and Rhys,' Gil said, sitting up, his eyebrows almost mashing together on his head.

———

ELIS SHOWED them the channelling system, collecting the gallons of cow manure and pushing it all towards a common point at the back of the holding barns. 'Mind your feet. We wash everything down, but even so.'

They had to navigate another tractor, this one with a front loader scoop attachment, along a narrow, concreted area with high walls. Even if they couldn't see the glistening surface of the lake of manure in front of them, they could smell it. Christ, you could almost taste it.

'Let me fire up the tractor so we have some light.' Elis climbed up on the machine and it kicked into life. It showed them a slipway leading out from the concreted funnel they now stood at the edge of. Beyond, a large area about the size of two or three tennis courts took up most of a field. And though the stained and putrid area around where the concrete slipway met with it left nothing to the imagination in confirming that this was a lake of effluent, the fluid itself appeared oddly tidy and regimented, covered in what looked like small pebbles that bobbed and shifted in the wind.

Elis left the tractor running and came back to join them. 'New regulations mean we have to put covers on our slurry lagoons. That's what those little balls bobbing about do.'

'So, all that is manure?' Rhys had a hand up over his mouth and nose.

'Manure and water, yes.' Elis grinned. 'You get used to the smell. What floats on top is a bulk ceramic material that controls the release of methane, hydrogen sulphide and ammonia. Of course, we still have to stir the whole thing to get bacteria to work. On those days it's best to be away from the farm.'

'That's a lot of… manure,' Rhys said.

Elis shrugged. 'More than usual. As I said, the wet season means we couldn't spread as normal.'

Rhys coughed under his hand. Elis picked up on it right away. 'Enough of this. Time for a cuppa or something stronger. What do you say? Hana won't be long now, I'm sure.'

'Good idea,' said Warlow.

Elis clambered back up into the tractor cab, pausing only to look back as both Warlow's and Rhys's phones signalled a message. They both read at the same time what Catrin had sent them:

Hana Prosser out of the country at the time first pendant bought.
Likely her name and address used by third party.

Warlow read it twice. He looked up to see confusion all over Rhys's face. But he suspected what the DC saw etched all over his would-be exasperation as the truth came flooding in. South America. It had almost come to him then when Elis had mentioned it. Something he'd read in Hana's CV. Her post-university trip to the southern hemisphere and the dates thereof.

Stupid. He'd been a complete idiot. It hadn't been Hana who'd bought the pendants. They'd been bought by someone else as gifts for two young men.

As gifts, perhaps from an older lover to an excited new and younger gay partner.

An older lover who had carte blanche to travel all over parts of Wales and England as an active Farmer's Union rep while contractors did the milking on the farm. Time away under camouflage of business. And ample time to meet young men with a similar interest away from prying eyes. Meet them… or prey on them.

Rhys had worked it out on his own. One glance at his

open face showed first, surprise and then suspicion as his head whipped up towards the tractor.

It was then that Warlow realised that the engine was still running. He heard a gear engage as he looked up and saw Elis Prosser glaring down with a look of pure hatred from the cab as the machine accelerated straight at them.

'Run,' Warlow yelled, and both men headed down the slipway towards the slurry pit.

CHAPTER THIRTY-SEVEN

THEY SPRINTED FORWARD. The only direction they could take, with the sides of the concrete walls on either side of the slipway getting higher as the ground angled down towards the pit.

In front of Rhys by no more than a foot or two and with the tractor roaring behind them in the enclosed space, Warlow reached the edge of the lagoon. Ahead, nothing but darkness and the lake of filth. To either side, a smooth fence around a concrete bowl where the pit had been dug.

'Left,' Warlow bellowed. 'Go left.'

They had to go down. It was the only way.

Scrabbling for a foothold, Warlow edged around the wall and almost lost his footing. Beyond the funnel slipway, the lagoon's walls fell to ground level, the slurry three feet below it. Warlow lunged for the edge of the concrete and his hands met with a three-inch rim. Beneath him, his legs splashed into fluid that felt thicker than water. But even as he tried not to think too much about what it was, the stench that battered him left no doubt. Legs dangling and with no purchase, Warlow shimmied across on his forearms and elbows, three inches of concrete was all that spared him from the disgusting lake beneath, his face an inch away from a solid concrete panel that protected the lagoon from outside.

Rhys followed him, but misjudged his reach. He floundered and slipped. Warlow threw out an arm and grabbed the material of Rhys's coat with his left hand. The sickening noise of legs flapping wildly followed by a fresh wave of stench, told Warlow that Rhys was going in. But Warlow's hand slowed the descent long enough for Rhys's hand to come up and find that same rim, and the DC hauled himself up before he fell any lower.

In that instant, the tractor's front loader came through the gap they'd moments before occupied. It stopped there, the dark metal coated with stringy slivers of cow manure.

'Rhys, you okay?' Warlow shouted over the noise of the tractor engine.

Rhys's breathing sounded odd and laboured. 'Yes, sir. Oh, God, the smell.'

'Try breathing through your mouth.'

It helped. A little. But there was no escaping the awful ammoniacal reek.

A breeze ruffled Warlow's hair momentarily and, for once, he thanked whatever God might be listening for sending it as the gust wafted the noisome vapours away for an instant's respite as both men sucked in air.

To a casual observer on a different day, in different circumstances, or perhaps in a maniac's dream, the two men hanging on for dear life looked just like holidaymakers at the edge of a pool, resting after swimming a length. Except that this pool wasn't crystal clear and chlorinated, this was teeming with bacteria and gasses and was one hundred per cent lethal.

Rhys's mistimed jump and his desperate efforts to find purchase had agitated the slurry beneath him much more than Warlow's lunge had. And yes, the smell was enough to make anyone vomit. But what terrified Warlow was what they couldn't smell.

People died in farming accidents all the time. And slurry deaths were all too common. He could detect the eggy hydrogen sulphide in the sickening mix. A disgusting enough aroma, but one that in the here and now he almost welcomed. Because he knew from the tragic incidents he'd had to deal with in the past that high enough concentrations knocked out your sense of smell and caused breathing difficulties and disorientation. That hadn't happened. Not yet.

Next to him, Rhys made a retching noise.

'Don't let go, Rhys. Do not let go.'

'The stink, sir… The stink it's…' Rhys retched again.

'Keep your head up as high as you can and lean forward towards the fence.'

The tractor's engine slowed to an idle and the cab door slammed.

'Move Rhys. Move across, away from the tractor.'

Warlow edged away from the slipway gap and Rhys followed. They'd got beyond arm's reach when Elis Prosser's head appeared next to the tractor's front scoop. He stared at them, silhouetted against the tractor's lights, a dark malevolent shape.

'Might as well let go. Get it over with. I can get up to the other side of the fence with a gaffe. Or pour some petrol on you. Or drop a weight on your head. Easy as whistling.'

Warlow shuddered. 'Who else is in here?' His voice sounded strained and when he shifted his weight, the movement made him a little giddy.

Breathe, Warlow, breathe.

Elis shook his head and his words were more poisonous than the miasma from the lagoon. 'You'll never find out.'

'People know we're here,' Rhys croaked.

Warlow heard the effort it took and winced.

'Do they?' Elis said. 'Ah well, once you're in, we'll get a grappling hook and hide you somewhere else on the farm. I have lots of room.'

'Is Aeron in here? Is this where you chucked Robert and Joseph?'

Another gust gave Warlow a moment's respite from the stench. But Elis's words brought a new horror to his heart. 'Rotten flesh all looks the same after six months under there, believe me. Let go. Find out for yourself.'

'You bastard—'

'Dad?' A familiar voice on the far side of the tractor made Elis jerk around. Warlow turned, too, and saw Hana Prosser, still in uniform, holding a shotgun pointed at the floor. 'Dad, what's going on?'

'An accident, Hana, they fell. I was showing them around and—'

Warlow yelled across. 'They're all in here, Hana. Robert, Aeron, Joseph. He's put them all in here.'

'It's the gas, Hana,' Elis said. 'They're losing it.'

Hana's eyes were wide with shock, flicking her bewildered glare between Warlow and her father and back again, shaking her head. 'What is this?'

Rhys retched again.

'It's him, Hana,' Warlow shouted. 'He forced us in here. Ask him, Ask him to his bloody face.'

Elis had his back to Warlow. He reached out a hand. 'Put the gun down, Hana. We can talk.'

'Oh, my God. Oh, my God.' Hana's words rushed out of her. 'Dad… how can it… Dad?'

'These men are liars. Desperate for someone to blame. I can explain.'

Hana screamed. She brought the gun up and squeezed both triggers, aiming out over the blackness of the lagoon. Rhys flinched and ducked, as did Warlow. When he looked again, Elis had gone and Hana stood, shaking, the gun once more pointing down at her feet.

Elis was not to be seen.

'Hana…' Rhys's desperate voice sounded full of pleading.

She dropped the gun and moved across the front of the tractor, ducking lithely under the scoop to stand where her father had stood moments before. Once more the tractor lights threw her form into silhouette, but this time the arms that reached out were helping, not intent on murder.

'Move back, Rhys. Come on, you can do this,' Warlow urged. He could sense the world slipping away. The tractor lights were changing colour as he inched his way behind Rhys, urging the younger man hip to hip. The stench was easing though. That was a good thing…

No, it wasn't.

Warlow shook his head, sucked in air through his mouth.

'Move it, Rhys,' he croaked.

The tractor's front loader, the very thing that Elis had meant as a tool for their destruction, now proved to be their salvation. Hana jumped into the tractor's cab, the engine revved and slowly the loader's scoop descended to a point where it was low enough for Rhys to reach. With a grunt of effort, he grabbed the metal and the machine inched backwards, Rhys holding on for dear life, his legs from the waist down dripping and covered in slick, thick, slurry as Hana dragged him from the pit.

Warlow waited. He could try to reach up for the smooth vertical concrete wall, but his hands and arms were shaking badly. He doubted he had the strength. The tractor had reversed out of sight, but he heard Hana's voice from somewhere, then the tractor engine revved once more and the scoop appeared in his wavering vision. Why had she changed the lights? They were purple now and the reek... the reek was finally going, too.

Perhaps the easiest thing would be to let go, sink back-wards and float until rescue came. Warlow glanced behind at the strange bobbing lake and pushed up with his trem-bling arms.

Hana's shout shook him out of it.

'Mr Warlow? Sir? Reach across. I'm here, sir.'

He swivelled his face and saw her reaching hand. He half turned, lifted his arm and touched the cold steel of the scoop under his palm. He let go of the concrete rim and swung his other hand around.

Hana was gone, but then he was moving as the tractor reversed, pulling him out of the pit's clutches, his hands grasping the machine as he fought against the slurry's suction around his legs and the lake's reluctance to let him go.

In his altered state, there were voices, too. Calling for him. Begging him to stay. Were these voices from under the lake of filth asking him to fight for them? To get justice for those forgotten.

The rough edge of the slipway's walls pulled him around and then there was solid ground beneath him and cleaner air in his nostrils. He let go of the scoop and fell to his knees, sucking in the air and letting the world reset around him.

Rhys sat against a wall, legs coated in muck, his face as pale as milk, Hana on one knee next to him. Rhys retched and brought up the rest of what he'd eaten for lunch onto the concrete floor. He spat, retched again, heaved in air. 'How does anyone work in this?' he huffed.

Warlow pushed up, sagged to his knees once more and sucked in three huge lungfuls of air.

Rhys was right, of course. This was no place for the living. And no place for the dead.

'Call it in,' Warlow ordered, as he got to his feet.

Hana nodded, her face wet from crying. Her world was crumbling around her.

'Can you do that, Hana?' He stared down at her.

She nodded and Warlow felt a surge of pride and admiration for this girl who was, at her core, a copper. He allowed that one tiny fragment of satisfaction to break through his anger before he turned away.

Hana frowned. 'But sir, where are you—'

Warlow didn't hear the rest of it. He'd already started running.

CHAPTER THIRTY-EIGHT

ELIS PROSSER KNEW his world had ended with that shotgun blast from Hana. He'd seen it in her eyes. She'd believed that *ffwrch* of a DCI. She'd wanted to shoot him then, her own father. But she was still his daughter and a tiny spark of what had once been her love for him made her turn the gun away.

It was over. All of it. He'd been expecting this day ever since his wife confronted him about what he'd been caught doing with one of the farm workers all those years ago.

The boy had come down from up north for work experience and been a willing participant, but Sara had looked into the barn and seen something she should not have seen. He knew then there'd be no explanation he could give that would be acceptable. Sara was a staunch Hermon attendee. That lot could find nowhere in their hearts or minds for unbiblical acts or those who perpetrated them.

She'd wanted him to atone.

To confess his sins.

Her accident had been easy to arrange. Farming remained the most dangerous of occupations, after all. Tragedies happened every day. He'd received sympathy and an outpouring of love for himself and Hana. And having the beautiful blue-eyed daughter to look after had made it all so much easier after that.

No one questioned the grieving widower's reluctance to involve himself with another woman.

In fact, they'd considered it *parchus*. Respectable.

No one questioned his work and his trips to the cities for committee meetings. Places teeming with people where he could be anonymous. Where he could meet partners and do what he needed to do. Bad luck that he'd met Robert Lloyd in one of those clubs. Worse luck that the kid had actually thought they had a future.

He'd dealt with that minor problem well enough.

What he hadn't bargained for was that Robert had let Joseph in on their little tryst. So he'd had to spend good money to keep Joseph sweet. Wine and dine him. Buy him presents. Until he too had believed that Elis actually meant what he'd said about love and companionship.

He was almost thirty years older than Joseph, for God's sake.

He allowed himself an icy smile. God had no place in any of this.

He'd found a solution for Joseph, too.

But he hadn't bargained for this.

Damn that bastard Warlow.

Still, he had a chance to get away. He'd prepared. Another car parked up on the eastern edge of the farm registered in a farmhand's name. From there, he would go north and east. The continent, perhaps. He ran for the house and the rucksack he'd kept packed for this moment.

All he needed to do was take the Land Rover across country to an old storage shed full of winter silage bales and the fuelled and serviced Renault.

He got to the house, ran upstairs, one wistful look

around and then back out to the yard, thumb on the key fob, the Land Rover's lights flashing as it unlocked.

The wind gusted around him. He glanced at the now starless sky. Heavy rain was due. Good, it would help blot out his tracks. He felt no remorse. No regret. Never had.

All he wanted now was to get away from them all. The police, Hana, the petty, claustrophobic attitudes. And it was within his grasp now. He was ten steps away from the car when something came out of the darkness at speed and drove all the air out of his lungs. He fell heavily on his shoulder in the cobbled yard. Something pushed him violently onto his face and a knee bored into his back, pinning him to the cold stone yard. His wrist pivoted back and his shoulder twinged with excruciating pain.

He heard a click and then his other wrist got yanked backwards. A second click and his arms were secured. And then the smell hit him. and he knew in an instant who it was that was pinning him to the floor.

'Lie still,' said a male voice, 'or, so help me, I will break both your arms. And believe me when I say it would give me the greatest of pleasure to do so.'

'You wouldn't dare.' Elis's words emerged as a wheezy rasp from his distorted lips flattened against the floor.

'Oh, I would,' Warlow said. 'I get DCI's privileges.'

CHAPTER THIRTY-NINE

THE ANGLER'S laid on a late supper. The kitchen had meant to close at nine, but by the time they got Elis Prosser in custody and themselves back to Newtown, it was late.

Once away from the lagoon's disgusting fumes, Rhys recovered quickly. Hana found something for them to change into at the farm and bagged up their clothes. She did all of it on automatic, fussing over them, not wanting to think too much about it all, Warlow guessed.

That would come later when she was alone in her bed. Her partner had been contacted and was on the way back from his course. She wouldn't need to be totally alone. But sometimes having that physical presence of someone else in the bed with you was not enough. In the wee small hours, it was only you and your conscience. And that could be a very lonely place indeed.

Even with their clothes double bagged and tied securely, an oozing reek of leaking gas permeated the back of the Jeep all the way to the hotel. When they got there, Warlow made an executive decision, took the bag and asked the manager to put it outside but to make sure it wasn't thrown out, on the off chance it might be needed as evidence.

He'd already decided that if Kapil didn't want it, the lot was going into the landfill.

Rhys had looked appalled at the suggestion, but Warlow was insistent.

'In fact, I'll get Superintendent Buchannan to stump up for some expenses.' He told the DC when they were sitting in the bar with their first round of drinks and the rest of the surrounding team. 'You can always buy a new suit, Rhys. Good DCs are much more difficult to come by.'

Rhys blinked, his mind trying to read the subtext in the compliment. 'Does that mean me, sir?'

Warlow noted, 'It does. But do not let it go to your head.'

Rhys shook his head. 'I didn't think I'd been much use, sir. I couldn't cope with that slurry. I...' A dark memory clouded his features.

'You can't train for a situation like that, Rhys. Besides, you never lost faith in Hana. And you were right. So take that as a positive.'

Warlow bought the first round. IPAs for him and Gil, a bottle for Rhys, gin and tonics for Lowri and Catrin.

'What's that you're drinking, Rhys?' Gil asked, smacking his lips and wiping away his froth moustache after a healthy swallow of beer.

'It's Jemima's Pitchfork, Sarge. Named after a Fishguard woman who rounded up French soldiers armed only with a Pitchfork.'

Gil raised an eyebrow. 'Think I met her once on a night out in Tenby.'

'1797, Sarge.' Rhys shook his head.

'Must have been her sister, then.' Gil nodded and turned to the DCI sitting next to him, sniffing gently.

'What the hell is wrong with you?' Warlow growled.

'Thought I saw a bit of something stuck to your scalp. Green with a bit of straw in it.'

Warlow's hand went to his head. 'I've had two showers.'

'Exactly my point.' Gil grinned.

'Not funny, Sarge.' Rhys took on a pained look.

'No, it isn't,' Warlow added.

'That mean it's off limits for taking the piss, then?' Gil looked from the DCI to the DC.

'Well,' Warlow mumbled.

'Good.' Gil took the wavering and ran with it. 'Because I've got them all lined up. It's a shit job, but someone has to do it. These are all crap jokes. There's a mushroom burger on the menu you might both like, shit-takey of course.'

Rhys winced.

'No, don't poo-poo it until you try it,' Gil said.

Lowri lost her cool with that one and almost choked on her drink.

Catrin, with her trademark straight-faced delivery, asked, 'Who is it you follow in the premier league now, Rhys? Manure-nited is it?'

Everyone turned to stare at that one, owl-eyed.

'What?' Catrin instantly took umbrage. 'It's okay to laugh at Gil's rubbish puns, but not at mine?'

'Manure-nited?' Gil gaped and then laughed softly. 'Genius.'

The waitress announced their food was ready, so they took their places in the restaurant. And, inevitably, the change of venue brought a change of subject. The case itself.

Elis Prosser admitted to killing Robert Lloyd and Joseph Randal. Aeron Randal was nothing but collateral damage, because he turned up with his son. He also confessed to slaughtering Hari Gregory's sheep to bolster the rustling theory. As for Julia Lloyd, he'd wanted to make sure there was no evidence in her home and saw the fire as a way to kill two birds with one stone. He'd taken Joseph's clothes on a quad bike cross country to the Falls at Pistyll Rhaeadr and hung Aeron's jacket on the bridge at Habberley to ensure it would be found. All aimed at getting the police going in every direction but the right one.

All designed to confuse.

'He actually said that?' Lowri asked.

'He did,' Warlow told her.

'What about Robert Lloyd?' Catrin asked.

'They're going to drain the slurry pit. I have a feeling they'll find his remains in there. It's a question of how many others.'

Catrin drew her lips back at the idea of it. 'I can't imagine doing that job.'

'You think he may have killed others?' Gil asked.

Warlow stared at his glass. 'I would not be surprised. I suspect Elis Prosser has been doing this for a while.'

Rhys cleared his throat. Everyone looked at him. 'Would it be alright if we stopped talking about this until we've had our food?'

Warlow nodded. 'Good idea, Rhys.'

'Absolutely. That suggestion deserves a pat on the back,' Gil said, then caught himself. 'Sorry, you've already had one of those this evening.'

Catrin groaned.

'But,' Gil continued, 'and all jokes aside. I propose a toast to a job well done and an unscathed team.' He raised his glass, and everyone drank.

Warlow regarded his colleagues. The old stagers and the young blood. They'd done well, all of them. And Lowri showed real promise. He'd be speaking to Buchannan about her. And then he wondered about Hermon Chapel and of people's misguided faith and of the damage that could do. He couldn't blame the Chapel for a monster like Elis Prosser, but he wondered how much comfort a place with so much hateful baggage could provide.

Bread had been passed around and Rhys was tucking in, already better after his ordeal. He'd glimpsed his own mortality this evening. Something Warlow caught sight of every time he picked up his ART pills. But for a young man, being so close to death had been traumatic. Being in a team undoubtedly helped. Gil knew that, and his insistence on delivering dark humour was a salve for the young DC's mental wounds.

Warlow picked up his glass and studied them in turn over the rim. Gil was a tonic wherever you were. Catrin didn't suffer fools at all, and Lowri had been the spark that lit the fuse. Warlow didn't do faith, but he believed in this lot. What they stood for.

He raised his glass. 'I'd like to say thank you, too, for a job well done. And to remember absent friends.'

'She'll be glad she missed this one, sir.' Catrin grinned.

'*Mam fach*, yes.' Gil nodded. 'DI Allanby doesn't do bullshit.'

Everyone groaned but drank the toast anyway.

———

WARLOW SPENT the following morning writing up what had happened at Caemawr. It had already been decided to take Elis Prosser down south to a bigger and better custody suite on the patch. Warlow and the team would continue the interviews down there. By late morning, he'd done the needful and headed for the Jeep. But he had one more thing he needed to do.

Hana Prosser had been taken off the case for obvious reasons. They'd offered her leave, all paid for, while the 'dust settled'. Tomo delivered this phrase with a roll of his eyes that said a lot about management's clueless appreciation of just how seismic a case this would turn out to be. And also a lot about how the young PCSO must be feeling.

No one would blame her for hiding away in a cave, but, to her credit, Hana had turned up for her shift the next day, suited and booted. Warlow found her in the station at Welshpool, doing paperwork.

He found a room upstairs and kicked the secretary out on the promise he'd be no more than fifteen minutes. If she even thought about objecting, one look at Warlow's scuffed and bruised face courtesy of last evening's adventures soon sent a bullet of cooperation into the good sense bit of her brain.

Warlow stood. So did Hana. 'I'm not going to insult you by asking you how you're feeling.'

Hana nodded. She looked tired and drawn. 'Thank you, sir.'

'You don't need to be here, you know?'

'I'd rather keep busy.'

Warlow nodded. For now, the press knew sod all about Elis Prosser and what he'd done. But that would change, and Hana had a whole new world of pain ahead of her, courtesy of the hyenas that would begin circling soon enough. On one level, she'd be aware of that. On another, she had no idea.

'You did a good thing last night, Hana,' Warlow told her.

She nodded. But the tears that would never be far away started running almost immediately. 'He has said nothing about my mother, has he?'

Warlow shook his head. 'He may never. He may consider that taboo.'

'Why? Because it might upset me?' Anger flared, but she bit it back, regretting it almost immediately.

Warlow shook his head slowly. 'Who knows what he's thinking. Will we ever truly know?'

She pulled herself upright and wiped the tears with an already crumpled tissue.

'The next few months will not be easy. I'm not going to pretend to say I understand what it must be like, either. I don't. Few people in this world will. But I'm here if you need any help.' Warlow handed over his card. 'Ring me any time.'

'Do you think they'll let me stay in the police, sir?' Hana sounded distraught. 'I shared things with Da… with him. I told him what I was doing. He knew things he shouldn't have known.'

'You've done absolutely nothing wrong, Hana. There'll be an investigation, obviously. He was one step ahead of us all. But if you need anyone to come to any interviews, ring me. If I can't make it, Gil or Catrin will come. We'll leave Rhys out of it, because you don't want him drooling in the seat next to you.'

A smile began, but soon faltered. 'It'll be hard for them to keep a killer's daughter in employment.'

'Harder for them to get rid of you if you want to stay. Constructive dismissal is a bugger of a thing. But now and again you have to admire the clever sods who dreamt it up. Only thing I know that's guaranteed to put the willies up any HR suit.' Warlow smiled. It wasn't a difficult thing to do in this young woman's presence. 'You're a good copper, Hana. This world needs good coppers.'

Hana looked at the card and then walked over to Warlow and he held out his hand. She ignored it and pulled him into a hug. 'Thank you,' she whispered. 'I needed that.'

Warlow pondered if she meant the words or the hug and decided it mattered not one iota either way.

Before opening the door, Warlow had one more thing to say. 'We all need help at some time, Hana. Make sure you make use of it.'

With that, Hana Prosser nodded, and Warlow headed for home.

CHAPTER FORTY

WARLOW GOT the text on a deserted stretch of road between Builth Wells and Beulah. His plan had been to head straight to the Prince Philip Hospital to at the very least stick his head through the doors of ITU to check on Denise. And whereas, by all things lawful, he probably should not have been checking his texts while driving, in the throes of a major investigation into what would undoubtedly be a serial killer case, he needed to stay in touch.

He had the phone on a cradle on the dash, as hands-free as was possible to be. But when Martin's name popped up as a WhatsApp notification, Warlow decided to pull in. Easier said than done on this stretch and it took him a mile to find a spot next to a steel and Perspex bus-stop shelter devoid of waiting passengers. He doubted too many buses passed this way anyway.

He jabbed at the touch screen and read the message – all in capitals.

RING ME AS SOON AS. MARTIN

Warlow plucked the phone from its holder and pressed

the phone icon next to Martin's name. He answered on the fourth ring.

'Hi. It's Evan.'

'Christ, Evan. I've been trying to get you for an hour.'

'Middle of nowhere, I'm afraid. Crap signal. What's up?'

Martin didn't answer right away and the sound of his ragged breathing filled the space left by his voice, punctuated by the odd sound of a sucking inhalation. Warlow suspected he was outside somewhere smoking. 'Whoa.' Martin huffed. 'I thought I'd be ready when you rang but… ah, shit, she's gone, mate.'

'Denise? Gone where? They transferred her?'

'No, no transfer. Everything packed up. Multiple organ failure. It's a thing.'

Warlow heard the words and tried his best to put them all together into something coherent. He zeroed in on the words 'multiple organ failure' and 'gone'. When he did, a cold ripple ran through him.

'Martin, what's happened?'

Another ragged breath. Another toke of smoke. 'Denise is dead, Evan. Her heart packed up two hours ago. They got nowhere with resuscitation.'

A huge cattle truck roared past the bus stop doing sixty and the Jeep shook in the vortex of its wake. 'But I thought…' Warlow's words trailed off. It didn't matter what he'd thought.

'The pancreatitis,' Martin said. 'It's a real nasty bastard. One doc told me it rots the insides.'

'Was she in pain?'

'No, not at the end. They had her on the good stuff since yesterday.'

Warlow nodded. There was no one to see it, but it felt right. 'Who've you told?'

'No one. I wanted you to know… They've moved her to the mortuary and…'

'So, Tom and Alun haven't heard yet?'

'No. I was going to, but…'

Warlow heard the lie but didn't pass comment. 'I'll take care of that, Martin. I'm sorry. About Denise, I mean.'

'Thanks, Evan. Yeah… hard to believe she won't be around hassling me anymore.' He let out a dry laugh.

'It is hard to believe. You did a good job of looking after her. There'll be a lot to organise now and I won't interfere, but if there is anything I can do…'

'Thanks, Evan. I appreciate it. I'm a bit numb now. Give me a day or two.'

'Of course. You know where I am.'

Warlow rang off and sat. Numb seemed an appropriate enough word for what he, too, felt. Numb and… yes, there could be no denying it, shocked and saddened. Not for himself particularly; Denise had been dead to him for a long while. No, his remorse was all for the boys. They'd both had their challenges coming to terms with their mother's alcoholism. And Alun especially laid some of the blame for it at his father's door. But Denise had been their mother and before the vodka took over as her significant other, she'd been a funny, loving, wonderful mum.

She would always be their mother and her death would still leave a big hole in their hearts. And he would have to be the one punching that hole. Being a dad wasn't all that easy, either.

Another lorry rumbled past and once more the Jeep shuddered in the buffeting after-draught.

He ought to move from this spot. But not yet. No point putting this off.

He picked up the phone and found Tom's number.

'Dad? Everything alright?' Like his father, Tom's

instincts told him a mid-afternoon call usually meant business, not pleasure.

Warlow attempted a dry swallow and wished he'd bought some water. He took a breath. 'Tom, I've got some bad news. It's about your mother.'

THE END

ACKNOWLEDGMENTS

As with all writing endeavours, the existence of this novel depends upon me, the author, and a small army of 'others' who turn an idea into a reality. My wife, Eleri, who gives me the space to indulge my imagination and picks out my stupid mistakes. Sian Phillips, Tim Barber and of course, Martin Davies. Thank you all for your help. Special mention goes to Ela the dog who drags me away from the writing cave and the computer for walks, rain or shine. Actually, she's a bit of a princess so the rain is a no-no. Good dog!

But my biggest thanks goes to you, lovely reader, for being there and actually reading this. It's great to have you along and I do appreciate you spending your time in joining me on this roller-caster ride with Evan and the rest of the team.

CAN YOU HELP?

With that in mind, and if you enjoyed it, I do have a favour to ask. Could you spare a moment to **leave a review or a rating**? A few words will do, but it's really the only way to help others like you discover the books. Probably the best way to help authors you like. Just visit my page on Amazon and leave a few words.

FREE BOOK FOR YOU

Visit my website and join up to the Rhys Dylan VIP Reader's Club and get a FREE novella, *The Wolf Hunts Alone,* by visiting:

www.rhysdylan.com

You will also be the first to hear about new releases via the few but fun emails I'll send you. This includes a no spam promise from me and you can unsubscribe at any time.

AUTHOR'S NOTE

Suffer The Dead takes the team to the very Northernmost part of the Dyfed Powys territory. Literally to the foothills of the Snowdonia National Park. I've been lucky enough to have travelled a lot across the middle of Wales, heading north to Manchester and beyond on many an occasion. Often I have thought how wonderful it would be to have a straight dual carriageway that would get me there faster. Or even a train-line up the middle, but then I'd miss all the stunning scenery and the tracts of emptiness that some-times ignite the imagination. In my case with ideas of unspeakable crimes of course. And in this case, it's a different mountain range that forms the backdrop to the unpleasantries and not the Black Beacons themselves.

But we're still in the ancient kingdoms of Powys and Dyfed, stretching from the eastern borderlands to the wild western coast.

It's an amazing part of the world, full of warm and wonderful people, wild coastlines, golden and craggy mountains. But like everywhere, even this little haven is not immune from the woes of the world. Those of you who've read *The Wolf Hunts Alone* will know exactly what I mean. And who knows what and who Warlow is going to come up against next! So once again, thank you for sparing your precious time on this new endeavour. I hope I'll get the chance to show you more of this part of the world and that it'll give you the urge to visit.

Not everyone here is a murderer. Not everyone... Cue tense music!

All the best, and see you all soon, Rhys.

READY FOR MORE?

DCI Evan Warlow and the team are back in Book 5 ...

GRAVELY CONCERNED

Turn your back for just one moment and...

In broad daylight, on a quiet rural road, six year old Osian Howells disappears from his own front garden. In the blink of an eye he's a missing person, taken, in the words of a headline hungry press, for nefarious purposes.

DCI Evan Warlow knows that the first hours after an abduction are crucial. Decisions have to be made quickly. Evidence can be lost or compromised, persons of interest need to be interrogated. And more than one has the team's antennae twitching.

Worse, the abductor's deviousness seems to know no bounds as cruel taunts pepper the investigation. With emotions at boiling point, and under pressure from family, the press and his superiors are all 'gravely concerned' for the boy's welfare.

As always in such cases, the clock is ticking. Warlow and the team need answers and soon, before a kidnapping turns into something infinitely worse.

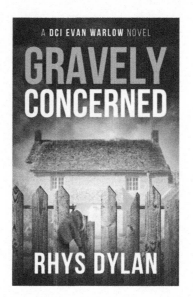

Made in United States
North Haven, CT
09 July 2024

54544498R00193